"Stop," she whispered.

"Stop what?" he asked, his hands continuing to roam.

"This game you're playing."

"But you like playing games, Diana, isn't that why you married John? You wanted to see me grovel. Better yet, did you want to see me crumble? But you and I already know that you sold that sweet little body of yours to the highest bidder."

Diana blanched and slapped him hard across the cheek. He froze. The air in the room seemed to turn bitter cold. Shock made him immobile. Breathing hard, her eyes swelled with tears.

"Don't you ever speak to me like that again!"

Trace's eyes locked on hers in disbelief. "You believe in living dangerously, Diana," he said in a venomous tone. "There was always heat between us. No matter how much you despise yourself, there's a hunger you need me to feed. There's a thirst I see in your eyes that begs for me to quench it. It's inevitable that we'll become lovers again and...soon."

The Heart Knows

Renee Wynn

Genesis Press, Inc.

INDIGO LOVE SPECTRUM

An imprint of Genesis Press, Inc.
Publishing Company

Genesis Press, Inc.
P.O. Box 101
Columbus, MS 39703

ISBN-13: 978-1-58571-444-5
ISBN-10: 1-58571-444-5
Manufactured in the United States of America

First Edition

Visit us at www.genesis-press.com
or call at 1-888-Indigo-1-4-0

Dedication

To Jacqueline Harris, my critique partner and BFF, whose encouragement keeps me writing. To Steve Follman, the best bud in the world, thank you for helping with all my computer stuff, knowing that I'm completely helpless on the thing. To my son, Derek, who reminds me to write. And to the love of my life, my husband, Michael, who is the wind at my back.

Acknowledgements

To my other BFF, Velma Ricks, the sun shines brighter because of you. My sister, Beatrice, I can't imagine my life without you.

Chapter 1

Diana Hamilton Pisano stood in the doorway of the library at Raven's Nest and looked at the people scattered throughout the room. Some were close to the front waiting for the lawyer to tell them what was in John Pisano's will.

John had passed away a year ago, and still there were times she found it hard to believe he was gone. He'd died peacefully in his sleep without fanfare, just like he lived his life. He always hated pretentiousness and couldn't abide people who fawned over him.

She wasn't surprised at how many people were gathered in the room. Practically everyone in attendance was there because of one thing: the expectation of money. A slight, ironic smile graced her lips; everyone had a little greed, even the most humble person.

People who attend a funeral are usually ones who cared about the deceased, but the reading of a will brings out the vultures.

Her sister-in-law, Crispina Pisano Montgomery, who wore her Italian heritage and wealth with regal pride, was talking in hushed tones to a Pisano cousin. As usual, she was dressed impeccably in the latest designer suit. Her dyed jet black hair was coiffed in beautiful style that should've softened her face and eyes, but didn't. She always hated the fact that her only brother—and heir to the mass Pisano fortune— took an African-American woman to be his wife. On the outside, Crispina looked perfect. But in reality, she was a cold-hearted woman with a viper's tongue. Diana should know; she'd been on the receiving end one time too many during her marriage to John. Crispina hated her, and the feeling was mutual.

She grasped her small son's hand, straightened her spine, forced the muscles in her face to relax, and turned to the waiting flock. She took a deep breath and moved forward. They were waiting for their meal, and she was the main course.

All eyes were on her as she walked toward the empty chairs at the front of the room. She felt the burn of their stares but she refused to stumble. Once seated, she exhaled, releasing the tension in her shoulders.

Martin Smythe, her husband's long-time lawyer and friend, was seated at the long mahogany desk facing her. It was John's favorite piece of furniture in the mansion. His great-grandfather had brought it over from Italy when he came to America with his young bride.

The lawyer cleared his throat and started the proceedings. Halfway through his reading, he stopped nd stared at her in surprise. Diana blinked, realizing she had cried out in distress. She took a deep breath to try to stop the tears that flowed unhindered down her cheeks. Through her tears, she saw Martin standing in front of her holding out a handkerchief. She took it and he waited while she composed herself. Diana knew she'd made a tactical error; emotion displayed in public wasn't something a Pisano would ever do. During her marriage to John, she'd learned not to let her emotions show no matter the pain or fear she felt on the inside. She was a young black woman who'd married an aristocratic billionaire, who happened not only to be white, but forty years older than she was. She'd endured a lot.

"Would you like a drink of water?" the lawyer said.

"No, I'm fine, please continue."

Martin Smythe gave Diana a smile, resumed his seat, then looked at Crispina over the rim of his glasses and frowned. "To my beloved sister, Crispina, who has everything, I don't leave money because she doesn't need it." Crispina hissed an angry snort. "However, I leave to her something she has always wanted and coveted all our adult lives...my collection of ancient coins." Crispina gasped with pleasure.

"To Nicodemo John Pisano, the sweetest little dynamo I've ever encountered, I leave a trust fund of five million dollars. I also leave him ten percent of the Pisano Bank shares. The executor of my estate will hold the proxy for these shares and administe[r] his trust fund until Nicky's twenty-fifth birthday. A separate fund has been established for all of his living and educational expenses."

"Now for my lovely and beautiful wife…"

There was a sound as the library door opened slowly. Diana didn't turn to see who'd come in. She pulled Nicky close. He squirmed, trying to loosen her hold. She relaxed her grip and let him lean back in his chair.

The lawyer continued, "Diana, you've been my sun during the day and light at night. Because of you, I was a better person. You and Nicky brought me more joy than I could've ever imagined. I often wondered how an old crusty bachelor like me could get so lucky. I know how much you love Raven's Nest, so I'm leaving you half ownership of the mansion."

Martin paused a moment and cleared his throat. "Now for everything else. The entire investment portfolio, controlling interest of Pisano Bank and Pisano Industries, my seat as chairman of both corporations and—" Martin stopped abruptly and took a deep breath before he continued, "fifty percent of Raven's Nest goes to my nephew, Trace Randall Montgomery." A loud gasp went out in the room.

Diana stood up and screamed, "No!"

"Yes!" Crispina's voice echoed through the room.

"Mrs. Pisano, please sit down so I may continue," the lawyer said.

Shaking, Diana sat down. Shock and slow anger vibrated through her. Why would John do this to her?

Martin continued reading. "Diana, I know you'll be very angry with me, but know I did this for you. You've no need to worry; you'll be taken care of. As the executor of my estate, I have complete trust Trace will take care of you and Nicky. I want you to be happy, and this is the only way you can achieve true and complete happiness. All my love, John."

Martin took off his glasses and placed them upon the papers. He folded his hands on the desk in front of him and looked around the room before bringing his eyes back to Diana. "Although he did leave a personal letter to be read by Trace Montgomery only, this was the last will and testament of John Nicodemo Pisano. He was of sound body and mind when he asked me to prepare the will." His eyes traveled to the back of the room. "Some of you may not understand what John did, but he had his reasons." There was silence as Martin spoke to the people gathered. "The will can't be contested. If you try to do so, Raven's Nest will be liquidated and all the proceeds will go to charity."

Diana sat numb with disbelief. Her husband had left her without a penny. Crispina must be enjoying this. How many other people in the room were smirking at her ill fortune? She squared her shoulders and refused to give them the satisfaction of seeing her defeated.

"Mrs. Pisano?" Luca, Nicky's nanny, stood at her elbow. "It's time for Master Nicky's nap. It's been a long day for him," she said softly.

Diana forced a smile at Luca. In the chair beside her Nicky was asleep, leaning against her arm. She stroked his face and gently woke him. Her heart contracted with the fierce protectiveness she felt for her son. He was such a beautiful little boy. A small catch formed in her chest as he trained his eyes on her. Nicky's small, light brown face had a few remnants of baby fat that would eventually disappear, as he grew older. Each day he reminded her more of his father, the same sleepy-eyed look and the slight dimple in his cheeks when he smiled brought memories of a happy time in her life. Shaking her head to clear her mind, she hugged him close and then let him go. She didn't want Nicky to feel her stress. He was a very bright and intuitive four-year-old.

"I don't wanna sleep." He rubbed his eyes. Diana bent toward him and whispered, "If you go with Luca and take a nap, I promise you a big surprise when you wake up."

Nicky hated to nap but loved surprises. It was summertime. Diana's parents were picking him up in a few days to spend time with them. They felt it was good for Nicky to be around his cousins and be a normal little boy. Diana agreed. He needed to learn to value and respect the simple life. There was more to life than living in luxury. Diana grimaced. Her mind went back to another man who thought money could buy him anything. Closing her eyes, she cleared her mind, not wanting to think about him, nor that period in her life.

"Okay," Nicky said as he rubbed his eyes again. Diana smoothed his curly mop and engulfed him in a hug. His small arms reached up and around her neck. A rush of emotion filled her, and she hugged him tight.

"Tight, Mommy!" Nicky cried and Diana let go. "I'm sorry, sweetheart. Mommy didn't mean to hug you so hard." Sighing, she kissed the top of his head as he scrambled out of the chair and grasped Luca's hand. Diana stood and watched them walk out the side door of the library with a feeling of unease.

A chill suddenly ran through her, and the hairs on the back of her neck stood to attention. Diana turned around to scan the room to see what had caused the sensations. Her gaze connected with a pair of piercing blue eyes. She felt the color drain from her face and she froze in her spot. She quickly turned to see if the side door to the library was closed. It was. She sighed with relief. The library was huge and could easily hold a hundred people comfortably. She was in the far corner at the front of the room. No one watching could see her clearly, unless she was facing the person. Thank God she wasn't.

Trace Montgomery, a man she thought—or rather hoped—she would never see again stared unflinching at her. A gamut of emotions ran through her, making her weak. She prayed her legs wouldn't give out from under her. Pulling from strength she didn't know she had, Diana refused to look away. Trace was one of the most eligible bachelors in the world, relentlessly pursued by hopeful women. A man of strength, high intelligence, and power, hard, tough, and of little patience, he brushed aside people who had the audacity to approach him without permission.

His arresting, wide-set dark blue eyes projected the hardness of a man who took what he wanted without question. Jet black hair, inherited from his Italian ancestors and rumored gypsy blood, was smooth and layered around his head. He wore an elegant black suit, a crisp white shirt, and a dark tie. A tall man with broad shoulders, his body was muscular but lean, and he walked with a natural, languid grace. His thirty-eight years looked good on him. He was arrogant, ruthless, and charming. Women wanted to consume him and men wanted to dissect his brilliant brain. Everyone, male and female, recognized the cosmic energy and power he projected upon entering a room. He was seemingly unaware of the speculative interest in his tall, broad frame. She stood motionless as he moved toward her.

❥

Trace Montgomery straightened, moved away from the wall, and strolled toward the woman he had been watching intently for the last hour. His gaze slid over the tailored blouse that hugged her breasts and the black straight-leg slacks clinging to her hips. With a choker of white pearls around her slim neck and matching pearl earrings, she'd never looked more feminine and beautiful than she did right now. Only Diana could pull off wearing bright red toe polish at such a somber occasion. He stared at the smooth cinnamon skin of her face. Time was not her enemy. She was unbelievably gorgeous and still managed to capture his attention and hold it, even after all these years. It angered Trace she still had an effect on him. He hadn't been prepared for the instantaneous avalanche of emotion and uncertainty he was experiencing. Although he was careful to betray nothing, he felt everything inside him tighten. Something hot and fierce gripped his body and, for a moment, his mind took him to a time when he and Diana had explored a hidden cave. The sound of the waterfalls echoed against the entrance as she frolicked in the water. The day had been magical, ending with them making love for the first time. He grabbed hold of his runaway thoughts. He needed to focus.

The proud tilt of his head, the cynical glint in his eyes, was sufficient to keep the other people in the room at a respectful distance. He ignored their stares, knowing they were wondering about the prodigal heir who'd returned home after a five-year absence.

"Hello, Diana." Trace gave an arrogant inclination of his head. "It's been a long time."

"Hello, Trace," she said in a calm and clear voice.

He smiled slightly at her apparent calmness. Her lovely face was devoid of expression.

Diana moistened her lips. "What brought you back, Trace?" she asked.

"A lot of things," he said in deep, cultured tones.

"You didn't attend John's funeral."

"No." He moved closer. She stepped back. He liked the fact that she wasn't as calm as she appeared. "You've grown more beautiful, Diana." His voice dropped low as his eyes traveled slowly down her body. He wanted to make her uncomfortable. Up close, her skin was like fudge, smooth and delectable. Her hair flowed across her shoulders like dark coals of fire, vibrant and lustrous. He knew from experience how soft it felt against his skin. Her full lips were bathed in a shade of lipstick that gave an added light sheen to her lips and made him remember how it felt to kiss her. How he'd missed her. His body hardened and he shifted his weight from one leg to the other. Damn. He needed to stop. He was here for one reason, and it wasn't that.

"You could make it for the reading of the will but you couldn't make the funeral?" she said with irony. "But you always did find the time for what you felt was important to you."

His mouth tightened. It was because of her he'd stayed away. "We need to talk."

"Why?"

He cupped her elbow. "It's important."

Surprise flashed in her eyes, but was quickly quelled. "I can't think of any reason you would need to talk to me."

"Let's go into the study," he said. She pulled slightly away from his touch. He followed her down the long hall to the study. At the door, he allowed her to turn the knob, noticing the slight tremor of her hand. Trace followed her through the door, taking in the contemporary decor and plush carpet. "You changed the room," he said as he closed the door.

Diana walked to the large window and stood with her back to the manicured grounds and the mesmerizing view of the Smoky Mountains.

"Yes, I did." She crossed her arms, her face closed. "You can forgo the small talk."

She was still the same in that regard, no nonsense. Diana never did like beating around the bush. She'd always been a bit reserved, a mixture of fire and ice. He had loved that about her. He inclined his head at the long floral sofa in front of her. "Why don't you sit down?"

"I would rather stand," she said.

Trace knew she wasn't going to like what he had to say. There was no easy way to say it. "The year before John died he visited me in London." He watched surprise flash across her face.

"Why?"

"He was starting the process of passing the reins of the company to me. Because the bank is a privately held company, it's in the bylaws that the chairmanship must pass to a male descendant of my grandfather, meaning me. What surprised me was the division of Raven's Nest. I thought for sure he would leave it to your son."

"It surprised me as well. Besides business, I didn't know you and John communicated personally."

"Even though you were married to him, Diana, he was still my uncle," he snapped.

"I'm sorry. I didn't mean to imply—"

"You meant to imply exactly that, Diana. My relationship with John was civil, though the bond we once shared when I was a small boy was severed."

She winced. "I didn't—"

"Drop it, Diana. I didn't come here to relive what is dead."

"Then why did you come, Trace? John left you everything. I'm sure Martin could have sent you John's instructions for the estate and the companies."

"Martin informed me last week that it was imperative I attend the will reading."

"Martin and John apparently knew what would get you to return to Raven's Nest."

"Believe what you will." Trace paused, wanting to say more but deciding against it. He took a deep breath, hoping to give her time to adjust to the news. "I thought it was important you know what John wanted, but if you—"

"As usual, everything stands still until the great Trace Montgomery sees fit to make an appearance."

"Sarcasm doesn't become you, Diana," he said drily.

"Oh, really, and how do you know what becomes me? You haven't seen me in more than five years; you have no idea who I am."

"You're right, I don't. When I last saw you, you were a woman I thought I could completely trust. You were my lover, my best friend, and the woman I lo—" He pinched the end of his nose, took a deep breath, and placed his hands on his hips. "There's no need to beat a dead horse."

"You're right. It's the past. There's no need to dredge it up."

Running his hand wearily over his face, he said, "I'm sorry. I didn't bring you in here for that."

"Then why did you?"

"Raven's Nest is now jointly owned by you and me. What you don't know is that for it to be legally ours, you and I must live in the mansion for two months... together." He saw the blood leave her face. A small moan escaped from her throat, and she couldn't hide the shock in her eyes.

"Oh, God," she murmured, and finally sank onto the sofa. "I can't live here with you!" Diana was visibly shaking. There was more to it than just living in the house with him.

"What are you afraid of?" Trace asked.

Diana blinked. "What?"

"The mansion has thirty-five rooms. I'm sure we can stay out of each other's way for two months."

Hands clasped tightly together, she looked at him. "It's not that."

"Look, Diana, if you are worried I might make some sort of advance toward you, forget it. You have nothing to worry about on that score. I'm not interested. Whatever we had died on the day you married my uncle."

A choking sound escaped. "Leave John out of this."

"How can he be left out? His death and his will are what brought us together today." He observed her ashen face. "You never did like to talk about unpleasant matters."

She jumped up from the sofa. "I'm not going to discuss John with you."

He had never seen this side of Diana. She was even more beautiful when she was angry. Hating himself, he tried to rein his thoughts in. Now was not the time to rehash a dead relationship. But he couldn't seem to stop.

Anger and his past hurt controlled him. "You were the one who left me and married my uncle within weeks of ending our relationship. That's something I'll never forgive."

"Did you ever think I might have a few things I can't forgive, either?"

He studied her for a long moment. "Such as?"

A tired look suddenly entered her eyes. "It doesn't matter any longer. It's all in the past."

He heard the resolve in her voice. He wouldn't let himself soften toward her. The anger simmered. She'd hurt him deeper than anyone in his life. His mother's indifference and desertion didn't compare to Diana's betrayal. It had cut to the core of his being and left him wounded. For the first time in his life, he'd doubted himself. She wouldn't get the chance to do it again. He would spend the required two months in the house and then leave. With steel in his voice, he said, "You're right. It's the past and it's dead. Again, I apologize."

Her gaze dropped from his, and she smoothed her palms on the front of her slacks. "Trace, it's been a long time since we have seen each other." She took a deep breath and continued, "Five years ago, I made a decision to marry John. I never regretted it."

Trace released his breath in a slow hiss. Her declaration caused a slight ache in his chest and made him realize that she still had the power to make him feel things that were alien and uncomfortable. He'd allowed her to get under his skin in a way that no other woman had ever done before or since. It made him feel angry and out of control. He'd wanted to spend his life with Diana, but she had left him and married his uncle before he could make the mistake of asking her to marry him. The wound to his heart and pride still festered like an open sore.

"You made your choice." It was time to end the walk down memory lane before fury consumed his mind. Diana had walked away from him and left him devastated. He never told anyone of the gut-wrenching pain he felt when she married his uncle. Never would she get the chance to do it again.

"Yes, I did."

"I won't question your motives, but you must've loved him at least enough to marry him," Trace said roughly. Even though he knew it sounded cold and distant, his voice harsh and angry, he didn't want to soften it. Why did she leave him? The question resonated through his mind but he didn't ask the question…afraid of what the answer would be.

"Trace, I don't want to live with you. There must be another way." She wrapped her arms tightly around her midriff.

"I don't want to live with you, either, but John had an ironclad will drawn up."

"I don't believe you." Her voice grew desperate. "Montgomery Enterprises and Pisano Industries have tons of lawyers on the payroll; there must be a way around it."

"It was examined thoroughly. It's ironclad." Trace moved closer. "Diana, Raven's Nest is a landmark mansion. It's been in my family for many decades. A registered historical site, it's been a part of Asheville's history for over a hundred years. I practically grew up here. I'll not see it go to charity because you're too damn immature to spend two months with me in this house. If you don't want to honor the will, you can always forfeit and leave, in which case I will make an offer to buy it from the charity."

"You would love that, wouldn't you? You believe money can buy you anything. If I leave, then I'll have nothing. It must give you immense pleasure—"

"Diana, I didn't know the full content of John's will until today. Believe me, it gives me no pleasure to have to take care of you."

"How dare you! Go to hell."

"Whether you like it or not, you're my responsibility."

"I'm no man's responsibility. I have a job."

"I believe at Pisano's."

"Are you threatening my job?"

"As long as you continue to do a good job, it is yours."

"There's never been any complaint about my work."

"Then I guess you still have a job."

"I'll not be bullied by you."

"Bullied?"

"Yes. I won't have you create problems because you want revenge." She took a deep breath. "I'll live at Raven's Nest to satisfy the will, but I don't have to like it."

Trace shrugged. "Well, I guess we're stuck with each other." He trained his blue eyes on her. "At least for two months." Conflicting emotions battled on her face. He loved Raven's Nest and knew she did also. Even when they were together, Diana had expressed a sincere awe for the beauty of the place. He didn't want it to go to charity.

"If we must live together, I don't want my son to be affected by what's going on between us. He's very smart and will pick up on our mood."

"I'm not a monster, Diana. I would never say or do anything to hurt a child."

"I believe you," Diana said slowly. "I didn't mean to imply you would harm my son. I don't think you would knowingly cause a child pain."

"Stop, Diana, while you're ahead."

"I wasn't trying to belittle you. Anyway, I think enough has been said today."

Trace's voice was surprisingly calm when he spoke. "I agree. Any further discussion between us will only compound the situation. I'll move into the mansion tomorrow. If you need to reach me, I'll be at the penthouse."

"Penthouse?" she questioned.

"Yes. I never sold it."

"I assumed you would stay with your mother."

"What made you think that?"

She shrugged. "She would expect it."

"Diana, I haven't lived with my mother since I was six years old and I'm not about to start now. I'm my own man; I come and go as I please. Crispina is my biological mother. That's something I can't change, but I decide where I sleep at night."

His mother, Crispina Pisano Montgomery, was possessive when it came to him. It was partly because he was an only son and she hadn't been the best mother when he was growing up. For years Crispina had been trying to make up for his adolescence, when she practically ignored him, turning him over to boarding schools and nannies for rearing. If it hadn't been for his father and his uncle, he would've been a lonely little boy. But his father and uncle's presence had made Crispina's absence not so painful.

There was a long silence. Finally, she said, "I'll get Rosa to prepare one of the suites in the east wing for you."

"I haven't been gone so long, Diana, that I have forgotten the east wing is seldom used. I think you're trying to put as much distance as you can between us before I even move into the house." He gave her a crooked smile. "I'll use my old suite of rooms in the west wing."

Trace wasn't going to let her pretend he didn't exist. She'd had five years to erase him from her mind, and it was too bad if she hadn't because he refused to be dismissed now.

"Okay. I'll ask Rosa to prepare your old suite." She moved to walk past him to the door.

"There's no need to rush," he said as she continued walking. "Diana." She stopped but didn't turn to face him. He moved in close to her. The light jasmine scent of her perfume tantalized him, and he inhaled deeply.

"Diana," he said her name again, his cultured voice rasping slightly, "I'll be here tomorrow at noon. You can tell Rosa to have the rooms ready by then."

"Okay." She continued walking to the door and he followed.

"Aren't you forgetting something?" Trace said softly, his breath grazing the back of her neck. She shivered in sharp reaction to his nearness. The need in him tensed; he waited for a response. None came. He ran his hard fingers lightly against the smooth, soft contour of her slim neck. She spun around sharply and stepped away from him. Her breath came in sharp, quick gasps. An array of emotions crossed her face. He moved his hand to her face and brushed his thumb slightly over her full top lip. Trace barely touched her, but she stiffened and lifted her chin, her eyes opening wide in confusion.

"What did I forget?" she said.

He captured the small space between them and gave her a slight, twisted smile, "You forgot to say, 'Welcome home.' "

Diana's breath caught in her throat and her eyes grew wide. Confusion marred her features; a look of fear flashed across her features and quickly disappeared, replaced with a frown. If he hadn't been watching her closely he would've never seen it. Diana was a master at hiding her feelings. She breathed deeply and stared at him. Silence hung between them. They were like two warriors waiting for the other to make the first move. Finally, she murmured a quick, inaudible reply and slipped through the door.

Trace cursed as his eyes followed her until she disappeared from his sight.

Chapter 2

Diana closed the door on her parents and leaned against it. She had called them quickly after the meeting with Trace and asked if they would come and pick up Nicky tonight. She had scheduled dropping him off in Charleston next week, but with Trace moving into the house she had to expedite her plans. She'd given her parents some mundane excuse for the urgency. She could tell her mother was curious about the impromptu call. Diana hoped she was successful in disguising the panic in her voice. She was grateful her mother hadn't asked any questions. Diana wanted Nicky out of the line of fire while she and Trace maneuvered around each other.

Diana's thoughts were troubled as she walked toward her bedroom. From published reports, Trace was still regarded as one of the world's most eligible bachelors. Gossip magazines published articles about scores of hopeful women relentlessly pursuing him, trying to get him to the altar. Financial magazines named him as one of the most powerful and richest entrepreneurs in the world. It was reported he could be deadly when it came to negotiations; when he took over a company, he would strip it to the bone, leaving nothing behind. Diana believed every word.

Time had made him an even more handsome man than she remembered. He was more powerful and certainly more dangerous than before. The high, slanting cheekbones were more defined. There were a few lines around his eyes and mouth, but they didn't diminish his sexual appeal.

She needed to be careful. The episode in the study had been stressful. One thing Trace always liked was a challenge. Her hand unconsciously strayed to her neck. The warmth of his breath still lingered on her flesh. With them living in such close proximity, she needed to guard her emotions and most definitely her heart.

He shouldn't have touched her, Trace told himself as he arrived at the mansion. The scent of her skin was still in his nostrils. Disgusted and berating himself for being a fool, he exited the car and headed to the front door. Five years was long enough to get over someone who had hurt you badly. The pain of losing her had dulled in the years since their relationship ended, or so he told himself. The lie settled in his mind.

Using the key he'd had since his childhood, he entered the mansion, walked down the wide corridor to the winding stairs, and looked up. Diana stood at the landing.

He wasn't prepared for the clinching of his gut at seeing Diana, a beautiful, graceful, astounding beauty. He was early; he'd intended to be. He wanted to catch her off guard, to see her unprepared reaction to him. However, he was the one who wasn't prepared for her effect on him. She looked even lovelier this morning, dressed in a pair of white shorts that showed off the smoothness of her long, brown legs and a lime green sleeveless blouse. Her lustrous, dark, thick hair was pulled away from her sculptured face, caught up in a ponytail that brushed her shoulders. She glided down the stairs, her feet bare. He enjoyed the breathtaking sight. When she reached him, he could see she was visibly upset.

"You're early," she said, looking down at his hand. "I see you still have your key."

Displeasure furrowed his brow. "You knew I was coming."

"Yes, but you said noon, not eight o'clock in the morning."

"What difference does it make? You're safe with me, Diana." He captured her eyes with his. "Are you afraid of what you might want to do?" Sardonic amusement touched his mouth. "Ah…I believe it's yourself you aren't so sure about."

Her swift intake of breath caused him to smile. He enjoyed rattling her. She tried to brush past him, but he took hold of her arm to stop her. "I'm here, Diana, and it's best if you get used to it."

25

"It's only for two months," she stubbornly reminded him.

A satisfied look crossed his face. "A lot can happen in two months," he said. Noticing how her comfortable outfit showed off her small, compact figure, his breath caught in his throat. Her flat abdomen showed no sign of her ever carrying a child…his uncle's child. His mouth tightened at the thought. She was uncomfortable with his survey, but he didn't stop. He homed in on her nipples pushing against the thin fabric of the blouse. She wasn't wearing a bra. Showing up early certainly had its rewards.

"Let's not play games, Trace. We find ourselves at an impasse. I know how much you want Raven's Nest; it's been in your family for over a hundred years. I know you would do anything to make sure it stays in the family, including seducing me." Diana inhaled deeply and continued. "We can live in the same house, but it certainly doesn't mean we have to spend time together. There's no need to pretend a relationship exists when we both know it doesn't."

"So the girl has grown into a fiery woman with fangs. I believe I like it," Trace drawled.

"This conversation is finished."

"Not by a long shot," he said. Her eyes blinked and the pulse at her collarbone jumped. Swallowing, he fought the impulse to place his lips against her neck.

They were so close. Breaking the trance, Diana stepped back. She wrenched her arm from his grasp. This time he let her go. She spun on her heel and ran up the stairs. Soon, he thought, she wouldn't be able to run.

❧

Trace watched Diana across the dining room table. The dinner so far had been a quiet affair, each acutely aware of each other. She nibbled at the steamed broccoli. Taking a piece of lobster drenched in butter, she put it in her mouth and used the tip of her tongue to catch the excess drippings. How could she put out such a sexual vibe when she was eating? He took a sip of red wine to calm his feverish blood but it only fueled it.

He sensed his presence made her uncomfortable, which upset him. They used to be very comfortable around each other. Trace leaned back in the chair and tried to relax. Although she pretended to be interested in the food, he knew she felt tension between them.

He mused over the fact that John had left her without a penny. The revelation had been a surprise. As far as the world knew, John had been enamored with his young wife. So why hadn't he provided for Diana in his will?

John had inherited millions upon his grandfather's death. With the banks, the companies, and shrewd business decisions, he'd quickly become a billionaire.

27

John wasn't a stingy man, but he had left the care of Diana and his son to Trace. That fact puzzled him. He intended to get to the bottom of it, and soon.

Trace glanced at Diana, stopped eating, and pointed to her plate. "You've only taken a few bites." He put down his fork. "You've mostly moved the food around."

"I guess I'm not really hungry."

"It's grilled lobster."

"Huh?"

Again, he pointed to her plate. "Grilled lobster. I remembered how much you loved it. I asked Cook to prepare it especially for you."

"Oh, thank you, it's delicious."

"Good. I'm glad you like it."

He resumed eating and so did she, but he felt her gaze on him. He allowed himself a small smile. She was definitely curious. Good, he wanted her to wonder about his next move. All day he'd thought about her as he worked in his uncle's study at the far end of the mansion. Realizing she was somewhere in the mansion and he could locate her any time had made his heart beat unusually fast. But he had left her alone and given her space.

When he asked Rosa, the housekeeper, to inform Diana he required her presence at the dinner table, he had expected her to balk at the request, but she'd arrived without argument. It was a turning point. She just didn't know it...yet.

"I'm really not that hungry," she said huskily, and sat back in her chair.

He poured more red wine for himself, then reached for the white wine chilling in the side bucket and re-filled her glass. He raised his glass in a toast. "To you and to me."

Her eyes widened. "Us?"

Trace smiled. "Yes, to putting aside our differences and forging an alliance to save Raven's Nest."

He was pleasantly surprised when she picked up her glass to clink against his. "To Raven's Nest," she said.

He laughed. "Okay, to Raven's Nest." Studying her, he said, "You've developed poise and elegance." Silence filled the air as they both conspicuously observed each other. Finally he said, "Tell me about your son."

Her eyes widened in shock. "My son?"

He rested back against his chair. "Yes. I saw him leaning on your shoulder at the reading of the will. I couldn't see his face, but he seems to be young."

"Why do you want to know about Nicky?"

"I see that you named him after my grandfather, Nicodemo."

"Yes. John and I decided on the name together."

Leaning forward, he placed his glass on the table and stood up. He came around to her chair, took the glass out of her hand, set it on the table, and assisted her out of the chair.

"Let's go into the sitting room where we'll be more comfortable." He put his hand at her elbow and guided her out of the dining room.

Diana went without protest then sat on the sofa. Trace sat across from her on the loveseat. He leaned back, crossed his legs, and waited for her to answer his query. When she didn't, he broached the topic again.

"I haven't heard your son all day. Where is he?"

"My mother and father picked him up last evening." She weighed her words carefully. "Nicky's spending a few weeks with them."

Trace frowned, remembering the first time he was shipped away to boarding school. He'd been only six. "Isn't he a little young to be spending that amount of time away from you?"

"Not really. Since my parents live in Charleston, they don't get to see him as much as they do the other grandchildren."

"I can't understand why parents get rid of their kids. If they want to have time alone, they should've never had them."

Diana bristled. "Aren't you making assumptions? I'm not getting rid of my son. I let Nicky spend as much time as possible with my parents because he loves it."

She smiled, and he caught his breath at the brightness of it. "Plus, he loves his cousins. Both of my brothers have small children. I would never send Nicky somewhere he didn't want to go."

"I knew that Terrence was married, but when did Morgan get married?"

"About four years ago he took the plunge." She grinned. "I can't believe he is a father. He was such a die-hard bachelor. But to see him with his little girl is enough to make you believe any man can reform."

Trace gave her a long look. "Even the mighty can fall."

"Yes." She ran a trembling hand over the long silk belt that hung from her dress. She was nervous about something, he thought.

"Your little boy," he said, bringing the conversation back to her son. Her eyes became guarded as Trace continued, "John was very proud of him. In a short conversation we had, he mentioned him."

"John talked to you about Nicky?" she asked, surprised.

"Just once. I think he mentioned the boy because our conversations were always strained. It was his way of making small talk." He paused. "Why are you surprised?"

"He never mentioned talking to you."

His mouth tightened. "I saw him twice a year when I flew to New York for the board meetings." He shot her a hard glare. "I never solicited any personal information about you or your life together." He didn't want her to know how much he craved any news about her.

"I didn't know if you were still on the board."

"The board seat rightfully belongs to me. Why would I give it up?"

"I didn't expect you to give it up. John never discussed it, but I know there was tension between you and him. He was quiet and a little sad whenever he came home from a board meeting. It hurt me to see him hurt. The estrangement was hard for him. He thought of you as a son."

"Well, his marriage to my faithful lover severed the bond between us," he sneered.

She blanched. As soon as the words left his mouth he knew he shouldn't have uttered them, but he would be damned if he would let her know how much their breakup had affected him. He opened his mouth to apologize, but decided against it. He was not sorry for what he'd said.

Diana rose and walked to the small table where the housekeeper had placed a pot of coffee, along with small individual iced cakes, and cheeses on a serving tray. She poured coffee into a cup, turned around and bumped into Trace.

"Ah!" she said as the hot coffee spilled on her fingers.

He reached out a hand to steady her. He took the cup and set it on the table behind her. Every inch of her slim frame stiffened at his touch. A slight flush tinged her cheeks. She inhaled deeply. Trace held her gaze, then took both her hands and examined them for burns, blowing cool air on them to relieve the pain.

He saw the beginning of a small red mark and brought her hand to his mouth. Taking the fingers one by one into his mouth and gently sucking them, his gaze locked with hers. Diana's breath caught in her throat. He stared into her brown eyes, not breaking contact.

"What are you doing?" she demanded. "Please stop!" Diana's breath came in shallow gasps. He released her fingers, but not before giving each finger a final lick. He moved in close, using his hand to skim the softness of her cheek.

"I should've thought it was obvious what I was doing. I'm relieving the sting."

So close—too close. He felt a whisper of her breath on his face. It smelled slightly of the wine she'd had at dinner. His heart raced, sending blood pounding through his veins.

He needed to kiss her. He moved in closer, remembering how it had been with her. He needed to know her again. He wanted to be able to laugh with her again, talk to her in the wee of hours of the morning while they fought against sleep, not wanting their time together interrupted.

He struggled to resist her seductive pull. After looking at her for a long moment, he pulled back, spun on his heel, and walked to a chair. He rested his shaking hands on the back of the chair and fought for control. He couldn't believe he'd almost kissed her. This wasn't how it was supposed to be. He was losing control all over again. Frustrated, he ran a shaky hand through his hair, trying to cool his hot blood. Damn. He wanted her…bad.

He turned and faced her. "I'm sorry. I didn't mean to startle you. You'll need to put something on the burn so it won't leave a scar."

He groaned as Diana ran her tongue over her lips. Had she been as affected by the near kiss as he was? She refilled her cup with more coffee. The cup shook as she raised it to her lips.

He took a deep breath, trying to calm his feverish blood. "We need to talk about the living arrangements," Trace said.

"I don't foresee a problem." Her eyes didn't meet his and her voice was filled with sarcasm. "I know you want to get this over with as much as I do."

He stared at her for a long moment. "You're angry."

"What?"

He strolled close to her. She stepped back and walked aimlessly around the room; his eyes followed her. He stepped in front of her.

"You're upset because I didn't kiss you." She tried to move away but he stopped her. "There're some things that the passage of time doesn't change. It's still there between us," he said softly, lifting a hand and brushing her cheek gently with his fingers.

"There's nothing between us. It's dead, Trace."

He smiled. "It's useless to deny what the body says so clearly." He reached for her and she shivered. He gave a soft laugh and slid his hands over her shoulders with an ease that brought back vivid memories of their love-making sessions. Although a virgin, she had been an excellent lover. It seemed like only yesterday that they had made love with a passion that had stolen his breath from his body. Only Diana had the power to render him helpless during their lovemaking.

"You're even more beautiful than I remember," he murmured, his hands sliding down to her hips. The sexual tension between them continued to build, over-whelming him, making him forget she'd left him to marry another.

"Stop," she whispered.

"Stop what?" he asked, his hands continuing to roam.

"This game you're playing."

"But you like playing games, Diana, isn't that why you married John? You wanted to see me grovel. Better yet, did you want to see me crumble? But you and I al-ready know that you sold that sweet little body of yours to the highest bidder."

Diana blanched and slapped him hard across the cheek. He froze. The air in the room seemed to turn bitter cold. Shock made him immobile. Breathing hard, her eyes swelled with tears.

"Don't you ever speak to me like that again!"

Trace's eyes locked on hers in disbelief. "You believe in living dangerously, Diana," he said in a venomous tone. "There was always heat between us. No matter how much you despise yourself, there's a hunger you need me to feed. There's a thirst I see in your eyes that begs for me to quench it. It's inevitable that we'll become lovers again and... soon."

"You can go to hell. You think I would let you touch me again? Don't flatter yourself." She pushed his hands off and spun away, heading toward the door. She turned back toward him and sneered, "You want me, Trace, but you'll never, and I mean never, have me."

Trace answered with confidence and determination. "You think not? Hell, Diana, I smell the aroused scent you put off every time you come near me." His mouth turning up with a sardonic grin. "It's only a short matter of time before you crawl into my bed."

"When hell freezes over," she hissed and then slammed out of the room.

His mouth tightened at her rejection. He would let her go for now. He wanted her to feel she had the upper hand. When she least expected it, she would become his. Again.

Chapter 3

Diana retired to her bedroom fuming at what had almost happened. She took a long shower, hoping it would relieve her anger. She stepped out of the shower and wrapped a large bath towel around her body. With irritated, hurried movement, she began her nighttime routine, applying exotic herbal lotions to her body. What was wrong with her, letting Trace get that close? She refused to think of it as being any more than what it was, a moment of insanity, a meaningless encounter with a man who wouldn't pause a second when it came to destroying her. Moreover, she knew Trace would continue this game of seduction to exercise his overactive libido. She grimaced at the prospect of falling victim to his appeal. She would be damned if she'd let him hurt her again. She reminded herself that she would be strong, and only in his presence when necessary. She was totally in control... this time around. And she'd make sure he knew the ground rules.

When Diana stepped into the kitchen the next morning, Trace stood at the counter with his back toward her, drinking a cup of coffee. She must have made a sound because he whipped around and trained his blue gaze on her. A soft, fleeting look quickly passed over his face, then disappeared.

"You're late," he drawled, his eyes going over the pale pink sleeveless dress cinched at the waist.

She must have imagined the softness that briefly crossed his face because his face was now a cold mask. She shook her head. What was wrong with her? Trace was not, nor had he ever been, a man that showed softness.

"I'm not late." She forced herself to ignore the pull of his smothering blue eyes as they followed her. She poured a cup of coffee and leaned back against the counter, careful not to get too close to him.

"I've already eaten breakfast, but if you want something, Rosa has quite a few dishes on the warming table in the dining room. We have a few minutes before the car arrives."

"You don't need to wait for me; I usually drive myself to the office."

"Why take two cars when we're going to the same place? I'll ask Rosa to delay the car for a few minutes while you eat."

"I'll grab something at the office. I usually share a croissant with Susan while we go over the day's schedule."

"Dominic told me you were in charge of the marketing department." He paused. "He said you were very good at your job." He emptied his cup and set it on the counter.

"I love it," she said as she sipped. Again, there was a moment of silence.

"You look very lovely this morning, Diana."

Something in his voice caused her to look up and she found his eyes sliding over her again, making her nervous. She swallowed, took a deep breath, set the coffee cup down with a shaky hand, and tried to act casual.

"Thank you."

"You're welcome."

She cleared her throat. "I apologize for hitting you last night. I have never hit another person in my life and I deeply regret it."

"Diana, I—"

Rosa entered the kitchen. "The car is here, Mr. Montgomery."

"Thank you, Rosa." The housekeeper exited the room as quietly as she came in.

Trace stood in front of Diana. "I'm sorry for what I said to you last evening. I was out of line, and I apologize."

"Thank you. We're both under a lot of strain and we said some things that were regrettable. I do want this to work."

"It'll work, if you let it." His voice became so soft that she wasn't quite sure she had heard him correctly.

Diana didn't respond. Instead she headed to the car, not looking to see if he was following her.

They didn't speak in the car except for a moment when he asked if she wanted a bottle of water. The elevator ride to the top floor was silent also. Stepping off the elevator, Diana hurried towards her office. Trace stopped her by touching her arm. Surprised, she spun around.

"Would you come into my office for a moment?"

Diana arched a brow at his referral to John's office as his, but didn't say anything. Taking a deep breath, she followed him to the other side of the building and into John's office. Trace opened the double doors and allowed her to precede him. Everything was still in place as John had left it. A calmness she hadn't experienced since his death settled over her as she moved further into the room. Diana felt John's presence in his office, and it made her feel more peaceful than sad. She walked toward the large mahogany desk and stood waiting for Trace to speak. Diana didn't have to wait long.

"I was reading over the Australia project notes and saw you're leading the project yourself."

"Yes, I am."

"Why isn't one of your reps doing it?"

"Because I want to do it. I did the marketing design and the ads."

"I can understand that, but there are more pressing matters."

"Such as?"

"I want you on the team for the Japanese bank."

"Why? I put Susan on that project and she's doing well."

"I'm sure she is, but the project is too important for any screw-ups. I want our best team on it."

Diana bristled. "Susan is the lead and the best. I'm not going take her off the project. I trust her to do the job."

"I've chosen you," he said stubbornly.

"No." Diana became angry. "Susan doesn't need a watch dog, and you aren't going to use me to be one for you."

"This is not to be debated. I've made my decision."

Diana tried to be calm and not let her anger consume her, but she was pissed. "It gives you great pleasure to have this control."

"You need to calm down. This is business. It has nothing to do with control."

"Like hell it doesn't."

"You're being irrational."

"Right," she sneered.

"My role in this company is to make sure everything is running smoothly."

"I'll not have you dictating to me and my people. My department ran smoothly before you got here, and it'll continue to do so." Her voice dripped with sarcasm.

"I have made my decision and I'm not changing it," Trace said.

Diana was so furious that she knew if her skin were two shades lighter, her face would be beet red right now. "I don't give a damn about your decision. Now you have told me, and I'm leaving," she croaked as she pushed passed him.

He stopped her. "You're being defensive and childish, Diana."

"You're doing this for some sort of revenge. Well, it isn't going work. John never had a problem with the way I ran my department."

"I'm not John."

"That's for damn sure," she said nastily. "You're nothing like him. You're a little boy who has to get his way in everything. Better yet, the devil disguised in a fancy suit. I don't align myself with the devil." For a moment, Diana thought she had pushed him too far. Trace stood there with a pulse ticking in his jaw.

"I'm a devil?" he growled. "I guess I have to prove you right." His movement was swift and smooth and came without warning. He grabbed Diana and pulled her up against his chest.

"Trace! Let me go!"

"Not a chance." His hold tightened. She pushed at his shoulders. He powered her back against the desk and trapped her mouth under his with such ferocious passion that it devoured her. She reached blindly for the edge to keep from falling, but she didn't have to worry, he had a tight hold on her. His kiss turned gentle, then deep, searching for a connection.

Her skin tingled; heat exploded deep, and every inch of her trembling body screamed out for him. She tried to fight against the tide that was consuming her.

His hard body came between her legs, hiking up her dress. With a sweep of his hand, he cleared the desk. Trace lifted her and sat her on the desk, sliding up her dress as he went. She moaned as he held her captive with his weight and the heat of his mouth.

Dragging her mouth from his, she wordlessly breathed his name. He captured her mouth once again and his tongue delved between her parted lips.

The need was a powerful driving force that blasted everything from her head except the primal urge for sexual fulfillment. It had been too long…five years too long.

In confusion, she watched as Trace stopped and started to pull her dress down. Sanity returned and she pushed his hands away and smoothed the dress over her hips.

"The door is not locked. Someone could walk in on us." No one moved to lock the door.

Embarrassment and shame flooded Diana's face. It had never crossed her mind that someone could walk in on them. She was mortified and sick about what she'd almost let happen.

"When the time is right, you'll give yourself to me and it'll be good. But not right now." His voice was rough with need.

She lowered her eyes and he stepped away. He was giving her time to collect herself. Nothing about his body language suggested that only moments before they'd been on the verge of indulging in hot, mindless sex on the desktop in her dead husband's office.

Torn between utter humiliation, disgust, and the aching frustration that he still had the control to pull away, Diana smoothed her hair and hoped she would be able to walk out of the office with some pride left intact.

As usual, his expression gave away nothing. Diana raised her hand and touched her lips, which felt swollen and hot. Her legs were shaky, but she would be damn if she would fall at his feet. She wasn't going to give him the satisfaction of knowing how deeply she was affected about what just happened between them.

44

"I hate you," she said with venom. "This was a mistake. It'll never happen again."

Trace gave her an arrogant smile. "It's not me you hate, Diana, it is yourself. You like pretending that there is nothing between us." He shrugged. "If that is how you can justify your powerful reaction to me, so be it. You can continue to deceive yourself. But there'll come a time when you'll come willingly to my bed."

Her laughter was raw and brittle. "You are crazy! What just happened was a colossal mistake." She wouldn't let him think he had the upper hand.

"It was bound to happen," he said.

She fumed at his audacity.

"We haven't seen each other in five years, and although we never had a problem when it came to sex we needed to test the waters to see if the chemistry is still there. It is. Now we no longer have to wonder about it."

Trying to ignore the insistent throb that beat against the very center of her body, she moved away from him.

"Lust is something that can be controlled. I'll not let it dominate me. I have more sense than to enter into another affair with you."

He frowned, obviously irritated at her choice of words. "We weren't having an affair. We were in a relationship."

"After what you did to me, I would be insane to let myself be seduced by you."

"What have I ever done to you, Diana?"

She couldn't believe he had the nerve to act innocent. She looked away from him, trying to control the fresh rush of anger that consumed her.

"I'm not going to discuss it. It's water under the bridge, and I've moved on with my life."

"I see."

Would he ask her what she meant? Knowing Trace he wouldn't, and he didn't.

"We'll be good together, just like before. I can feel it, and so can you," he said with confidence and a smirk.

She refused to rise to the bait. Her flesh still yearned for his touch. She shifted on her feet, denying the insistent throb deep in her pelvis.

"Like hell we will. That was five years ago, and this is now."

"You deny what happened."

"No, but it was only sex. You can get that anywhere."

Trace moved closer to Diana and put his finger on her swollen lips.

"Yes, I can. But I have what I want right here."

His beautiful blue eyes drew her in; she felt as if she were drowning. She needed to remind herself that Trace wanted revenge. He had some warped belief that he was the injured party.

She dropped her eyes to his lips. Trace's tongue darted out, touched her lips gently, and then pulled back. Strong hands cupped her face, bringing her mouth closer to his. Trace lowered his head. Her eyes watched his mouth as it descended toward hers. She put up her hands to ward him off.

There was a quick knock at the door and it was flung open.

Diana felt the loss of Trace's hands as he dropped them and turned to face the intruder.

"What are you doing here, Mother?" His voice was agitated.

Crispina Pisano Montgomery walked in with a flurry of elegance and poise.

Diana uttered a soft expletive. *Just what I need right now, a barracuda baring her teeth.* Crispina hated her guts, and the feeling was mutual. She inched around Trace's broad shoulders to get a peek at his mother, but he moved to shield her from his mother's keen eyes.

Crispina Montgomery was a member of North Carolina's elite society, and she sat on the board of directors of her late husband's company, Montgomery World Enterprises, and her family-owned company, Pisano Industries. She was old money and wore it well.

Her motive for marrying Trace's father was that Randall Montgomery was extremely wealthy, and could trace his aristocratic lineage back to fifteenth-century England. After wealth, family lineage was the most important thing to Crispina. The blue-blooded Montgomery family hated her because of the callous way she'd treated Trace and his father. Although Crispina looked every inch the aristocratic Southern lady, she had an iron will. She was controlling, and had a sharp tongue she didn't mind using.

She looked at Trace and smiled with fake innocence. "I came to welcome you on your first day. And I want to take you to lunch."

"There's no need," Trace said.

Crispina stared at Diana for a long moment, a deep frown on her face. "I thought you worked on the other side of the building, Diana."

Warning bells rang in Diana's ears. Crispina's remark was clearly a challenge.

"I do, Crispina. I was on my way out."

Trace put out his hand to stop her, but she moved away from him and walked to the door. "There's no need for you to leave," he said.

"Yes, there is. Your mother came to see you. I have a lot of work to do." Diana walked past Crispina without looking at her or saying a word. She was not in the mood to be polite to the woman. She'd made her life a living hell for the five years she was married to

John. He was now gone, and she refused to take any more crap from her. Diana walked out the door and closed it firmly.

Chapter 4

As soon as Diana closed the door, Crispina started in on Trace.

"Have you lost your mind?" Crispina raged. "Didn't she do enough damage to you five years ago? Are you going to let her destroy you again? She had one Pisano man, must she have you, too?"

Trace slid his hands deep in his pockets to control his simmering anger and glared back at his mother.

"Are you finished?"

"Don't get brusque with me, Trace. Remember I'm your mother."

"Unfortunately, you don't let me forget it. But it's nice for you to remember after all these years."

She gasped, but he didn't take back the words.

"Your father would be ashamed of you right now."

"Don't bring my father into this."

"Your father was proud of you. I just don't believe he would like this trap you're falling into."

He ignored the comment about his father. He would not discuss him with her. And he refused to let her play the dutiful mother role all of a sudden. It was too many years too late.

"What trap is that, Mother?"

"She's not the right woman for you."

"What type of woman is the right one?"

"She isn't one of us."

"Us?"

"Don't be obtuse, darling. She doesn't have the right pedigree. For God's sake, she comes from the back woods of South Carolina."

"I wouldn't call Charleston, South Carolina the back woods."

"Well, whatever, she certainly isn't the—"

"What may or may not happen between Diana and me is our business. It certainly doesn't have anything to do with you," he said in a hard voice.

Crispina's eyes widened at his tone. "It's because of that girl you're talking this way to me."

He stiffened. "Mother, I just realized how much you dislike Diana."

"She's not for you," Crispina said. "That girl will never be your equal."

He cocked his head and stared at her intently. "Why are you really here? I don't believe you came just to take me to lunch." Not waiting for her to answer, he abruptly walked around the desk. He tried to get a grip on the anger that was rolling through his veins. He observed the woman who had given him birth. After all these years, it still surprised him how cold and unfeeling she was. Melancholy passed over him. It was hard to believe his father had loved her. Did she ever love his father...or him? He gave himself a mental shake. Crispina had never loved anyone but herself.

"The meeting for the building of the hospital wing isn't until next week. I want to know the real reason why you came to Pisano," he said.

She avoided his eyes. "You're vulnerable right now. I know John's death was hard on you. He was like a father to you."

He stiffened. Her words hit a wound he thought had healed. "His death stunned a lot of people. He left a void that will never be filled."

She blinked and cleared her throat. "Ah, yes, I can imagine it might. However, I was in the room during the reading of the will. I saw what happened when you saw her again. I don't understand why my brother left that creature the mans—"

"Mother, watch your tone. She has a name, and it is Diana. Use it."

"You dare defend her to me?"

"You have a viper's tongue. It can be poisonous," he said with barely controlled disgust.

Crispina continued as if he hadn't spoken. "I just don't know why John did such a thing. Raven's Nest has been in the Pisano family for over a hundred years. It was built as a carbon copy of our ancestral home in Italy."

"I know that," he said with little patience.

"I'll not stand by and watch a stranger inherit my ancestral home."

Fury built up in him, threatening to strangle him. He had to breathe deeply before he could speak. "You're stepping over the line, Mother. There is only so much I'll tolerate from you. Diana isn't a stranger. She was married to your brother."

"Your main concern should be Raven's Nest, and not that woman."

"Are you forgetting John has a son? Although it bothers you to have Diana at the house, her son is a Pisano, and he belongs there."

Trace saw that she seemed oddly disoriented. A hand went to her temple. "I don't know if the boy is John's." She shot him a look. Her voice was innocent enough, but there was an underlying current.

Trace didn't flinch, although the comment surprised him. He wouldn't let his mother put doubts in his mind. Crispina was a master manipulator. It gave her immense satisfaction to control people. He needed to tread carefully. She was on a hunt, and Diana was the prey.

She shrugged. "I'm sure a young girl like her married to a man old enough to be her grandfather must have found solace outside of her marriage."

"Be careful of slanderous remarks, Mother, they could get you in deep trouble."

"I'm only repeating what others have said, or thought."

"Did John tell you the boy wasn't his?"

"Oh, goodness no. My brother doted on the boy... and her." He glared at her as she tried to backpedal. "John once told me she made him happier than he'd ever been. She changed him." Her tone was snide. She paused and smoothed the already perfect French knot. Trace knew this to be a gesture to gain control of her thoughts.

"However, he did tell me when the boy was born that without a doubt he was a Pisano. I thought maybe he was trying to convince me, but my sources tell me John had a DNA test performed on the boy." She snorted, not looking at him. "He probably did it to squash the rumors."

"What rumors? he asked, but not too eagerly. He wanted to know more about Diana, but he wouldn't give Crispina the power to examine why he needed to know. Trace watched her as she strode aimlessly around the room looking at pictures on the wall. Frowning at one, she snorted. "I told John to get rid of this picture. It does nothing for the decor," she said.

"Mother—"

She glanced at him and lifted her brows at his tone. "Well, there was a lot of talk when he married her, and there was even more when she became pregnant. Everyone talked about it. No one knew about the marriage until after it happened, and then the day after he announced the marriage he took her on a honeymoon trip?"

She paused and watched him closely. "They didn't return for months. When they did, she was visibly pregnant. It was a total shock. I just couldn't believe he would have a child at his age. It was bad enough he married an outsider, but to bring a child into the marriage was unspeakable."

"For God's sake, they were married," he snapped. "Married people do have children. You called Diana an outsider, but what you meant is that John married a black woman. It really bothers you."

She looked surprised. "Well, yes, darling. This sort of thing is just not done in our circles. However, your uncle didn't seem to care about the talk, but it bothered me. It's been quite hard to hold my head up in this town. For the last five years, I've spent most of my time in New York so I wouldn't hear the snide remarks."

Trace didn't reply. He knew if he did, it wouldn't be pretty. If he spewed what he was feeling, the words would erect a wall higher than the one already in place between him and his mother.

Crispina sighed. "My main concern is you. I just want you to be okay."

"When have you ever been concerned about my well-being? I've taken care of myself since I was old enough to walk."

The color drained from Crispina's face. Then she arched her back and gave him a direct stare.

"I'm your mother. I have always had your best interests at heart."

"Passing me off to nannies and teachers was best for me? It certainly was good for you. It alleviated you of any obligations."

Crispina stiffened, lifted her chin, and shot him a cold look. "You've had the best of everything that life could offer. I'll not be judged by you."

Trace refused to debate what type of mother she had been. It was too many years too late, and he honestly didn't care anymore. When he was younger, he'd wondered why she couldn't love him and wished she at least cared about him the way she cared about her jet-set lifestyle and friends. He had excelled at academics and sports, but it had never seemed to impress Crispina. She acted as if he didn't exist. Many times, he'd wondered why she took the time to have him; she certainly didn't desire to be a mother. He gave her a hard, unflinching look. Silently, connecting with the coldness in her eyes, he stood still with arms folded across his chest. It always made her nervous. This was one time he was glad it did.

Her hand shook as she absently touched the pearls at her neck, indicating she wasn't as in control as she appeared. "Trace, I couldn't believe what I saw when I walked into this office. I don't begrudge you some sort of entertainment, but, darling, there are so many respectable and eligible women in our circle who would be more than glad to have a relationship, or at least a date, with you."

"What bothers you the most, Mother, that you saw me kissing Diana or the fact that I might have already taken her to my bed?"

She blanched. "Don't be vulgar, Trace."

Trace lost patience. "Look, I'm not fooled by your concern or your excuses. I'm warning you, only once; don't poke your nose into my private life. I'll not tolerate your interference."

"Are you threatening me?"

He placed his hands at his waist and gave her a cruel smile. "You know I never threaten in business or life, but I do make good on a promise."

Crispina threw him a look that would have most men cowering. She was angry. He knew she would be a worthy opponent in battle.

"You expect me to sit back and watch you run after that woman and sully the Montgomery name? I watched my brother do it to the Pisano name, but I'll be damned if my only child will do it, too."

"I expect you to stay out of my business."

"When it comes to her, I can't."

"I know you've never liked Diana, but five years should've given you enough time to overcome your dislike."

"I barely tolerated her marriage to my brother," she sneered. "I'll never accept that woman for my son." Disgust was evident on her face. Trace came from around the desk, his hands stiff at his side.

"When Diana and I first starting dating, you showed your dislike. I never said anything, trying to give you time to see what a kind person she was."

"Kind?" she said nastily. "That woman dropped you to marry a billionaire. How dare you defend her to me?"

Trace shook his head, knowing Crispina would never change. "I'm not going to defend Diana to you because you have already made up your mind. I always knew you were a snob, but a bigot is another thing."

"We are descendants of royalty. Your father's family can be traced back to the fifteenth century. If that makes me a snob or bigot, so be it. I'll not apologize for it," she said haughtily.

He stared at his mother as if she were a stranger. In many ways she was just that…a complete stranger. Ending the conversation, she walked toward the door. The coldness of his voice stopped her in her tracks. "I won't let your poison touch Diana or her son."

His mother turned and looked at him. "I'm warning you, Trace. Don't for one minute think that woman will become a part of the Montgomery family. I won't allow it."

"Don't wage a battle with me. You won't like the odds." Trace's tone was hard and controlled.

Crispina's lips tightened. "Well, I guess I received my answer." The door closed firmly behind her.

He stared into the empty space and slowly released his anger. He rubbed his tight jaw to relieve the tension. How far would she go to protect what she perceived as his best interest? His father had been a strong man, but his love for his wife had made him more accepting of the things she did. Trace hadn't been quite two years old when Crispina left his father in England to move back to the States. She hated the isolation of the countryside and the damp weather. It didn't matter that she'd broken her marriage promise to live six months of the year in Britain. That was the beginning of the twenty-year separation. Randall Montgomery had held out the hope that Crispina would eventually come back to him. She never did. Trace had talked his father into dissolving the marriage. He'd started the divorce proceeding, but was killed in a boating accident before it was finalized. Trace vowed not to be like his father when it came to a woman. Crispina's coldness and disregard for her husband's feelings had almost destroyed Randall Montgomery. Trace frowned. He no longer loved Diana, and therefore she had no power over him. He wasn't in danger of losing his heart or becoming weak.

Chapter 5

Trace stood in Diana's office doorway and observed her while she focused on the large global map on the wall. She was concentrating and unaware of his presence. Diana had been avoiding him, and he didn't like it. He knew she didn't want to face him after what had happened in his office. To accept the pleasure she'd felt in his arms would mean surrender, and one thing Diana wouldn't do is surrender.

It had been a long couple of weeks; he had been busy running both companies, and by the time he returned to the mansion it was usually well past midnight. In the morning, she was normally on her morning jog by the time he descended the stairs at 6 a.m. She stayed clear of the house until he left for the office.

After his mother took leave of his office that fateful morning, he had tried to smooth things over with Diana, but to no avail. She was even more wary of him now. Crispina's untimely entrance had Diana retreating.

He needed to regroup and devise a new plan of attack. He wanted her, but he wanted revenge more... or did he? He didn't love her. His brain rebelled in confusion and his heart raced at the revelation that he could still love her. He breathed deeply, trying to gain control. No, he wouldn't allow himself to love her again.

He caught his breath when she reached for a push-pin on the map and her dress rode up a little, revealing the smooth contour of the back of her thighs. A rush of desire hit him full force as he remembered what had transpired in his office. God, he couldn't get over how she'd responded to him. *Stop torturing yourself. It's only lust.* Is it really? He closed his eyes to clear the traitorous thought.

In the past five years he'd made love to other women—some more beautiful than Diana—but none ignited him the way Diana did.

"I see you're busy," he said as he stepped through the open door and closed it. "I hope you don't mind me stopping by unannounced."

Diana spun around, her face showing shock that she quickly masked. Confusion marked her lovely features for a moment, but was quickly replaced with a frown. She was good at covering her feelings, but she hadn't been quick enough. She was happy to see him. Trace knew she expected him to be in New York and not standing in her office.

She smoothed the wrap dress that hugged her curves. Her fingers ran through her hair. The gesture stretched the fabric across her breasts and accented their fullness. Her long hair was loose and feathered around her face. She looked young and innocent, but he knew better. His breath caught in his throat as he remembered a time when her hair was wild across his pillow as he made love to her. Trace knew she favored dresses over slacks. This was one morning he was glad she did.

"Yes, I'm a little busy planning the ad campaign for the new wines that are coming out in September." She bit her lips. Trace smiled, glad that he had an effect on her. "When did you get back?" She licked her lips drawing his attention to them.

"An hour ago." His eyes roamed the soft lips he had kissed so often in the past and still craved. He cleared his throat. "I heard from Dominic that your ideas for the new ads are great."

"I'm glad he approves. I value his opinion."

Dominic Mello was a Pisano cousin in charge of all of the Pisano wineries. He was revered all over the world for his expertise in the winemaking field.

"It seems John made a good decision appointing you the VP of Marketing."

"I worked hard for the position, Trace. Contrary to what people may think, John didn't give me the position because we were married. People forget that I graduated from the Wharton School of Business."

"I wasn't implying that the job was given to you, Diana. I'm on the board of directors. I know your worth."

"Thank you."

"You're welcome."

He looked around the room, walked to the outer office, and turned toward her. "Where is Susan? I heard she's your right hand. I haven't seen her since I've been back."

Susan Torres had worked for Pisano since she was eighteen. Now thirty, she was Diana's senior marketing manager. Susan had started out as a receptionist and had gone to college at night to earn her degree.

A smile came to Diana's face, mesmerizing Trace.

"Sunday is her parents' thirty-fifth wedding anniversary. I gave her today off to finish the loose ends for the surprise party she is giving them. She wants everything to be perfect."

"I want you to know you were right about Susan. It's a huge responsibility but I heard she's doing a fantastic job on the Japanese project. She doesn't need a watchdog."

Diana gave him a wide smile and look that said 'I told you so.' "Is that an apology?"

He grinned. "I've already given you a pound of flesh. What more do you want?"

"Thanks for apologizing. I knew everything would turn out to be perfect." Her smile was infectious, and he was blinded by its invisible pull.

"I can understand wanting everything to be perfect," he murmured. His gaze held hers and wouldn't let go.

She exhaled nervously. "Thank you for telling me about Susan. I knew she could handle the job."

He gave a faint smile at her prim and proper tone. "I also came to take you to lunch."

She blinked. "Why?"

"I want to go over the marketing strategy for the new high-rise." His eyes watched her face, taking in her consternation.

"Isn't the design department in charge of the project? I've already sent over the preliminary ad and promo."

"I know. I've already seen what you sent. However, I had a meeting with them and gave some input. I'd now like to share my ideas with you."

"You seem to be up to speed."

"For the last few months, I have been overseeing Pisano and Montgomery operations from the London office. Using Webex, I was kept abreast of what was going on."

"I see."

He saw she was hurt at the fact she wasn't consulted on the decision. "I don't think you do. The board and I made a decision to keep things quiet. Our competition can be vicious. If they thought for one minute that Pisano had suffered a weakness due to John's death, a hostile takeover could've been imminent. With me running the business, there was never a dip in our strength."

"I do understand. However, you don't need to take me to lunch." She turned back to the map and began to remove some of the pushpins, dropping them into a box on her desk. "Just send me a memo with your ideas or whatever revisions you want done."

She was uneasy and appeared to be desperate to keep him at arm's length. He realized she didn't trust herself with him. It gave him pleasure to know that.

"Are you afraid of being alone with me, Diana? I promise we'll lunch in a crowded restaurant."

She glanced at him. "I'm not afraid. I just don't see the need."

"You're still running."

She bristled. "I'm not running. I'm extremely busy."

"So busy I haven't seen you in days."

"You've been in New York."

"Only for two days."

"Raven's Nest is a very large mansion," Diana declared.

"Excuses, Diana?"

"I'm not going to play this game with you, Trace."

"What game?"

She ignored his question, but he waited. "I'm not having lunch with you."

"Why not? It's only lunch."

By the tightening of her lips, he could see she wasn't happy. He could always tell when he pushed her too far. Right now, she was pissed. And it made him smile. He liked it when Diana let go and showed emotion instead of giving him a cold stare.

"You can have the revisions sent to me. I'll make the necessary changes and send them to design," she said.

"Dismissing me?" He had forgotten how much she hated confrontations. She had a habit of changing the flow of conversation when she was cornered or felt uncomfortable. She could do it so smoothly that most times it went unnoticed. "I won't be dismissed."

"No. You probably won't. And that's always been your problem. You don't really care or listen to anyone. It doesn't matter to you that I want to be left alone. You don't see me as a woman who just doesn't want to become involved with you. You have absolutely no idea who I am or what I want. You've never taken the time to find out."

To his surprise, her beautiful brown eyes clouded and she blinked feverishly. She took long breaths to get control. It wasn't like Diana to be so emotional. Something was going on with her. He wondered what it could be. Sooner or later he would find out. Her tears wouldn't make up for what she'd done, but it might be a small start.

Abruptly, he moved around the desk to stand in front of her. She took a step back, putting a small space between them. He closed the gap and reached to stroke a finger lightly across her cheek. Just touching her, the electricity vibrated through his hand and up his arm. Again, his mind betrayed him as he remembered how much he had loved her once. He shook with the force of it and fought hard for control. He wanted to banish her sadness and see her genuine smile.

What was wrong with him? This was the woman who'd betrayed him and married another man...but he still wanted her.

"I'm not going anywhere, Diana. No matter how much you protest I know you want me. You proved it in my office."

"I knew you'd bring that up."

"I won't let you pretend it never happened."

"It was a mistake that I'll not be repeating."

"Diana, don't throw down the gauntlet and expect me not to pick it up. We started something and it will be finished." He paused. "We could be perfect together. Remember how it was five years ago?" His voice was husky as he moved in closer to her. "After a night in my bed, you'll never want to leave it again."

"This is about sex."

"That and more."

"Are you saying you've spent the past five years pining for me?" There was a hint of sarcasm in her tone, but the tiny pulse beating at her throat told him she wasn't as indifferent as she pretended to be.

"Our relationship was too much for you five years ago. Too powerful. Too consuming. You were barely twenty and didn't know how to control the fire that burned between us. You were scared, so you ran," he explained. "You weren't ready for us." He grinned. "Never has any woman affected me the way you do."

She frowned. "Don't expect me to fall at your feet."

He laughed. "I don't expect you to fall at my feet, just into my arms."

"This is no laughing matter, Trace."

The look on his face turned serious. "Are you still so naïve that you don't recognize powerful chemistry between a man and woman? When the time comes, you won't have a choice. Your need for me will out-weigh your desire to run from me."

She shook her head in awe. "Your arrogance is un-believable. You think all you have to do is say the words and it will happen. You'll not control me. I won't let it happen."

Trace looked at Diana and realized it wasn't going to be as easy as he'd thought. Since Diana, women in his life had been interchangeable, actresses and mod-els hoping to snag him, even society debutantes and royal princesses with the right pedigrees, but they had all left him empty.

"You think not? I want you in my life again."

"What?"

"I'm the heir apparent to two corporations. Although there are many cousins, your son will eventually inherit Pisano. He needs to be groomed for the position."

"Is this some sort of joke?" she asked, a deep frown marring her features.

"Wouldn't you like for your son to be my heir? Just think, Diana, with my shares he will control everything."

"You don't know anything about Nicky."

"But I know you, and that John was his father. He helped raise me, and I know what kind of man he was."

"What do you get out of this?"

"The chance to know you again."

She ignored his comment. "Nicky might not want Pisano. Besides, you'll marry one day and have children."

"No, I won't." He'd only wanted to marry one woman. He ran his hands through his dark locks. "Look, your son has Pisano blood. As my heir, it'll make him next in line to inherit everything."

A twisted smile lifted the corners of her mouth. "And what would your mother have to say about this?" For a brief moment, he saw a flash of pain in her eyes.

"My mother has nothing to do with this. She'll accept my decision." And she would, he thought, because she didn't want to lose him.

Diana laughed cruelly. "It's no secret that Crispina and I don't like each other. You honestly believe your mother would meekly accept her only son being with a woman she detests? She barely tolerated me five years ago. Do you think she'll let you enter into a relationship with me again? You need to think again, Trace. It's not going to happen." She took a step from him. "Your mother will never accept this. But whatever happens, I won't back down from Crispina, not this time."

"I am my own person. Crispina doesn't rule me."

She laughed again. "I'll not change for anyone. I love being who I am. I come from generations of strong, proud, hard-working people. Your family could never understand why John married me. But John loved me and I loved him." Trace stiffened. "I was a misfit in the midst of money, power, and an old lineage. I wasn't accepted, nor was I liked. I learned to survive, and it made me stronger. I'll not go through that turmoil with your family again."

He cupped her face gently with one hand. "I don't want you to change. I like you just the way you are. When I first saw you sitting in John's office, my interest was piqued and I wanted to get to know you. I know you felt the instantaneous connection as much as I did. You were the first woman who had ever truly interested me. I didn't see a black woman, but a woman I wanted to get to know a whole lot better. Your no-

nonsense attitude and outspoken ways captivated me and your beauty made me hotter than hell."

She moved slightly and his hand fell from her face. "Too much has happened between us. I have too much at stake."

With mounting exasperation, he realized she was determined to keep her distance. He had forgotten how stubborn she could be. However, he refused to give up. He wanted her...badly. She would be his.

"Diana, we were once lovers, but we were also friends. Give me the chance to prove we can at least be friends again. You ended our relationship prematurely. We were good together, and I believe we can be again. Give me time to prove it. If your feelings change, we'll move the relationship to another level. If, at the end of the two months, you want to remain friends, we will."

She stared unblinkingly at him. "Have you been drinking or something? You can't be serious."

"I'm very serious, Diana. I made a mistake not to come after you, a mistake I regret. I want a chance to rectify things."

"Why?"

"I need closure," he said.

She chuckled. "Shouldn't that be my line? What kind of relationship do you want?"

"What do you think, Diana?"

"Maybe you want me as your mistress again. It would put me in a humiliating position, and you would have your revenge."

He frowned because she was closer to the truth than she could imagine. "Five years ago, we were lovers in a relationship. You were never my mistress."

"You didn't love me then, nor do you love me now, Trace."

He looked at her and persisted. "I want you."

Confusion clouded her eyes. "Why me?"

"I like you, Diana. You're smart and I admire you. You never let adversaries stop you from making your life successful. We used to laugh together and really enjoy each other's company. I want to explore that again."

"What about what happened five years ago? Are we going to pretend it never happened?"

He shrugged. "The past is where it belongs. Let's keep it there."

"Just like that we pick up where we left off five years ago?"

"Diana, we never made promises."

"But—"

Holding up his hand, he stopped her. "Look, we both made mistakes. I think this is a second chance for the both of us."

"I have a request."

"What is it?

"At the reading of the will, you inherited everything of John's. I don't want to be beholden to you. I want control of my son's inheritance."

"Your son's inheritance is set up to be administered by me."

"You can relinquish your role."

"Your son is a Pisano. He'll one day be running a billion-dollar company and will need to know how to rule. I can teach him that."

"I'll not be under your thumb. I can provide what he needs."

He inhaled deeply. Irritated, he ran his fingers through his hair, making the ends stand to attention. "You're not under my control, Diana."

"Really? John left money and shares to Nicky, but I didn't receive anything but half of Raven's Nest. Saying it was a shock is an understatement. He knew I was capable of administering Nicky's trust."

He paused and looked at her with new conviction. Diana was a lot tougher than he'd thought. He would have to tread lightly with her if he intended to get his revenge. He wanted his fill of her, and then he would drop her just as she'd done him. He had every intention of getting her to fall in love with him. He wanted her to feel the pain and devastation he felt. Thinking about her in his bed made his heart beat at an alarming rate. He had to be careful he didn't fall into the trap he had set for her. He couldn't let that happen.

"I'll compromise. I'll make sure I get your input when it comes to your son's trust."

She stared at him without blinking. He knew she wanted something else. He didn't have to wait long.

"I want it in writing," she said.

He bristled at her words. "My word is my bond. But to make you see my word is good, I'll ask Martin to draw up the papers on your behalf."

"Good."

"You're a good negotiator."

"I had the best teacher, my husband."

"Yes, you did." He was silent for a moment. "We'll start this new friendship with dinner tonight."

"Are you asking or demanding?" she asked with a frown, her hands planted on her hips. She looked ready to do battle.

He grinned. "I'm asking."

"Since you're asking, it doesn't have to be cozy, just good food. While you try to make something develop between us, I might as well get a good meal out of it."

Trace laughed. "If you want to fool yourself, be my guest. I'll see you tonight."

He turned to leave her office but she stopped him. "Trace, don't think you'll seduce me. What happened in your office will not happen again."

He gave her a crooked smile. "If you believe that then I know you are fooling yourself." He walked out and closed the door quietly behind him.

Chapter 6

Over the weeks that followed, their conversations became more complex—a little guarded but stimulating. The past was never brought up for discussion, which meant unanswered questions lay between them. By the end of the first week, they had enjoyed heated and serious talks and long walks; a new friendship formed, with a tenuous trust beginning to evolve.

Trace indulged her love for the arts and ventured to the theatre with her one night. Afterwards, as they shared a quiet, intimate dinner at the famed Biltmore Hotel, they encountered friends of Crispina. A surprised look crossed their faces on seeing them together. It quickly turned to displeasure at their obvious intimacy. Trace held her hand and didn't release it. Self-conscious, Diana tried to remove her hand, but Trace held it firmly but gently. After a few moments of uncomfortable chit-chat, the couple said their goodbyes.

Trace reached for his wine glass and swirled the liquid around. He seemed fixated on its movement. "Are you enjoying the music?" Finally, he took a swallow and set the fragile stemware on the table in a controlled matter.

"Yes. It's lovely."

He leaned back. "Why are you uncomfortable?"

"I'm not."

His voice was strained. She could tell he was angry. "Come on, Diana. You can pretend with yourself but not with me. You tried to withdraw your hand when Crispina's friends arrived."

Taking her time to answer, she took a sip of her drink. "I was surprised to see them."

"Really? Or was it the fact that you were with me?"

"I don't have anything to be ashamed of," she said.

"I didn't know if you were going to get up and run or slide under the table," he said sarcastically.

"You're being overly dramatic."

"I don't think so. It matters to you what they think."

She sighed. He was vying for a fight, but she refused to get angry. He didn't want her to have any doubts about their relationship. But she wasn't comfortable in public, and it showed. "Of course it matters what people think. I have to live in this town. But I don't let it dictate my life."

"Who are you trying convince, me or yourself?"

"Trace, we had a relationship in the past."

"I know. And you never had a problem being with me in public. Why now?"

"I wasn't John's widow."

"Ah, I see. Being married to John made you more aware?"

"It wasn't easy being a younger woman married to an older man. I never got used to the stares and the whispers, but I never let them see me sweat."

"You liked having them call you the Ice Princess."

She inwardly cringed. "I heard people called me that. I didn't care because I know who I am." No one knew how much the words wounded her.

"If you say so."

"Look, I have nothing to hide. I just didn't expect to see them."

"Are you sure there isn't more to it? John has been gone a year. I believe it's appropriate for you to date."

"He wouldn't want me to be alone. Anyway, I would never do anything to embarrass his memory."

"And being with me does that?"

"I didn't say that. You're putting words in my mouth."

"Then what are you saying?"

"People can be vicious. Words can be damaging. I have a son to think about. I don't want my decisions to hurt him."

His tone serious, he said, "No one will dare to say anything to you. You have me now."

"Do I?" She paused, giving him a sharp look. "For how long?"

"For as long as you want, and in more ways than you can imagine." His voice smooth and hypnotic, he reached over and took her hand. She tried hard to ignore the heat simmering between them, but each passing day it was getting harder to avoid the need to recapture the magic they'd once enjoyed. The attraction was stronger than before, and trying to fight it was becoming a losing battle. Although Trace wanted more than the occasional touch, he kept his distance and never made a move. At times she would catch a strange look on his face, but it would pass so quickly she would wonder if she had imagined it. It was hard to interpret a complicated man like Trace, who didn't generally show emotion. He'd made it obvious he wanted her in his bed. Want and need were a part of Trace's persona, but love wasn't in the equation. Being a red-blooded man who enjoyed women was normal for most men, but for Trace it was even more so. Resisting Trace's allure was a full time task. His magnetic pull was strong and addictive.

"I'll not tolerate anyone hurting you, Diana. If they do, they will have me to answer to."

She shivered. He was still classified by many as a hard and ruthless businessman. When it came to running Pisano, he could be unrelenting, making sure the executive board was on top of their game. He didn't take kindly to people who took their jobs for granted. His explosive temper had showed itself when an executive came unprepared to a meeting. Even the strongest person would cringe at one of his cold and direct glares. Enemies were many, and friends were few.

What people thought of him didn't faze him. Despite it all, he was respected as a man of great strength and intelligence, a force to be reckoned with.

"Thanks, but I can take care of myself."

He let loose his gorgeous smile. She caught her breath at the brilliance of it.

"I'm certain you can. But humor me and let me have the pleasure of protecting what belongs to me."

She bristled, as he'd known she would at the remark. She prided herself on being strong, highly intelligent, and, yes, sometimes stubborn, but she knew she was no match against Trace's power. His ability to eradicate a person, whether it was business or personal, was legendary. One didn't cross Trace, nor ask for forgiveness or another chance to do business with him. He could be a cold and rancorous man. However, marriage to John had taught Diana not to back down from a fight, and for that she was grateful. Trace wouldn't find the naïve young girl of five years ago. He was in for a very rude awakening.

For a weekend trip, they sailed down the coast. They watched the dolphins jumping high out of the water, gasping with excitement and joy at seeing the beautiful animals at play. Then Trace let her take a turn behind the wheel of the huge motor yacht. He taught her to steer. It was a lot different from driving a car. The exhilaration of the experience was powerful and liberating.

As the sun disappeared, they sat on deck watching seagulls as they flew over searching for a chance to grab food from unsuspecting boaters. It was a beautiful evening and very relaxing and peaceful. Leaning back against the lounge chair, she sipped a chilled glass of fruit juice and closed her eyes, enjoying the evening air.

Although relaxed, they were acutely aware of each other. Accepting Trace's weekend invitation had been a major step. She was nervous, wondering about what would happen next. She blew hot and cold and was angry with herself because she couldn't make a decision to be with him or not. They were enjoying themselves, and she saw a side of Trace he had never shown before. Had he really changed that much in the last five years?

Trace lay in the lounge chair beside her looking handsome and virile. His blue polo shirt enhanced his well-built body. With his arms stretched above his head, his eyes concealed behind sunglasses, and his breathing slow and even, he appeared to be asleep. The white shorts showed off his tan and muscular legs. He always tanned easily, and being in the sun most of the morning had given a beautiful golden hue to his skin.

The last bit of sun lit his face. He made a physically potent picture and she felt a tremor inside. She was losing control—fast.

He turned and caught her staring at him. He removed his Giorgio sunglasses. Blue eyes stared back at her with a burning intensity. "Are you glad you came?" he asked, not breaking eye contact as he swung his legs to the side of the lounge.

"Yes, I am." She took a sip of her drink. "It's beautiful out here."

"Good. I want you to enjoy yourself. You've been working hard."

Surprised, her mouth gaped open. She didn't realize he knew the effort she'd put into making sure the two major marketing segments due in a week were completed. "Are you feeling empathy for me?" she quipped with a smile.

He grinned. "No, you have a team of marketing managers and graphic designers who work for you. You don't have to do everything yourself."

"I enjoy what I do."

"Everyone on your team knows how dedicated you are," he drawled, lifting his glass of lemonade. "You don't have to prove anything to anyone."

She raised her glass and touched it against his. "Here's to a great marketing strategy."

"And to us," he added.

She pulled the glass back. "There's no us, Trace. There's you and there's me. Two separate entities."

"Really?" His voice was low and seductive. "We're together—alone on the ocean."

The pit of her stomach began to churn. "We're not *alone*. There are crew and staff on board."

"For all intents and purposes, we are alone. The staff and crew work for me," he emphasized. "No one would dare disturb us."

She gave a small laugh. "I've always known you were arrogant, but you continue to astound me," she said, and caught a look of surprise on his face. That in turn surprised her. He really had no idea how arrogant he was. He expected everyone to conform to his wishes, commands, and dislikes as if they were the norm.

"I'm confident. I don't see anything wrong with that."

"There is a difference between being confident and just cocky." She leaned back against the chair and raised her face to the fleeting sun. She inhaled deeply, smelling the saltiness of the water as the breeze gently blew across her.

He gave a hearty laugh. Diana raised her head up and looked at him, spellbound. She didn't believe she had ever heard him laugh with such robust abandon.

"You amaze me, Diana. Five years ago you would've never said that to me. You were such a nice girl," he teased.

She rolled her eyes at him. "I'm still a nice girl." She leaned back again and closed her eyes.

There was a comfortable silence. "Are you ready to concede?" he asked.

"What?"

"That we have moved to the next level in our relationship."

She turned toward him and searched his eyes. He was waiting for a response. She started to act as if she didn't know what he was talking about, but decided against it. She tilted her nose in the air and gave him a haughty look. "I concede to a tenuous friendship and nothing else."

He grabbed his heart. "Oh, Diana, you wound me."

She frowned. She wanted to stick her tongue out at him, but it was a childish gesture. Instead, she rolled her eyes at him again and tilted her nose in the air. "You haven't convinced me I want a relationship with you, and you won't."

He threw back his head and laughed again. *He is going to disrupt every sleeping creature in the ocean if he keeps that up*, she thought.

"We'll see. I still have time left before the will is satisfied," he said.

Despite his relaxed posture, those piercing blue eyes studied her thoughtfully for a moment, giving nothing away.

She wasn't fooled. Trace had set out to get her in bed. Once he'd made up his mind to do or to get something, it was accomplished come hell or high water. How long could she evade him? She was afraid she would succumb, no matter how much she fought the inevitable. But she wanted to be the one to control when and where it happened.

Her nose picked up his masculine scent. He had ventured near without her realizing it. He leaned closer to her. The dark stubble on his jaw seemed to intensify his masculinity; she swallowed, trying to clear the lump that had formed in her throat.

"It's time for dinner." He offered his hand and waited. A warm rush came over her when she placed her hand in his. Feeling she had crossed over another threshold, she stood. Too close, they stared at each other, breathing in deep breaths. Diana was the first to break the connection.

"I didn't realize it was that late. I'm starved." She slowly pulled her hand from his.

"I see nothing has changed. You still love to eat," he said, leaving her no doubt that he was referring to more than food.

Her heart flipped. Every angle of his strong, handsome face was concentrated on her. The arrogant prince of an extremely rich family with ancestry that could be traced back centuries, he represented his legacy well in his demeanor. These past weeks in his presence had been savory torture. Both of them were aware of each other but hadn't given in to their desires. They'd redirected their energy into building their relationship. He hadn't tried to seduce her, not once. But she wished he had—didn't she? She was afraid to answer the question.

"Food is my weakness. I'm a certified foodie, but I try to be careful what I eat. The pounds can sneak on without you noticing."

His eyes glided up and down her body. "There's nothing wrong with your body. In fact, you could stand to add a couple of pounds. You're beautiful." He paused. "No, let me correct that. You're perfect." His voice had grown husky. It brought a warm flush to her face and a tingle in the lower part of her body.

She tried to hurry past him and stumbled. He caught her arm. "Thank you. I'm going to shower and change. Give me thirty minutes and I'll meet you in the stateroom."

He chuckled and released her. "I remembered it usually takes you thirty minutes to shower and two hours to dress."

"Having a small child changed all that." She reached for her sarong and wrapped it around her hips. The entire time he watched her movements. Finally, she grabbed her sunglasses, put them on, and walked away.

She released a nervous breath when she reached the bottom of the steps.

Chapter 7

Trace swirled the amber liquid in the bottom of the glass and leaned back against the sofa, listening to the soft jazz piping into the room.

Diana sat at the far end of the sofa, her eyes closed and bare feet tucked under her dress. She held a glass of wine in her hand. She looked peaceful and relaxed, but he could tell how tense she was by her grip on the glass.

She came to dinner in a flowing white sundress. The bodice dipped low enough to give a peek at hidden treasures beneath the fabric.

Diana's hair hung to her shoulders in a cascade of curls. White high-heeled sandals adorned her slim feet.

She had kept her promise and met Trace in the stateroom within thirty minutes. He was amazed at what she'd accomplished in such a small amount of time. Each time she inhaled, her breasts rose against the thinness of the dress. He understood why his body reacted but he refused to examine why his heart fluttered at her mere presence.

He wanted this woman, and this time it would be different. He would be completely in control of the situation. He would get her out of his system and then, just as she had, he would walk away.

❧

She could feel him watching her. She refused to respond to the pull of his gaze. Her mind was mulling over how wonderful the evening had been. Overall, it had been perfect. Trace had been considerate and charming.

She knew he wanted her. She could feel it at that very moment. He had asked for a relationship but she hadn't felt pressured to move their friendship along to something deeper. She inwardly smiled. Friendship; was that what they called it nowadays?

During dinner, they'd talked about many things. They laughed over the oysters Rockefeller and argued politics over the crème brulée. Now the evening was ending and they would retire to their separate rooms… or would they?

She shut off those thoughts for now; friendship was enough for her. Who was she kidding? She knew where she wanted the night to end. She wanted to make love with him just this one night, nothing more. If he made a move to seduce her, she wouldn't have the strength to stop him. She wanted to feel the pleasure only he could give her.

Get a grip, girl! She pulled her wayward thoughts together and tried to focus on other things. But she continued to drift. It was so intimate to sit together in the calm of night listening to music. It was something they'd never shared in their previous relationship. They had been lovers, but she couldn't honestly say they were ever friends.

They could never go back to what they had before. Too much had happened. For once, she was going to live in the moment and damn the consequences.

She stood and walked to the balcony overlooking the now dark waters. The moon was full and the stars twinkled, far brighter than on land.

Diana felt his presence before he reached her. It had been that way since the first day she met him. The connection they had was inexplicable.

"Are you okay?" he asked, studying her as if he was trying to consume her thoughts. It made her uncomfortable.

She nodded, still looking at the ocean.

He leaned against the rail. They were both silent, each deep into their own thoughts. Finally, Diana moved from the balcony and walked back to the stateroom. Trace followed. "What is it, Diana?" he said with a frown.

She walked to the counter, poured a glass of water, took a sip, and looked at him. She was silent for a moment. "Sometimes I wonder if I ever knew you." She placed the glass on the counter and entwined her fingers. "These past weeks have been good. We've both had fun, and some serious moments, too. But I don't believe I have ever seen the real Trace."

A smile twitched on his lips. "I believe you know me quite well."

She ignored his mockery. "Do you believe in love?" she asked abruptly.

He hesitated. "Do you want the truth or the romantic illusion?"

"I have my answer. If you have to ask that, you don't believe in love."

His eyes became guarded. "How do you know that? Because I don't come across the way you think I should?"

"You're a complex man, Trace. You don't feel emotion."

"You've been in my bed, Diana. Wasn't I expressive enough for you? "

Irritated, she frowned at him. "So, finally we're back to sex."

"Sex can be an expression of love."

She caught her breath at his words. He could be infuriating one minute and, just as quickly, become a charming romantic. He leaned toward her but she moved away from him and resumed watching the dark waters. He silently observed her for a long moment.

Finally, he walked away, leaving her alone on the balcony.

❦❦

Sprawled on the sofa with a drink in his hand, Trace watched as Diana strolled in from the balcony. She had been out there for almost an hour. She moved around the room in a restless manner. Finally, she lifted a magazine from the coffee table and sat in the chair opposite him. The strains of David Sanborn's saxophone flowed through the room, causing her to sway to the melody while she turned the magazine pages. When she looked up and caught him looking at her, her body became stiff.

The door opened and one of the staff came in with a tray of assorted fruit and cookies and coffee. When the door closed, Trace stood and moved to the counter.

"Would like dessert and coffee?" he asked without looking at her.

"No," she answered in a low voice and continued flipping the pages.

"You were on the balcony for a long time."

"A little bit."

"You had a lot on your mind?" He turned and rested his hands on his hips.

She laid the magazine on the table, stood and went to the wet bar. She poured a glass of water, took a sip, and set it down. "Somewhat," she said.

He moved toward her. "Anything I can help you with?"

"No." She picked up the glass again and took another sip. She kept her eyes on the liquid.

"Okay." Reaching her, his eyes swept her beautiful face. "You're a beautiful woman." He lifted a hand and ran it through her thick and lustrous curls, allowing them to fall unrestrained against her shoulders.

Her eyes shot to him and she cleared her voice. "Maybe we should have dessert and coffee."

He cupped her cheek and smiled. "I have no need for coffee, but dessert, now that is another matter."

"Why must everything be a game to you?"

"Game? Not a game. Need, want, desire, maybe, but definitely not a game." He pulled her to him and kissed her, pushing his fingers through the strands of her hair. He was consumed by fire and had no desire to evade its heat. It felt so right to have her in his arms and to no longer fight what they both wanted. Repeatedly, his tongue delved inside her mouth, claiming her, taking all she had to give.

Her scent filled him. Her taste inflamed him. His body physically ached to connect with her. He moved the straps of her dress, pulling the it down to expose her hard nipples.

"Trace." She called his name and it enflamed him even more.

"I have never wanted a woman as much as I want you. I burn, Diana, only for you." His mouth closed over her nipple and she bit her lip and groaned.

He lifted his head and looked deep into her eyes for confirmation. She raised both arms and wound them around his neck, pulling him against her, tasting him with the desperate urgency of a dehydrated person finding water.

He pulled back, sucking in a deep breath of air. She followed suit, her lungs struggling for needed air.

"I'm taking you to my bed." His voice was barely recognizable. Diana nodded.

"I want to hear you say it. I don't want any misunderstanding about what is going to happen."

"I want you to make love to me, Trace."

He paused, giving her the chance to change her mind. "Are you sure?"

She smiled at him and said with conviction, "Yes."

With one swift movement, he scooped her in his arms, as though she weighed nothing, and headed out of the stateroom to the master suite. Finding the bedroom was easy. The wide double doors were flung open, as though ready and waiting to invite them both in. The lights in the plush, gigantic bedroom were dimmed and the moonlight streamed through the open balcony door. The white sheer curtains swayed seductively with the breeze from the ocean as he strolled with her in his arms toward the bed.

The bed was wide and high and covered in a white and beige duvet. A mountain of pillows was stacked against the brass headboard. He cursed and pulled the duvet cover from the bed, sweeping the pillows heedlessly to the floor. Then he deposited her on her feet, again giving her time to change her mind. She didn't. Her eyes burned into him. He wanted this woman like no other, but he was unsettled. He had slept with her years ago, but tonight felt like the first time.

Biting down on her bottom lip, Diana lifted her hands to the front of his shirt and undid the buttons. While he stood there unmoving, she pushed the shirt off his shoulders and down his arms to the floor. Then her hands slid across his chest. He inhaled sharply as the soft brush of her fingers glided over the hair that covered his torso. He almost exploded when her thumbnail stroked the tip of one flat nipple.

He grabbed her hands to stop her exploration. There was only so much he could take. His mouth came down on hers with a fierceness that surprised even him. He was desperate. His tongue parted her lips, and she opened for him. Their tongues twisted together in a heated dance that was only a taste of things to come. Her breath caught in her throat, and her head swayed to the side. Diana's knees buckled and she fell back onto the bed.

He stood watching her, trying to gain control of his emotions. He didn't want to spoil this moment by leaving her unsatisfied. His hand went to his waist and he yanked the belt free in one swift movement.

His hand hovered on the button of his trousers. Diana's eyes went to the fly of his pants and she licked her bottom lip. He nearly lost it. His trousers joined the shirt and belt on the floor, and the state of his arousal was all too obvious against the cloth of his black silk briefs.

He wanted to rip her clothes off and plunge into her, satisfy the need that had taken him over, but that, he knew, he couldn't do. He had never taken a woman to his bed without thinking of her pleasure. He wanted to pleasure Diana, very, very slowly.

In the dim light he stood at the foot of the bed, naked, showing her how much he wanted her.

"I want you completely naked," he said huskily. "I want to feel your skin next to mine."

He touched every part of her body. He wanted her to feel how much he wanted her. His self-imposed sexual hibernation was over.

He stripped her very slowly and looked at her as if seeing her for the first time. He kissed her mouth, her face, her neck, trailed his tongue along her collarbone, and suckled on her nipples while she twisted under him.

He shifted slightly, covering her with his lean, powerful frame as his mouth took hers again. His kiss was possessive and urgent. She arched in an involuntary movement. He groaned approval at her action as he lifted his mouth from hers and transferred his attention back to her breasts.

Mason flicked his tongue over her dark nipples and she pressed against him in an attempt to soothe the throbbing ache that was consuming both of them.

"You are mine." He promised in husky tones and proceeded to brand himself on her body. He kissed and caressed every part of her body except that one most intimate place that ached to be touched. He licked the top of her thigh, dragged slow kisses over her stomach, always withholding what she wanted most. She shifted and the ache inside him intensified until it was almost pain.

"Trace, please…" She reached for him, her fingers touching him intimately for the first time in five years. She gave a violent shiver of excitement as she felt the power of his aroused manhood.

Sensation merged and mingled until he thought he would explode before he could get inside her. His fingers moved with skill and awareness as he touched and teased until her entire focus was crushed and there was a blinding ache deep inside her.

He wanted her to be as desperate for him as he was for her. He paused to grab a condom from within the nightstand, and her eyes glazed as he rolled it over his member. She closed her eyes at the sight, groaning deep in pleasure.

He pulled her legs to wrap around him. She urged him on with her body and he slipped an arm under her hips and raised her.

"Look at me." His command was hoarse and urgent and her eyes flew wide as he thrust into her, sending them both into orbit. There was resistance and he stopped. She urged him on. He moved slowly. Her moans and whimpers became cries of ecstasy. It was just how it used to be. Just as shattering, just as glorious, and just as fulfilling. He had almost forgotten the feel of her enclosing him in her warmth the ultimate pleasure only she could bring him.

"You're tight." He looked strangely uncertain if he should continue.

She wrapped her legs tighter around his waist. "Don't you dare stop."

He didn't.

He began to move with powerful and long strokes, bringing her to the edge, then pulling out, and then slowly entering her again. The pleasure was too much. He began to move faster to outrun the sensation building to a crescendo in their bodies. He urged her to move and he guided them both towards sexual oblivion.

When the explosion came, it took them both together in a shower of sensation so intense that she clutched at him as if he were the one that could save her from the spiral.

He felt it too because he drove into her hard and then held her against him, murmuring against her neck while his body shook from the force of his release.

Chapter 8

Trace lay with Diana wrapped around him, her head on his chest, strands of dark hair spread over his arm. Throughout the night, he found himself reaching for her. Each time she willingly opened to receive him. He was tired but not sated.

Sex with Diana had always been good, but last night it had been magnificent and indescribable, so much that he was forced to re-evaluate his desire for revenge. He didn't like feeling protective toward her and he searched for the anger that had driven him to this point. He couldn't find it.

Five years ago he had been Diana's first lover, and he enjoyed knowing he was the first man to experience her passion. But since then she had been his uncle's wife. The mere thought of Diana giving herself to another man filled him with anger. Taking a deep breath, he exhaled swiftly. Damn. That was Diana's previous life, and it was over. She was his now. He needed to revamp his thoughts and think about now. He wouldn't lose her a second time. Pulling her closer to his chest, he drifted into a light sleep.

The next morning Diana woke to the slight rocking of the boat and inhaled the scent of the ocean through the open windows. She didn't want to face the reality of morning. She wanted to savor the moments of last night. Her hand reached for Trace. Where was he? The indentation in the pillow next to hers reminded her it hadn't been a dream. The rumpled sheets still held his cologne. She closed her eyes as memory provided a vivid image of what had transpired through the night with Trace. She blushed as her thoughts strayed to the things they'd done to each other. She was bolder than she was before. The first time she had taken him in her mouth it had shocked and excited him. She had been shy about doing it before and he had never pushed her. She glanced at the clock on the nightstand and saw it was nine o'clock. The shower was running. The aroma of the food drifted through the open doors of the sitting room that connected to the bedroom.

The shower stopped. Trace strolled out in a towel wrapped loosely around his hips; he was drying his hair with a smaller towel. When he saw she was awake, he threw the hand towel on the chair and gave her a smile. His black hair was wet and unruly and very sexy. He ran his fingers through it and the ends spiked. Immobile, she stared at him. The man was too gorgeous for his own good.

"Hi," he said as he strode toward her.

She blushed, pulled the sheet up to cover her breasts, and held it there. "Good morning."

He removed her fingers from the tight grip she had on the sheet.

"You don't need to cover up. I enjoy looking at you."

"I'm not hiding," she said with a nervous laugh.

"Really? Then you don't mind if I take my fill." He wrapped his arms around her waist and pulled her against his damp chest. And then he was kissing her, his mouth hard and hungry. And she was most definitely kissing him back. She promised herself one night. But what did it hurt to have at least another day? Strong hands held her head as he deepened the kiss and they fell into the rumpled sheets.

He pulled the towel from his waist and her arms slid around him even as her brain fought to stop her. His engorged penis sought the moist heat of her womb and thrust in to the hilt in one forceful movement. He waited until she caught her breath and then sought the rhythm that sent them both soaring to heights unknown, held them in a gripping climax, and then nudged them over the edge in a powerful rushing free fall.

After showering together they walked into the breakfast room. Enjoying the silence, they filled their plates. When they sat at the table, Trace poured cups of strong coffee for both of them and filled their glasses with freshly squeezed orange juice. His plate over-flowed with bacon, sausages, potatoes, and eggs. In addition, he had a side plate of silver dollar pancakes saturated with butter and syrup. She grimaced as she looked at his plate, then picked up her fork and cut into the assortment of fruit she'd selected for herself.

"You should try the fruit," she said between bites. "It's delicious."

"I'll try your fruit if you eat some sausage." He held a bite of sausage close to her mouth. She pursed her lips. Finally, she took the sausage from his fork and chewed carefully.

"Hmm. It's good." She took two links off his plate.

He chuckled and speared a slice of melon from her plate. "Are we going to talk about last night and this morning? Or do we pretend it didn't happen?"

"Is this your way of telling me that us making love was a mistake?"

She finished the last bit of sausage, took a bite of the buttered toast smeared with jam, and chewed thoroughly. "Is that what you think?"

"I asked you a question, Diana."

She stiffened. "Are you demanding an answer?"

He breathed deeply, placed his fork by his plate, and leaned back in the chair. "No. I didn't mean for it to sound like that."

"Good," she said. "Of course it was a mistake." His lips tightened. Then she added, "But I don't regret one moment we shared."

"I didn't seduce you, Diana. It was mutual."

"I know that. But I haven't had a morning after in a long time. I didn't know what you expected."

"What I expected?"

"I don't sleep around," she said in a raised voice.

"If you're hinting at my personal life, don't. My past relationships have nothing to do with us." He glared at her, picked up his fork and resumed eating.

"I'll not be another notch on your belt."

He threw down the fork and leaned over the table. She leaned back in her chair.

"For God's sake, Diana, how can you believe last night was nothing more than a fling?"

"It's been five years. I don't really know you anymore."

"You don't know me?" He stood up. "What the hell have we been doing for the last few weeks but getting to know each other? You talk as if I'm a stranger. We do have a past. My God, we spent an entire year together. You practically lived at the penthouse; hardly a day went by that we didn't see each other. How can you say you don't know me?"

"A person can change in five years." She stood and walked to the counter, her back to him. She could feel him staring at her. She turned and leaned against the counter. This man had been her first love. After all these years, her heart still yearned for him. She had come to him freely.

"This is not a game," Diana said.

"No, it isn't." He took a deep breath. "You need to stop acting like it is and tell me what's really bothering you."

Subconsciously, when she accepted his invitation to take a trip down the coast, she'd known they would end up making love. He was right. It was inevitable. But she also knew it couldn't last. She was going to enjoy the moment until it was over.

"I just want to enjoy the weekend. I don't want any pressure. Agreed?"

"Okay." He took her in his arms, smoothing away the wild strands of hair from her face. "I promise. No pressure. But we can't go back to how we were. I would like for us to move forward and see where it takes us." Diana opened her mouth to speak and he ran his finger over her lips, quieting her with his touch. "But for now, can we work on enjoying today?"

"All right. We'll take it one day at a time."

He dropped a fierce kiss on her lips. The palms of her hands flattened on his bare chest and his hunger hit her full force.. He increased the pressure of the kiss. It was desperate and hot. She felt consumed.

"I can't get enough of you," he whispered. Their tongues twisted together, battling for control. She groaned when Trace's hands slid inside the robe and covered her naked breasts. The robe fell open, baring her nudity. He let out a strangled sound and then dropped his head and latched on to her nipple. She threw back her head from the pleasure.

Trace released his hold, scooped her in his arms, and carried her back to the bedroom. He placed her gently in the center of the bed discarding his robe as he followed her onto the bed. She quickly removed her robe and threw it to the floor. Resting on his arms, he watched her for a very long moment. She averted her eyes, afraid of showing him too much.

Finally dropping his head, he closed his mouth again over one nipple and then turned to lavish the other one. Diana didn't think she would be able to withstand the pleasure; her breath struggled in and out of her lungs. Her hands slid up and down his broad, muscled back and her fingernails scraped over his skin. His kiss burned and demanded a passionate response. Diana lost herself willingly, she needed to connect and become one with him to drown out the weak voice of caution. This was what she wanted, what she needed now. She didn't care about the past, and she had no thought of the future.

She spent five years mourning the loss of what she had with Trace, hating the lack of passion in her life. Now, once again, she had the chance to experience the pleasure she knew only Trace could give her.

Those powerful hands were stroking her flesh, moving down to caress the core of her center. Soon his mouth took the place of his hands and she jerked against the heated flick of his powerful tongue.

"Trace, I can't stand it." She closed her eyes tight, arched her back, and grabbed his hair trying to move from the storm then finally abandoning herself to the sensual pleasure of his possession.

"Yes, you can," he said roughly. He pushed her harder to an orgasm. She felt it rushing to drown her in its depth. Orgasm after orgasm racked her body, and still Trace continued his feast. She lay open, lifeless, before him, and throbbing. After his fill, he planted light kisses on her stomach and her breasts, finally torching her with a deep kiss. She tasted herself on his tongue.

He probed the opening of her vagina. He was throbbing, thick, and heavy. She moved to meet him, spreading her thighs wider, lifting her hips while at the same time keeping her lips firmly attached to his.

"Can you take all of me?" he said in a hoarse tone, waiting to make sure she was ready.

"Yes," she said, her voice unrecognizable to her own ears.

He pushed into her and then held still, allowing her body to adjust to the invasion. She pushed her hips and he sank deeper, his body claiming her inch by inch. Her body stretched to accommodate him.

"Trace—" She let out a breath and gasped as he rocked his hips, pushing even further into her.

"I got you. Ride the storm with me, Diana. I'll keep you safe." Then he did the unexpected. He took hold of her waist and rolled her over so she was sitting on top on him. Still connected, he settled her down on his lap, so that his length was buried deep inside her to the very end of her womb. Diana looked directly into his eyes as he guided her in an easy rhythm.

"It's too much," she groaned. Moving on him, Diana found earth-shattering pleasure she never had expected. Her body and insides were straining, reaching toward the release that built within.

"Help me. I don't—" he said in a strangled voice. Her body trembled. She looked at him and knew he was holding back for her. He wanted her to find her release first. Balancing on her knees, she lifted up, exposing the base of his penis. She ran her finger along the edge, trying to make him lose control. He jerked and pushed into her, causing her to almost lose balance. He took control again and grabbed her by the arms. Then he flipped her over on her back, never losing the connection, and pushed deeply into her. He lifted her leg, placed it on his shoulder, and began long, hard strokes.

Teetering on the edge of something she couldn't control, she gripped his shoulders hard, trying to keep herself stable, keep from toppling over the edge.

"Come with me, baby," he ordered, his voice low and unrecognizable. "Now."

She surrendered to the rush of sensations coursing through her. They both rode the wave. A splintering orgasm hit her and her body shattered into pieces. He exploded inside her. She grabbed hold of him as they both fell over the cliff into immense pleasure.

❧❧

Diana was so happy it frightened her. They showered together, taking their time to explore each other again. The yacht had docked while they finished dressing. They left the bedroom and disembarked. She was eager to discover the sights of the historical southern town. They walked hand in hand down the street. Trace told her he had visited New Bern many times, but she had never been to the port town. She was a history buff and enjoyed reading about and visiting old places.

Excited, she said to him, "Do you know New Bern was discovered by the Swedes in 1710?"

"Yes." He grinned at her excitement.

She continued. "New Bern, North Carolina was a major port and trading center in the 1800s. It was captured and occupied by the Union army after a fierce battle."

"Yes, I know," he said, as he opened the door to an old antique store and ushered her in. "I'm so glad you brought me here." Diana clapped her hands as she spotted the Indian artifacts. "Oh, Trace. There's so much to see, I don't know where to begin."

He smiled. "Take your time. We have all day." She wandered through the store, picking up pieces and examining them. He encouraged her to buy things. Finally, she chose several pieces. He paid for her purchases and they left the store.

Next they went to the Tryon Palace Historic Sites and Gardens, which was a thrill for Diana. There was so much to see it took most of the morning.

They left the gardens arm-in-arm. "Are you hungry?" he asked.

"Yes."

"Do you want to go back to the yacht and eat?"

"No. Let's find a restaurant and eat here."

"Okay."

Trace took her to the famous M.J. Raw Bar and Grill. Happy and hungry, she splurged on a mixed meal of fried butterfly shrimp and scallops with a side of sweet and tangy coleslaw and a basket of French fries.

Trace was looking at her when she popped the last fry into her mouth. She took a long swallow of sweet tea and dabbed her lips with the napkin.

"Are you finished?" He laughed when she picked up the dessert chart. He held up his arms in mock surrender. "I will not come between you and your food."

She put down the menu. "Well, I'm kinda stuffed," she said sheepishly. "I'll have dessert after dinner tonight."

"Of course you will." He shot her an indulgent grin and he reached for the bill. He placed his black credit card on the bill and signaled for the waiter. "Do you want to continue exploring or go back to the yacht and rest?"

"No way. There's much more to see."

"Okay." He signed his name to the card slip. Standing, he held out his hand to her and bowed. "Your servant awaits your orders, my lady."

She stood, threw back her head and laughed, and then placed her hand in his.

"Lead the way, servant."

They browsed through a jewelry boutique. "Trace, look at these turquoise bracelets. Aren't they beautiful?" She pulled him by the hand to the case that housed the decorative pieces.

"Yes." His voice was strange. She turned, looked at him, and saw he was looking at her and not the jewelry. She smiled and leaned into him.

"You're supposed to be looking at the jewelry," she whispered.

"I am. I have the most beautiful selection in my arms."

She smiled wide. "Flattery will get you everywhere, my friend."

"Good. That is exactly what I'm hoping."

Diana laughed and reluctantly moved out of his arms to continue browsing. He took her hand in his and followed as she strolled around the store.

Trace insisted on buying her one of the turquoise pieces and a crystal bracelet. He hired a tour guide to finish their sightseeing. Mason was accommodating and patient even when she asked question after question of the tour guide and of him. In the past, patience had never been one of his virtues. Once she caught a faraway look on his face and wondered what was on his mind, but she never asked. She didn't want anything to ruin the day.

They enjoyed a quiet and romantic dinner at a quaint restaurant sitting at the edge of the water. From their table, they could look out over the water and see lights from the yachts anchored in the harbor. The food was delicious and the atmosphere reminiscent of their first date years ago.

Leaning back in her chair, she watched Trace, thinking about how good she felt. It had been a beautiful day. She didn't want to see it end.

"Do you want dessert?" he asked in a low tone.

Sighing, she lifted the wineglass and took a swallow. "I'm stuffed. I couldn't eat another bite."

"I'm glad you enjoyed your food," he said with a smile, glancing at her near-empty plate.

"I did. This is a beautiful place. I'm happy you brought me to New Bern. I have fallen in love with the town. It's so quaint, and the food is delicious."

"I'm glad you liked it."

"What's not to like? The history, the atmosphere, lights, music…a girl couldn't ask for anything more."

"And the company?" he inquired.

She gave him a soft look. "Most of all, I have enjoyed the company."

"I'm glad to hear that. The night is not over. I have more surprises for you."

"You know I love surprises. Please tell." She clapped her hands and laughed with glee.

Trace chuckled and then gave her a tender smile. "I know you love surprises. That is why it's going to stay a surprise," he said as he came around to assist her out of her chair. Grabbing the silk shawl, he wrapped it around her slim shoulders, his hands lingering at the pulse of her neck. She inhaled quickly, trying to fight the rush of heat that flooded her core. She had to get a grip. She was becoming addicted to his touch. Diana turned in his arms and saw the hooded look in his eyes. His uneven breathing indicated he wasn't as in control as he seemed. Trace took her hand as they moved to leave the restaurant.

His surprise was a carriage ride through the city pulled by four white horses. It was romantic and she felt like a princess.

"Oh, Trace," she said. She fought to hold back the tears that lodged in her throat. "You didn't have to, but I'm so glad you did. This has always been a dream of mine."

"I know." He lifted her onto the seat. She turned to him, waiting for him to explain. "I remember you telling me the things you would like to do."

She cupped his jaw in her hand. "Thank you for re-membering," she said softly and kissed him. His swift intake of breath let her know she had surprised him. She had never taken the initiative in the relationship. She liked the fact she could surprise him. She wanted him to know how much she appreciated his thought-fulness.

"I remember everything about you, Diana," he said softly. She pulled his head to her, placed her lips to his, and kissed him thoroughly. They were both gasp-ing for breath when he lifted his head.

"We need to get back to the yacht…quickly." Trace's voice was filled with need and desire.

"Oh, no, you don't. We're going to continue the ride. You'll not cheat me out of one of my dreams."

"I'll buy you all the damn white horses and car-riages you want. Then you'll be able to ride whenever you want."

"Uh-uh. Just think of what will come later. Now sit back and enjoy the ride."

"You drive a hard bargain."

"Hard? Hmm…" she teased. She placed her hand on his thigh and caressed it through the fabric.

"Diana, you'll pay for this." He gritted his teeth.

"I do hope so." She smiled and laid her head on his shoulder.

They strolled hand and hand back to the yacht. Not stopping for anything, he led her to the master suite. Without a word, he undressed her slowly, never taking his eyes from her face, and began to make sweet, passionate love to her. His touch was light as a feather that then turned fierce. She was drowning. When she found her release, she almost lost consciousness. She couldn't love him more than she did at that moment. Afterwards, he pulled her to him and spooned her to his body. She lay in his arms as he gently rubbed her to relieve the aftershocks and tremors of their lovemaking. The last thing she remembered before sliding into a deep sleep was the fleeting touch of his kiss as he cradled her close and whispered her name.

Chapter 9

Diana sat doodling on her notepad as Susan went over the budget for Pisano Wineries' newest ad campaign. As Susan spoke, Diana occasionally caught a comment she needed to remember and wrote it down. However, her mind was on other things, pleasant things. There was long moment of silence and Diana looked up at Susan with a question in her eyes. "What?"

Susan's dark eyes were mischievous. Her heavy jet black hair lay in layers around her beautiful olive face. "You weren't listening."

Diana grinned. "Yes, I was," she said. It was only a half-truth.

Susan pouted and crossed her arms. "Okay. Shoot. Go ahead and tell me what I said."

"You said we're going to do a preliminary test in New York to get a first reaction to the ad."

Susan leaned back and folded her hands.

"You were only half listening. I won't drill you on what was the rest of my brilliant presentation. Now that I have your full attention, what do you want to do about the hospital project?"

"It's really a family project, not a company one. However, I'll need to talk to Trace and see if he wants the marketing to be done by Pisano or an outside company."

"Speaking of Trace, you and he seem to be getting along quite well."

Diana's heart jumped. "Yes, we are. We both want what is best for Pisano," she replied. She tried to sound nonchalant with her response. She and Trace tried hard not to spotlight their personal relationship at work. Although Trace didn't want to hide their relationship, she didn't want to be obvious. She wanted to enjoy their time together without outside opinions and interference.

Susan was her best friend, but the relationship between her and Trace was too new, too private, to share with anyone. It wasn't that she was ashamed of them being together, but she didn't expect it to last. In addition, she had to think about her son. She didn't want to think of the ramifications when Nicky came back home.

"We agreed to be civil," Diana said.

Susan grinned. "From what I've seen, you're more than civil."

"What do you mean?"

"You and he smile quite a bit at each other."

"So?"

"It's a secretive smile. It's like the two of you have a secret that you're not sharing with the rest of us."

"Really? You must be imagining things."

"No, I'm not. I see very clearly." She looked at Diana without blinking. "John always put Pisano first. I believe it was a mistake. I don't think he fully enjoyed life until you came along. I don't want you to make the same mistake."

"I'm not. Believe me, Nicky is my first priority. Once he comes home, I will cut back to my normal two days a week in the office. I'm only coming in every day now because Nicky is away."

"Diana, I'm not talking about Nicky. Anyone who knows you knows you love that boy more than your own life. I'm talking about you."

"What about me?"

"You need a life."

Diana was silent. She didn't know where Susan was going with this, and she wasn't going to help her get there.

Finally, Susan said, "Are you enjoying being in the office every day?"

"Yes, I'm enjoying the excitement. Don't get me wrong. Working from home has its advantages, but coming into the office puts me in the middle of everything. It's exhilarating. I like being able to communicate face to face. I love my son dearly, but working and enjoying what you do is another type of love and commitment."

"I know that. I just ask that you don't lose who you are. You're a woman first."

"Meaning?"

"You need a man in your life." Susan paused for dramatic effect. "A tall, dark, handsome, *young*, virile, and sexy man."

Diana blushed. "I'm too busy taking care of Nicky."

"Yeah, right." She paused and gave Diana a sly look. "How's it going with Trace living in the house?"

Diana's heart lurched. For a moment, she was unable to speak. She should have known Susan wouldn't let the topic of Trace drop. She was like a dog with a bone.

"It's going fine. He's traveling quite a bit. I barely see him."

"Hmm…Diana, you forget that I was here when you first came to Pisano. I saw the sparks that flew between the two of you and watched both of you fall off the ledge."

When she'd started at Pisano, she and Susan had become fast friends. Although she never told Susan the complete truth behind the breakup, Susan knew how much she had loved Trace. During that horrific time in her life, Diana had told her Trace wasn't looking for a monogamous relationship so she'd decided to end it. A month later, she married John. Saying Susan was shocked was an understatement. She had relentlessly questioned her about her decision and wanted to know why. Diana told Susan she loved John and that was why she was marrying him, which had been the truth.

"Trace and I dated a long time ago. I was young and naïve."

"From what I saw it was more than dating. I would say you were head over heels in love with the man." Diana didn't answer, so Susan continued. "Diana, I see the way Trace looks at you now and I see how you look at him. Don't let what happened years ago, including your marriage to John, keep you from reaching for the happiness you deserve. Granted, John was a good man, but he wasn't the love of your life."

"But—"

Susan held up her hand to stop her. "I believe you have a chance again with the man you gave your heart to; I believe it stills belongs to him."

Sighing, Diana replied, "Too much has happened."

"Don't let the past shape your future. If you want it, you can have a life with the man you love. I wish I had the chance. I would not botch it."

Susan had lost her husband, a North Carolina state police officer, in a shooting two years earlier. Susan had met the handsome young Southerner when she moved with her parents from New York to Asheville at the age of seventeen. At twenty-one, Susan had married the love of her life. The pain of losing him was still fresh. Diana had encouraged her friend to start dating, but Susan had nixed the idea, telling Diana she was okay with her life right now. Diana hoped someday Susan would find happiness again. She richly deserved it.

"Are you talking about me or you?" Diana asked quietly.

"I'm talking about you. However, I deeply regret not having children with Tony. He wanted to wait until we became more financially secure. Granted, I agreed, but now it's something I wish I could change."

"Susan, I know how much you loved Tony and I'm glad I was here for you when you lost him. You'll find love again. I know it."

"Look at us." Susan smiled sadly. "We need to talk about happy times. Now back to you and Trace. What's happening between the two of you?"

Diana lowered her eyes. "What makes you think something is happening between us?"

"One, I'm not blind, and two, I know you. I'm your best friend and I can always tell when you are hiding something."

"I'm not—"

"Please, Diana, give me a break."

Diana sighed. "You're not going to let this go, are you?"

"Nope."

"All right, Trace and I have become close."

"Hmm. How close?"

"Real close."

"Your weekend away—was it with him?"

Surprised, Diana asked, "Why do you ask?"

"Diana, I never have known you to go on vacation by yourself. You would've asked me to tag along to keep you company, and you didn't."

"Maybe I was looking for change."

"You? A change? Diana, you're as anal as they come."

Diana glared at her. "I know that wasn't a compliment. Did anyone ever tell you that you're nosey?"

Susan chuckled. "Yes, you have, many times. Now tell me what happened."

Diana sighed and gave in. "He invited me to take a weekend trip down the coast. It was nice."

"Nice? I know there's more to it. Did you feel the sparks again?"

"They never left."

Susan rubbed her palms together. "Now you're talking."

"I went in with my eyes open." Diana was quiet for moment and then added, "I don't regret it. Not for one minute."

"Good for you, Diana!"

"What?"

"How many people get the chance to reconnect with their first love? I'm happy for you. I know you pretended to be happy—"

Diana interrupted her. "I was happy with John."

"Diana, I'm not disclaiming what you had with John. But it's not the same with Trace, is it?"

"No, it's not. It's not real with Trace. I'm just enjoying the moment. It will eventually end."

"Will it? I don't think so. Anyway, who're you trying to convince? Me or yourself?"

"My mind tells me it's not real, but my heart says something totally different."

"It's because your heart knows what your mind refuses to accept. Diana, you have a second chance to be with Trace. Go for it."

"He wants a fresh start."

"And you said?"

"I can't."

"Why? Diana, you have a man who loves you and wants to be with you. What in the world is stopping you?"

"Our past, for one thing. So much happened to drive us apart. We haven't ever discussed it. And he doesn't love me."

"Forget about it. And, yes, he does love you."

Diana rolled her eyes. "It's only sex."

"Has he said that's all it is?"

"Well, no, but he hasn't told me anything different, either."

"Do you think maybe Trace is waiting for you to define your relationship?"

"No, and I won't."

"Why not?"

"We haven't gone public with our relationship. Although two of Crispina's friends saw us in a restaurant, I'm sure they won't broadcast that they saw Trace holding my hand. Just think how devastated Trace's mother would be to know he was fraternizing with a *woman of color*." She sneered.

Susan sucked her teeth and exclaimed, "Who gives a damn what people think?"

"I have to take it slow. I need to think about Nicky and John."

"Did you think of Trace when you married his uncle so quickly?"

"That's a low blow, Susan."

"I didn't say it to hurt you." Susan took a deep breath. "In case you haven't realized it, you're already *hooked up* with him." Susan walked over to the built-in wall fridge, opened the door, and grabbed two bottles of mineral water. Handing one to Diana, she sat back down. "John would want you to be happy, and if Trace makes you happy, I say go for it."

Diana unscrewed the bottle cap and took a sip of the cold liquid. "That's just it, Susan. We have so much fun together. He makes me laugh. He voices his opinion and I certainly express mine. I love our time together—but it's not a real relationship."

"Diana, listen to yourself. He makes you happy."

Diana stayed silent, going over what Susan had just said. The time she'd spent with him over the last few weeks were some of the happiest moments of her life. This new Trace was a force to be reckoned with. Still, she knew the secrets she held could destroy any chance with Trace.

"There's still a lot that needs to be resolved."

"Well, you need to resolve it and move on."

"But the past—"

"Diana, forget it."

"How can I when the past affects the future?"

"Okay. I can tell you're holding something back. Do you want to share it?"

Diana told a deep breath and released it slowly. "Trace cheated on me with Lisa Davenport. That's why we broke up," she said.

"Whoa. Whoa. Back up. Lisa Davenport, the import/export heiress?" Susan asked, shocked.

"Yes."

"Are you sure?"

Diana frowned at her.

"What I meant is you never said a word to me."

"I was too humiliated to tell anyone."

"I knew he used to date her, but that was before you came to work at Pisano. I remember her coming to the office once. Boy, was she a drama queen. According to the rumor mill they broke up long before he started seeing you."

"I caught them at his apartment." Looking at the stunned disbelief on Susan's face, she gave her the complete story. "Trace was on a business trip. An assistant had called to let me know he would be returning a day early, but it would be late into the evening. I went to the penthouse that afternoon to set up a romantic interlude. Imagine my shock when I walked into the bedroom and found Lisa Davenport in his bed. Apparently, he had arrived earlier than scheduled. If I hadn't come unannounced to his place I would have never known about Lisa."

"It's hard to believe," Susan said.

Diana gave Susan a pointed look.

"What I meant is, Trace seemed to be deeply into you. Did you ever confront him?"

"Trace was in the shower. I was too devastated. I hurried out of the penthouse before he came out of the shower. I left North Carolina that evening."

"I remember you calling me. You were hysterical. You told me you broke up with Trace, but you never said why," Susan said.

"I needed to get far away from him so I could think. After hiding out for a couple of weeks, I sent him a letter ending the relationship."

"You never told me where you were until you came back."

"If Trace had asked you where I was, I didn't want you to have to lie."

"He did ask, but I told him I didn't know. From the look he gave me, he thought I was lying. He never asked again. Did you ever tell Trace about what you saw?"

"No."

"Diana, you must talk to him. I know you saw Lisa there but there are always two sides to a story."

"Please, Susan, let it go. Lisa made it a point to describe what they had just finished doing."

"Diana, that woman is a bitch—and that's a nice name for her. She wasn't happy when Trace broke off the relationship. It was in all the gossip rags how she tried every trick in the book to try to get him back."

"I know what I saw."

"Okay. Say what she told you was true. In the last few weeks you've been with Trace, haven't you seen a different man from the one you dated five years ago?"

Diana thought for a moment. "Yes, I do. This Trace is almost a stranger. Oh, don't get me wrong, he's still as arrogant as ever, but there is a calmer side to him. He listens when I talk. It's unnerving."

"My advice to you, my friend, is to give him a chance to explain."

Diana frowned. "So you're the cheering section for Trace Montgomery?"

"No, I'm your friend and I know you still love the man. If you don't talk to him you might regret it for the rest of your life. Look, Diana, we all make mistakes. Some mistakes can be rectified and some can't. I believe this is one that can be."

Diana stood and went around the table and gave Susan a tight hug.

Surprised, Susan asked, "What was that for?"

"For being the best friend any girl could have."

Flustered, Susan cleared her throat. "Well, of course I'm the best. Don't you forget it."

Laughing, Diana grabbed Susan by the arm. "Come, my modest BFF, let's go to lunch. The morning has gotten away from us. I'm starving."

Reaching for her purse, Susan headed toward the door. "Sushi or Mexican?"

Diana grinned. "You choose. I can do either."

Susan opened the door. "Mexican it is. We can stop on the way back and pick up a sushi platter for our afternoon snack."

Diana laughed as she closed the office door behind her. Having Susan for a friend made getting up in the morning worth it.

Chapter 10

Diana sat curled up on one of the large white Chelsea Chester sofas in the sunroom and lifted her face to the sun filtering in the room. Out of all of the rooms in Raven's Nest, the sunroom was her favorite. Bright with accents of black, white, and yellow, the room was large and spacious. Floor to ceiling windows with scalloped custom-made sheer treatments permitted breath-taking views.

Vases of white tulips were scattered throughout the room. Several huge mountains and trees surrounded the exterior of the mansion, protecting it from the eyes of any intruders. For Diana, the sunroom which John had remodeled especially for her, was her haven from the stress of everyday life.

She took a deep breath, reached for the cordless phone, and punched out a number. Her mother's soft southern drawl came over the line. "Hello."

"Hi, Mama."

"Hi, sweetie. How's everything?"

"Fine. You sound tired."

Laughing, her mother said, "I am tired, but it's a good tired. The kids and I have been in the pool all morning. I think I might have gotten a little too much sun."

"Are you okay?" Diana knew if her Mother was sick or not feeling good, she wouldn't say anything.

"Honey, I'm fine."

"Yes, I know but I don't…"

"Diana Estelle Hamilton Pisano, I'm fine. You know being out in the sun is draining. I just stayed out a little longer than I normally do."

"I hear you, Mama, but don't let the kids control you. You would never let us be in charge." Her mother laughed.

Diana took a deep breath. "Mama, I need a favor."

"Yes?"

"I was wondering if it's all right if Nicky stays a little longer."

"Is something wrong?"

"Oh, no. Uh…I'm a little behind on a project I'm working on and need a little extra time to finish." She stumbled over her words; she hated lying to her mother.

"Well, it's no problem. I'll tell you what. We'll drop him off before we go on vacation."

Diana's heart skipped a beat. "When…when will that be?"

"We're still trying to decide if we want to go to Hilton Head or Savannah. I have to check with your father, but I'm pretty sure it's not for a few weeks. Your father has a house project he needs to complete before we leave. It might be closer to a month or so before he is done. You know how slow he can be."

Diana sighed. "A few weeks…that is good."

"Good. Then it's settled."

"Thanks, Mama."

"No problem. Do you want to speak to Nicky?" her mother asked.

"Yes." Estelle called Nicky to the phone. "Hold on a moment, Diana."

She could hear Nicky whining about how it was his turn to choose the show to watch on the television. He asked his grandmother if he had to come. She responded with a firm yes before telling him it was his mommy on the phone. The sound of running feet was music to her ears.

"Hi, Mommy!"

Her heart caught in her chest when she heard his excited voice.

"Hi, Nicky. How is my baby?" She could tell he wasn't happy being called a baby.

"I'm not a baby. I'm a big boy," he shouted.

She laughed. "Yes, you are a big boy. But sometimes Mommy forgets and you have to remind me."

"Okay. I love you, Mommy." Diana heard a distant voice and thought Nicky must have dropped the phone. There was a moment of silence. Puzzled, she said, "Hello?"

Her mother's voice came through on the line. "Diana?"

"What happened to Nicky?"

"Sorry, but he's having such a good time. He ran off to make sure the other kids don't cheat him out of taking his turn."

Diana laughed. Although she missed him, she knew being with her parents at this time was for the best. Every day she talked to her parents, and still couldn't bring herself to tell them Trace was living at Raven's Nest. There would be questions, ones she didn't want to answer, so she remained silent.

"Diana, I love hearing you laugh. It sounds good. I take it everything is good with you?"

"I'm fine, Mama."

"Well, you sound happy, and I'm glad."

Diana sighed. "Believe it or not, I am happy."

"Does this happiness have anything to do with Trace being back in North Carolina?" Estelle inquired softly. Diana had told her parents when they picked up Nicky that Trace was now the CEO of Pisano. "I read in the paper that the financial world is excited about his new position."

"Yes, there seem to be a lot of new expectations for the company." Cautiously Diana added, "We're getting along, and that's good."

Estelle recognized the caution in her daughter's voice. "Honey, I do remember you and Trace have a past."

"I know that, Mama."

"You're a grown woman and it's not for me to ask about your personal life." Estelle paused. It seemed as if she was waiting for Diana to comment.

Diana didn't respond to her mother's statement. She listened to the happy screams of children in the background.

"Diana, I got to go. Joey has hold of Ashley's pigtail and won't let go." Before she hung up, Diana heard her mother say, "Joey, let go of Ashley's hair!"

Diana was laughing when Rosa came in the room. "Mrs. Pisano, you have a visitor—"

"I don't need to be announced in my own house, Rosa." Surprised, Diana stood immediately when Crispina entered the room. Crispina Montgomery was a very beautiful woman. She looked a lot younger than her actual age. Although she never divulged it, she was in her early sixties.

She took a deep breath. "Hello, Crispina."

She gave Diana a once-over without responding and turned to Rosa. "You're dismissed, Rosa." Rosa remained in the room.

Diana smiled at Rosa. "Rosa, could you please bring in a pot of tea? Oh, and could you see if Cook has some of those lovely scones she made this morning?"

Rosa shot Crispina a stern look and then said in a clear voice to Diana, "Yes, ma'am."

Crispina's cold eyes turned on Diana as Rosa left the room. "That woman never learned her manners. John was always lenient with the household staff, but he gave her free rein."

"Rosa has been at Raven's Nest a long time. She's more than an employee, she's family." Motioning to one of the chairs, Diana said, "Please have a seat."

"I prefer to stand. I don't plan to be here long."

Diana looked at Crispina's stance. "All right. But if you came to see Trace, he's not here."

"I know he isn't here. I came to see you."

Diana stiffened. "Me?"

"Don't be coy with me, Diana," she said indignantly.

"Pardon me?" Diana looked at her with puzzlement in her eyes.

"You know why I'm here."

"I do?" Diana was clearly confused. "Excuse me, but you need to enlighten me."

"I warned you to stay away from my son five years ago, but it seems as if you didn't clearly understand me."

Diana could tell by Crispina's tone she was vying for a fight. Diana's guard immediately went up. Crispina was here to do battle, and Diana was her enemy. Diana wouldn't back down, not today. This confrontation was a long time coming.

"Five years ago, I was a naïve girl. You'll find I'm no longer that girl. What Trace and I do is none of your business."

"So you admit you're sleeping with my son," she said with obvious disgust.

Holding on to her patience, Diana said in a calm voice, "I don't admit anything. If you want to know about Trace's personal life, I suggest you ask him."

"I'm not asking him. I'm asking you."

"Then I'm afraid you wasted a trip because I don't have an answer for you."

At that moment Rosa entered carrying a tray laden with a pot of hot tea, fresh strawberries, blueberry scones, and homemade whipped cream. She set it on the glass table in front of Diana.

Diana smiled at Rosa, letting her know everything was all right. "Thank you, Rosa. Mrs. Montgomery and I'll serve ourselves." Rosa hesitated but quietly left the room.

Diana sat down, which forced the ever etiquette-conscious Crispina to sit also. Diana busied herself handing her a napkin and then laying one across her own lap. She poured tea into two cups and offered one to Crispina. Good manners propelled Crispina to accept the cup; she took a demure sip and sat stiffly with the cup in her hands.

"Would you like a scone?"

"No."

Diana picked up a scone and bit into the slightly sweet biscuit. She leaned back on the sofa and brought her cup to her lips. Sipping the hot brew slowly, she savored the bold and rich flavor of the imported English tea. John had always had a shipment of assorted teas sent to Raven's Nest each month. Diana had fallen in love with the smoothness of the hot drink upon her first sip. She waited for Crispina to speak, but she only continued to stare.

Diana broke the silence. "The scones are really good. Cook knows how much I love blueberries. She made a fresh batch with berries from the garden. They're one of my weaknesses."

Crispina set her cup on the table and stood up; she looked at Diana with a look of impatience and annoyance. Diana couldn't help feeling the ice in the stare. Crispina disliked like her, but, until now, Diana had never known how much.

"I didn't come here to discuss berries or scones with you." Fury was evident in every word.

"Really? Well, since you can't stand the sight of me, I see no reason for you to be here," Diana said.

Crispina's eyes widened at the bold remark. Diana had caught her off guard. Crispina never expected her to be so direct. She wouldn't find the quiet and sub-dued girl she first encountered.

"Don't be insipid," Crispina remarked with an ar-rogant tilt of her head.

Diana slowly placed her cup on the tray and stood. "What do you really want?" Diana asked in a cool voice.

In the past, Diana was afraid that, if forced to choose, Trace would choose his mother over her. Her confidence and self-esteem had been at an all-time low and her fear of losing him had always been in her mind. Now she no longer cared what Crispina thought about her.

While married to John, she'd ignored Crispina, knowing how much he loved his only sibling. Not any-more. The woman couldn't hurt her. With John gone, the gloves were off.

Crispina shot Diana a cold look. "I know Trace is living here with you and I don't like it."

"Trace is living here to honor the terms *your broth-er* set forth in his will."

"And you are using it to your advantage. You al-ways wanted Trace," she added haughtily. "Now you see your chance."

Diana was surprised at the revealing remark. Crisp-ina was scared. She couldn't talk to Trace…or maybe she'd already voiced her objections to him. Knowing

Trace's arrogance, he probably told her to butt out of his life. She was relying on Diana's fear of her.

"You're running scared," Diana exclaimed. This little chat was getting more interesting by the minute. Understanding dawned in her mind and she felt lighter.

"I don't scare easily," Crispina sneered. "You think you can take me on in a fight? Believe me, you will lose."

"Why would I want to fight you? You showing up here today shows you have already lost the battle."

Crispina moved closer to Diana. Diana stared at her but didn't step back. Today she was taking a stand and not backing down. Whatever Crispina gave she would give it back. She knew her remark angered Crispina. She could see by the tightening of her lips that her comment hit home. *Good*, Diana thought. *I'm enjoying this.*

"Well, well, the little trashy nobody from the backwoods of South Carolina has a backbone," Crispina sneered. "I tolerated but loathed the sight of you for years. You wanted Trace but you couldn't get him so you put your hooks into my brother, a lonely old man who didn't know any better. I didn't see it coming, but not this time. This is your one and last warning. Stay away from my son."

"Or what?" Diana taunted. "Trace is a formidable man. There's nothing you can do to stop us from being together. Just imagine, Crispina, all those little brown babies running around with Pisano and Montgomery blood—your grandchildren."

Crispina slapped Diana hard across the face. The force of the blow snapped Diana's head to the side. Diana was stunned. All she could do was stare at Crispina in shock.

"You damn slut!" Crispina screamed. She was breathing hard and unevenly. The hatred was apparent in her eyes and voice. "I would never accept a child of yours. Do you hear me? Never in this lifetime. And don't you ever tell me what my son needs."

Although she wanted to touch her throbbing cheek, Diana kept her hand at her side. She refused to give Crispina the satisfaction of knowing she was in pain.

"I want you to leave my house," Diana said in a strong and controlled voice, although she was shaking inside. "Don't make me have to tell you twice."

"Don't you tell…" Crispina spat. Diana moved closer. She backed up a step, surprise and fear written on her face.

Diana was so angry she was afraid she would do bodily harm to Crispina. She grabbed Crispina's arm and turned her toward the door. "If you ever put your damn hands on me again, you'll wish you'd never been born." The fury burning inside threatened to consume her. Crispina jerked her arm, trying to get Diana to loosen her hold, but she held firmly.

Rosa stood in the doorway. Diana slowly removed her hand from Crispina's arm. It gave her a measure of satisfaction to the see the imprint of her fingers on her arm.

Rosa must have been on the other side of the closed door. She was standing guard the entire time. Rosa moved closer to Diana but kept a wary eye on Crispina. She noticed the redness of the welts beginning to form on Diana's cheek and sucked in her breath. Rosa started toward Crispina, but Diana put a hand on her arm to stop her. It surprised Diana to see the fury in Rosa's eyes. She knew this woman would go to bat for her. But she didn't want anyone else fighting her battles; she could do it herself. Crispina could be vicious and vindictive. She didn't want Rosa hurt in the midst of this.

"Are you all right Mrs. Pisano?" she asked stiffly as she kept her eyes on Crispina.

"I'm fine, Rosa. Could you escort Mrs. Montgomery out? She's leaving—now."

"With great pleasure." She put her hand on Crispina's elbow.

"Don't touch me. I know my way out," she snarled.

They watched as she turned and exited the room. She slammed the door to the sunroom behind her. Diana was surprised the door didn't groan from the force of the slam.

Diana took a deep breath and exhaled softly. Silence filled the room. She didn't want to make Rosa uncomfortable, so she started clearing away the refreshments, placing everything on the tray. Rosa remained silent. In the midst of Diana's stacking the teacups, Rosa looked closely at Diana's face and frowned. "I'll get an ice pack for your face."

"Thank you, Rosa." As she turned to leave, Diana said, "You're not to mention this to Mr. Montgomery. Is that understood?"

Rosa opened her mouth and then closed it. "Is that your wish?"

"Yes, it is." Diana patted Rosa's hand. Rosa was loyal and wouldn't mention the incident to Trace. Diana didn't want to widen the rift between Trace and his mother. "You don't need to be worried for me. I've been through too much to let that woman win the battle. Stop worrying, Rosa. I can handle Crispina."

"I truly hope so." Rosa moved toward the door with a worried frown.

Chapter 11

A week later Trace walked into the mansion, tired from overseas travel but anxious to see Diana. This trip had involved long negotiations to calm the banking market in Hong Kong. Everything had gone well. He could have settled his business and come home earlier, but he needed to stay away from Diana. He needed to keep his thoughts and emotions under control. He'd planned to get Diana to fall in love with him and dump her, but he had been snared in his own web. He realized that he'd never stopped loving Diana.

The house was quiet except for the movement of the staff going about their daily routine. Diana was probably still at the office, which gave him time to collect himself. He glanced at his gold Rolex. He wanted to make a stop at the mansion to shower and change before going to the office. Thinking of the information he needed to record, he decided to forego the shower for now and hurried down the corridor to his home office. He placed his briefcase on the desk. Then he massaged the knot in his neck and rolled his shoulders to relieve the tension. Walking to the small wall fridge, he retrieved a bottle of cold spring water. He sat on the sofa, propped his feet on the mahogany table, and laid his head against the cushion. He sipped at the water, his minding drifting. The minute he closed his eyes Diana invaded his thoughts.

She was in his blood. The thought of their weekend on the yacht made him smile. When he asked her to go on the trip, seducing her hadn't been his plan, at least not consciously. It was supposed to be a weekend for them to get to know each other again, but it had turned into a weekend of pure pleasure. Restless, he stood, moved to the window, and looked out over the manicured lawns. He sighed at the beauty of the land that belonged to him and Diana.

He smiled as his mind continued to fill with images of Diana. She could be very prim and proper when she wanted to be. He had taken her to one of the guest cottages on the property for an intimate and romantic interlude. He grinned, thinking of how they had christened the large in-ground Jacuzzi. Surrounded by the breathtaking mountaintop view of Asheville, he had made love to her. In the midst of his musings, the door opened and Henderson, the family's longtime chauffeur entered quietly. Trace turned from the window, set the bottle on the desk and addressed the man who had been at Raven's Nest as long as he could remember.

"Yes, Henderson?"

"Sir, Rosa told me she saw you come into the study. Are you ready to go to the office?"

Making a quick decision, he said, "No, I've changed my mind."

"Are you sure, because…"

"I'm sure. You can have the rest of the evening to yourself."

"Thank you." Henderson turned to leave.

"Oh, Henderson, would you please tell Rosa to buzz me in my suite the moment Mrs. Pisano arrives?"

"Yes, sir."

A loud buzzing sound brought him out of a sound sleep. Disoriented, he fumbled and reached for the phone on the table beside the sofa.

"Yes," he said in a gruff voice.

"Mr. Montgomery, Mrs. Pisano just pulled into the garage," Rosa said.

Becoming fully awake, Trace sat up straighter. "Thank you, Rosa. Please don't tell Mrs. Pisano I'm home."

Rosa paused before answering. "Yes, sir."

It would only take a couple of minutes for Diana to come through the walkway into the lower level. He must've been more tired than he thought. He couldn't remember the last time he'd fallen asleep sitting up. He rubbed his eyes, picked up the papers that had fallen to the floor, and put them into the briefcase in front of him.

Discarding his robe, he walked naked into the bathroom to run water over his face. He dried his face and quickly ran his hand through the dark thickness of his hair, making the thick layers look untamed and unruly.

Trace grabbed a pair of silk briefs from the top dresser drawer, took a pair of freshly pressed jeans from a hanger, and slipped them on. He chose a short-sleeved navy blue silk shirt and slipped his bare feet into a pair of Italian loafers. Finished, Trace strode out of the room and quickly headed down the long staircase. He wanted to see her reaction upon seeing him. He was acting like a schoolboy on his first date, but he didn't care.

The sunroom was secluded from the rest of the mansion. Because it was her favorite room, Diana always headed there for serenity and downtime. When she came from work, her ritual was to first take a shower, slip into what she called her comfy clothes and a pair of old flips flops, and head to the sunroom. Today he would wait for her there.

At the wall stereo system, he put on some jazz. Diana loved jazz and blues. To be so young, she had an old soul when it came to music.

At the built-in bar in one corner of the room he poured a glass of white zinfandel for Diana and a scotch for himself. Upon hearing the door open, he turned and watched as she entered the room. She closed the door behind her, insuring her privacy. She didn't notice him there. She was dressed casually in a pair of khaki shorts and a sleeveless shirt. He looked at her long, brown bare legs and smiled when he noticed she carried a pair of flip-flops that dangled from two fingers. Diana was truly a country girl. She loved to go barefoot.

From his side of the room he said, "Hello, Diana."

She dropped the shoes and whirled to face him, shocked. Then her eyes lit up. To think she was glad to see him made his heart swell. She remained rooted to her spot, so he walked toward her, carrying their drinks in his hands. He handed her the glass of wine. She took it, but continued looking at him as if he were a mirage.

He grinned at her. "I see you still like to go barefoot."

Coming out of a stupor, she said, "When did you get back?"

He smiled and took a swallow of his drink. Diana didn't like being caught by surprise; she liked to be in control.

Trace gently took hold of her elbow and guided her to the sofa. He removed the glass from her trembling hand and set it on the table along with his drink. He closed his fingers around hers and carried her hand to his mouth. He fleetingly kissed the fingers and the palm of her hand. "I arrived late this afternoon." His gaze caressed her face. "I have missed you."

Mason watched as she fought with her answer. "I missed you, too." The softness of her voice was his undoing. Diana reached up, took his face in her hands, and brought his lips to hers. He was surprised she took the initiative to kiss him first. Her tongue entered his mouth. With a swift intake of breath, he brought her closer and deepened the kiss as their tongues battled for control. Laying her on the sofa, he leaned into her and gave her what they both desired. He pulled her closer and took complete control of the kiss. Fire consumed him; he was fast losing control. Just a little bit more and then he would stop…at least that was what his head told him. His body had other ideas. Diana moaned and circled her arms around his neck, bringing him even closer. Her mouth melted beneath his.

Mason used his tongue to brand her as he moved his lips from hers to explore her neck. He moved aside the shirt and her bra and latched onto the brown nipple begging for his attention. He worshipped one breast and then moved to the other. He lifted his head and observed her as she thrashed her head side to side trying to escape the wave of passion rolling over her. She lay before him with her lips parted and her eyes heavy with desire. He slowly unbuttoned her blouse. Never taking his eyes from her, he removed her shorts along with the lace panties she wore. Trace lowered his head and brought his tongue to her flat stomach. He worked his way to her navel and moved lower. Diana grabbed hold of his head as his tongue latched onto her core. She tried to escape the storm, but Trace wouldn't let her. As her orgasm washed over her, she became motionless for a moment.

Then she reached for him. Her fingers fumbled with the zipper of his jeans. He covered her hands with his, helping her to undo the zipper. When they completed the task, his manhood sprang forth from its confinement. Impatient, he quickly discarded the jeans and the shirt. He threw the sofa pillows to the floor and placed her on top of them. His fingers moved in her center, preparing her to receive him.

"Look at me…" he said hoarsely. "I need you so badly. But if you want me to stop now, I will."

"I want you."

"This is our final turning point. I won't let you go. No more running."

She gave him her answer by reaching for him, and he followed her initiative. Bringing her legs to lock around his waist, he positioned himself between them. He tried to slow down, but she arched her body against him and pulled him closer. She moaned his name. He shuddered. She gasped. He thrust deeply to the tip of her womb. He didn't move for a moment. Her vagina squeezed his penis, wanting more. He closed his eyes to get control, but lost it when she bucked her hips.

He pulled out and then pushed back into her hard. She thrashed about, but he wouldn't let her escape everything he was giving her. She gently squeezed his scrotum, and he exploded. With a roar, he filled her with one deep, final thrust, spilling his seed into her. For several long moments afterward, he held her close. There was no going back for either of them.

Trace lay gazing at Diana's face and frowned when he saw a slight discoloration to the skin. He ran his fingers gently over the spot. He had noticed it before. Her makeup had concealed it well. He needed to ask her about it. Trace pulled her closer. He inhaled her musky scent and savored the feel of her in his arms. He had continually reached for her throughout the night. He felt at peace.

He cursed himself as he remembered they had made love in the sunroom without a condom, neither of them remembering until it was too late. This was the second time it had happened, the first being right after breakfast on the yacht. The idea of Diana being pregnant with his child didn't bother him. It stunned him because he would be happy to have the entire package with her. He sighed, tightened his hold, and idly he rubbed her naked back in a soothing circular motion.

"Trace?" Diana asked him sleepily. "What's wrong?"

In between stolen kisses, they had snuck through the mansion and climbed the stairs with their shoes in hand. They'd shared a shower together, he washing her back and she in turn doing the same. Afterward, they'd grabbed large white, soft bath towels and gently dried each other, all the while enjoying the nectar of each other's lips. When the kisses had turned fierce and their breathing labored, they'd discarded the towels, fallen into bed, and begun the journey once again. They had foregone dinner altogether.

"Nothing is wrong. I was getting comfortable."

Diana was sprawled over him and she seemed to have no intention of moving. "Are you saying I'm too heavy?"

Chuckling, he answered, "No. I've told you before you could stand to gain a few pounds."

She looked up at him, blinking the sleep out of her eyes. "Oh, yeah. Are you calling me skinny? You didn't seem to mind that last night."

He laughed. "I have no complaints." He pulled her closer and was quiet. After a few moments, he said, "I don't want you to have regrets tomorrow morning."

"I won't."

"We didn't use a condom in the sunroom. This is the second time. I'm sorry."

She continued gazing up at him with wide brown eyes. "I didn't realize we didn't use one in the sunroom."

"If you're pregnant—"

"You don't have anything to worry about."

"Believe me, I'm not worried."

She blinked up at him. "You're not?"

"No." He brought her closer to his lips and gently kissed her. He liked the softness in her eyes. She was opening up to him. He gently caressed her cheek. "I noticed this earlier and wondered what happened."

"What?" Her hand went to her cheek.

He removed her hand. "Did you hurt yourself?"

She shuffled in his arms and lowered her eyes. "I tripped and hit my cheek against a chair," she lied. Thoughts of the encounter with Crispina flashed vividly in her mind.

"It looks as if there was a cut." He examined the skin closely. "Please be more careful. You could've seriously been hurt."

"I'm fine. It's hardly noticeable now." She started to move off him.

"Where are you going?"

"I was giving you room."

Grinning, he pulled her to him. "Did I ask you to move?"

"No, but—" He brought his mouth down on hers, igniting the passion all over again.

"You're torturing me," she moaned.

"Not torture. Only pleasure."

Trace reached for a condom on the night table, reversed their positions, and straddled Diana across his lap. She gasped with surprise and gingerly took him into her body.

He knew she was sore so he lay still, letting her take the lead.

"Ride me, Diana," he said huskily.

She moved slowly on his shaft, each time taking more, finally taking all of him. He held his breath, slowly releasing the pleasure. Her muscles tightened around his shaft and it throbbed and hardened even more.

She quickened the pace. Bringing his hands to her hips, he pushed and helped her to the edge. With their cries of bliss mingling together, they reached an explosive climax. He knew he had fallen in love with her all over again, but he was afraid because he wouldn't be able to walk away this time.

Chapter 12

Trace's time at Raven's Nest was coming to a close. At first, Diana had hated the fact that they had to share a house together, but now she couldn't imagine him not being there. The anger she'd felt at the reading of the will, the feeling that John had betrayed her by leaving half of Raven's Nest to Trace, seemed so long ago and unimportant.

It was a warm Sunday afternoon. Diana and Trace were having lunch outside on the circular terrace. Raven's Nest was like a city unto itself. It had a breathtaking four stories. White pristine Italian marble columns guarded the front of the house. Bordering the length of the terrace were rose bushes and flower gardens that encompassed the exterior of the mansion, and swaying weeping willow trees ran the length of the house, like guards protecting it from strangers. A huge man-made waterfall and pond graced the middle of the huge lawn, giving it the look of paradise. Her breath caught at the sheer beauty of her surroundings.

Diana sat back in her seat, closed her eyes, raised her face to the sun, and inhaled deeply. She felt at peace. Feeling Trace's gaze upon her, she opened her eyes. "What?"

"Nothing. I was admiring the view."

"I know. I've lived at Raven's Nest for five years, and it still takes my breath away."

"I was admiring another view altogether."

"Are you getting romantic over chicken salad, Mr. Montgomery?" she inquired with a smile.

"Is it working?" He returned the smile.

She laughed heartily. "You should finish your lunch. You'll need your strength to play golf this afternoon."

"The execs can wait. Or I could cancel the outing?" he suggested.

"Uh-uh. Isn't that what you did the last time?"

He grinned. "I believe I was otherwise occupied."

"Oh, no, you don't. You promised you would play golf. I'll not be the one to distract you again."

"Rosa and most of the staff are doing their daily chores. I'm sure we could slip upstairs for a while." He shot her a sexy smile. "How about it?"

Diana's eyes widened with mock surprise. "Mr. Montgomery, do you want the staff to think that's all that we do?"

He chuckled. "Why not? You're young and healthy. I'm approaching forty and have to use every opportunity, while I have the energy, to make love to you."

"You make yourself sound ancient. You're in your prime."

His grin was wicked. "You're the one who knows it for sure."

Diana laughed. "You're crazy."

A serious look entered his eyes. "Yes. I'm crazy for you."

The laugher left her face. "Saying things like that will make me believe in fairy tales," she quipped.

"Then believe in them."

Diana was silent for a moment and finally said, "Maybe I'll take a chance."

He reached across the table and took her hand. "Close your eyes."

She did.

"Now I want you to make wish. I promise, if you let me, I'll do everything in my power to make it come true."

Diana's eyes flew open. "You're truly my hero."

"And don't you forget it."

She sighed and picked up her fork. "Now I know it's time for you to finish eating."

"Yes, ma'am," he said cheekily as he returned to his salad. He speared his fork into the greens and took a bite. He chewed and looked at her.

"What are you thinking about?" he said.

"I was going over the final details of the company picnic in my head."

"Is there anything I can do?"

"No, the caterers have been hired. Everything is on scheduled. Besides, Rosa and I have it under control.

"We don't have to have the party here at the mansion. We could set up tents and have it on the grounds of the Pisano office complex. It's large enough."

"I know, but it's more intimate to have it here. I think everybody looks forward to coming. I know I look forward to giving it."

"Are you sure?"

"Yes. We've had a little over four hundred responses."

"Wow."

"*Wow* is right. It's going to be a wonderful day with lots of food, music, entertainment, and games for everyone."

"I see the glint in your eyes. You're enjoying it."

"I am. Mama and Daddy came from large families. We always had a party going on. Whether it was a birthday, family reunion, or a holiday, we would gather at one of the relatives' houses to eat, laugh, and enjoy each other until our hearts were content. It was great."

"You had something I never had, a wonderful childhood."

There was a silence. Crispina needed to be crucified for neglect, Diana thought. The woman gave motherhood a bad name. Finally, she cleared her throat. "Yes, I did. I have beautiful memories. With both sets of grandparents gone, I'll always remember those times with joy, but a little sadness, too."

"This year will be even more special," Trace said.

"Why is that?"

"Because I'll be with you."

Diana was silent as she pondered his statement. At the rate they were moving—which was fast—it was only logical for him to assume they had a future together.

"Trace, about us…"

"What about us?

"I think we need to take it one day at a time."

"Why?"

"We need to try…" Seeing the closed look on his face, she stopped in mid-sentence, knowing she had offended him. "I can tell I have annoyed you." She pressed her palm to her temple to ease the sudden rush of tension. "This isn't a good time to discuss anything. You have to go and I need to really cement the plans for the party."

"I told you I'm crazy about you. That's something I've never told any woman. I'm not going to let you pretend what has happened between us is of little importance."

"I'm not doing that."

"Yes, you are. You're running scared." He was silent for a moment. "I didn't coerce you. You made the decision to be with me."

"I know that."

"Why do you keep running from me, Diana? Sometimes you are with me, and then sometimes, in the midst of a conversation, I see you slipping away."

"You're imagining things."

"Am I?"

"I don't want to get hurt, Trace. We're moving too fast."

"You believe I would hurt you?"

"Yes…no…I don't know. And I don't want to find out." She stopped, lowered her eyes, and absently fingered the white linen napkin in her lap. Taking a deep breath, she tried to explain. "I want to be in control this time. When and if you walk away I'll be strong enough to survive."

He would have no trouble and plenty of opportunities to indulge himself with any woman who caught his fancy. Although selective, she was sure he would have no problem finding a replacement for her…quickly.

He pushed his empty plate aside and pinched the bridge of his nose. He reached across the table and engulfed her hand in his. Diana's body reacted through instinct to the electric tension they created by just touching each other.

"I never left you the first time. Remember, it was you who left me," he said softly. Diana dropped her eyes and tried to pull her hand free, but he wouldn't let go.

Trace released her hands and ran his hand through his hair in frustration. "Diana, I want you in my life. This is real. Dammit, I'm not playing a game. It's not an impromptu request I'm going to retract. You're my lover and my friend. I have never wanted a long-term relationship with anyone but you. This isn't something I take lightly."

The man had stolen her heart long ago, and he still held it in his grip. Could she trust her instincts and give him another chance? She believed he wanted her, but she wanted him to love her. Granted, she'd never said the words, either, but she needed to know if he did. She couldn't commit herself to him without him loving her, could she? Did she have enough love for the both of them? She still had Nicky to think about; her son was her number one priority. Trace wanted answers as to why she left him. The last thing she wanted to do was rehash the pain. He extended his hand. Without hesitation, she placed her small hand into his huge one. He gently closed his hand around hers and pulled her from her chair. He held her loosely in his arms.

"Do you see how good we are together?"

"Mmm." Her skin tingled in remembrance of their lovemaking the night before and today. "I don't think it's something I could forget, even if I tried."

"Why even try?"

"Give me a little time, Trace."

"Your time ran out five years ago, Diana."

"I—"

He interrupted her. "Not discussing what is evidently between us and what happened to make you run from me won't make it go away. I want to be with you, and I know you want to be with me," he said.

She moved out of his arms and he let her go. She walked to the thick marble railing and looked out over the gardens. She wrapped her arms around her body. Trace followed her and moved up behind her, circling her with his arms.

"You're a stubborn and strong-willed woman. I like and admire that about you. It was one of the things that attracted me to you. But I won't let you run from this, it's too important."

"I need you to understand what I'm feeling, Trace. You came back into my life after a long absence. I thought you would fulfill the terms of the will and leave. I didn't plan or want to get involved with you."

"But you are involved. From the first moment years ago when I walked into my uncle's office and you looked at me with those beautiful brown eyes, you and I were connected. I've never ever had it with another woman. I know I can't let you go."

"Maybe we should rethink this…."

Trace turned her around so she was facing him. He blocked her from leaving by placing his hands on the rail and leaning into her.

"Don't think about running away this time, Diana. I'd search the corners of the earth and bring you back to me."

"Trace…"

"You trusted me enough to give me your innocence. I know you wouldn't have done that with just any man. I never told you, but I was honored to be your first lover. I don't understand why you married my uncle. I'm not going to lie, it still bothers me. I thought we had something strong and good. I know something happened to drive you from me, but I'm not going to press you to tell me…for now."

Diana opened her mouth to speak, but Trace laid his fingers on her lips. He cupped her face in his hands and gently kissed her, then again deeply. She leaned into him. His BlackBerry rang. He then leaned forward and gave her another hard kiss.

Cupping her face lovingly, he said, "Finish your lunch."

For a moment, it seemed as if he wanted to say something else. He kissed her again and walked away.

She wanted to pretend this was the ideal world, she and Trace enjoying lunch, happy and content. She forced herself not to think about what would happen if he uncovered her secret. Her heartbeat escalated. He wouldn't let her go this time without a fight.

This time she was afraid she didn't have the strength to walk away.

Chapter 13

Trace observed the endless stream of people that filled the grounds of Raven's Nest. The sun was shining bright, not a cloud in the sky. The caterers had turned the mansion grounds into a festive venue. A huge banquet spread held a plentiful supply fit for royalty.

A ten-piece band under a large tent played a foot-tapping beat. Some people danced and others frolicked in the two large pools. Lights were strung in the trees for when darkness fell. Diana had gone all out in planning this gathering, and it showed.

Trace was lounging in a chair, sipping a glass of lemonade, and wishing for something stronger. However, he needed his wits to play host to Diana's hostess.

While he listened to the chatter of his VPs, he covertly looked around for Diana and saw her talking to her best friend, Susan.

God, he couldn't get his fill of Diana. Granted the sex was unbelievable, but it was more than that. He enjoyed being with her. He heard her laugh and felt a catch in his chest. He loved her. This woman held his heart in the palm of her hand.

Diana's floral sundress flowed around her body in quiet elegance, draping her curves from the low neckline down to the smooth contour of her ankles. Tendrils of dark hair escaped the soft bundle of curls on top of her head, gently framing the smooth lines of her face. When she turned to speak to a passing waiter, he saw the sundress was almost backless.

Male eyes were trained on her from every direction, and he didn't like it one bit. He placed his lemonade on a passing server's tray, excused himself from his companions, and walked toward her.

A single lock of hair trailed down her cheek, brushing her skin as she tilted her head to listen to Susan. Diana's skin glowed, reminding him of the early morning lovemaking that had left them both surprised at the power of their combined climax.

"Hello, Susan," Trace called as he grabbed a stuffed mushroom off the tray of a passing waiter.

"Hi, sweetheart," he said softly. Popping a mushroom in his mouth, he reached for a napkin on the table behind her and wiped his hands. He then circled her small waist with his arm, pulled her tightly to his side, and bestowed a deep kiss on her slightly parted lips.

"Trace—" She frowned and leaned away from him, causing him to tighten his grip and press her even closer. Trace saw he had shocked her. Hell, he'd shocked himself by publicly staking his claim on her.

This was something he'd never done with any woman. What the hell was wrong with him? He didn't know and he didn't care.

Still frowning, she asked, "What's gotten into you?"

"What? I can't give my lady a kiss?"

"That wasn't a kiss. You were stamping me with your brand."

"Hmm. Now that is an idea."

Susan cleared her throat. "Trace, what you do think about having fireworks for the finale?"

"Sounds great," he said, not taking his eyes from Diana.

"I was telling Diana it was a lovely idea." Susan eyed them with ill-disguised curiosity.

He ignored the puzzlement on their faces. He wasn't sure why a burst of jealousy had propelled him to stake his claim. He'd never been jealous of a woman before, but the feeling felt natural when it came to Diana.

"Did you just get here?" Diana inquired.

"No, I have been here for a couple of hours." Trace looked around the backyard. "Large turnout."

"This is a small gathering compared to previous years, but a little bigger than last year," Susan replied.

"I haven't seen Crispina here," Diana said.

Trace frowned. "And you won't."

Diana shot him a surprised look. "As a board member, she was automatically invited."

"I uninvited her," Trace said, his tone cold.

"You did? But…"

"Let it go, Diana. Please."

Diana shot him a look that said *we'll-talk-about-this-later*. "All right."

There was a long, uncomfortable silence.

"Oh, well, I…" Looking over Susan's shoulder, he saw the arrival of his cousin. "I have a little business to attend to." He gave Diana a lingering kiss this time. "I'll see you later."

Diana and Susan watched him walk away. Susan turned and looked at Diana, surprise evident on her face. Diana took a deep breath and cleared her throat. Before she could think of how to explain Trace's possessive behavior, Susan spoke.

"I assume he and Crispina are at odds…again. But what was that?" Susan said.

"What was what?"

"Diana, Trace walked over here, grabbed you by the waist, and tried to make your body and his one. And then he drowned you with a kiss."

"I don't know what's gotten into him."

"You don't say," She planted her hands on her hips, a manner Diana knew meant *I'm-not-moving-until-I-have-every-detail*. "I thought the yacht weekend was a one-time thing that unexpectedly happened. I believe the man was stating his claim. I thought you said you two weren't in a relationship. But from where I'm standing, it looks like a relationship to me."

"We're not…not really. When he came home from a business trip, I kinda jumped him. I really don't know what came over me."

Susan was obviously in shock. "You've got to be kidding." Her friend's eyes were now huge.

"No, I'm not kidding."

"You?"

"Yes, me." Not liking the way Susan said it, Diana put her hands on her hips. "And what do you mean when you say, 'you'?"

"Well, you are so…" Susan shrugged and lifted her hands as Diana watched her try to find the right words.

"I'm so what?"

"Uh…nice. You're a good girl. I can't imagine you making the first move."

"Are you saying good girls don't enjoy sex?"

"No, but you have certainly taken charge and went after what you want."

"Trace is a hard man to resist." Finally admitting it to herself, she said, "I want to be with him."

"I know you do. It's wonderful. When you returned to work there was a glow to your face and a different stride to your walk. Now I know why."

"Susan, don't read more into it than there is."

"Hmm, if you say so."

"Susan—"

"I'm glad you listened to your best friend. Didn't I tell you you should give him another chance? The man is hot! hot! hot!"

"Don't get too excited about this…"

"You can't squash my excitement. I'm not even mad at you."

"You're not?"

"Nope. Eventually you would've told me."

"You think so?"

Looking at Diana with a strange look on her face, Susan said, "Why these questions? Are you sick or something?"

"No. I'm just concerned. I don't—"

"Stop it, Diana." Taking Diana's hand in hers, Susan gave it a light squeeze. "You must stop thinking you don't deserve to be happy."

"That isn't what I think…I'm just cautious."

"Yeah, right. You're always looking for the ax to fall."

"Not always."

"You're confident in your business ability and can hold your own in a room of chauvinistic piranhas. If I had graduated in the top ten percent of my class, you wouldn't be able to stop me from moving mountains."

"You're smart, Susan. Don't you ever let anyone tell you anything different."

"You're good for my ego, friend. Thanks."

"I'm telling you the truth. You're one of the smartest people I know."

Susan stuck her nose in the air. "I am, aren't I?"

Diana laughed. "Now tell me when you're going to stop being nasty to Dominic Mello?"

"Why are you bringing him up?" Susan frowned at Diana and put her hands on her hips. "We were having a great conversation, but you had to go and ruin it."

"He just arrived," Diana said slyly. She motioned to where Trace was standing and talking to a tall, dark, and handsome man.

Susan stiffened. "Who invited him?"

Diana shrugged. "He's Trace's cousin, plus his best friend."

Susan rounded on Diana. "I know you. You extended a personal invitation. Why in the world would you do that?"

"Probably because I like seeing him stare a hole in your back."

A red flush tinted Susan's olive skin. "Tell me you are kidding."

"Nope, I'm afraid not."

Susan abruptly turned around and caught Dominic staring. Diana noticed neither one broke eye contact. Finally he broke the contact when he leaned toward Trace to hear what he was saying. Dominic laughed and Susan flushed.

"Well, well, what was that look about?" Diana asked.

"I have no idea what you're talking about. The man is rude, arrogant, and a menace."

Diana laughed. "Oh, Susan, I do believe you protest too much."

"Diana Pisano, I'm not going to dignify that with a comment."

Slipping her arm through Susan's, Diana said, "I just bet you won't."

"Enough about that man," Susan said in a haughty tone.

"Come, let's go to the kitchen. You can help me to slice the pound cakes," Diana said.

Susan squealed. "Cook made pound cakes?"

"Yes, she did. Although the picnic is catered, no one can make a cake like she can."

"You definitely got that right. Lead the way!"

Chapter 14

In the kitchen, Diana and Susan found Mrs. Johnson, lovingly called Cook, slicing the cakes.

"Hmm, Cook, you really outdid yourself." Susan licked the icing from her fingers. "The 7-Up pound cake with the cream cheese icing is to die for."

"Thank you, Ms. Torres," Cook said with pride.

"Susan is right, Cook. The cakes are delicious."

"I'm glad to hear it. Now, if you ladies will excuse me, I'll go and make sure the servers are doing their duties." She turned and walked out of the kitchen.

"She's certainly a character."

"Yes, she is."

Breaking off a chunk of cake, Susan chewed and looked at Diana. "Okay, now you can tell me. When did you and Trace move to the next level in your relationship?"

"I told you." Diana fingered the icing and kept her eyes downcast.

"Diana, I like to pride myself on knowing you at least a little bit. I know there's more."

Sighing, Diana pulled out an island stool and sat down at the counter. Susan did the same. "I've decided that Trace and I need to take it slow."

"Did you forget to tell him? Because from what I saw, I don't think he's in agreement."

"Probably not, but it's what I want."

"Diana, I know you loved John, but it was obvious to me it was more friendship than a passionate marriage. It's time to move on."

"What?"

"John always treated you like a porcelain doll. Others would have taken it as a man deeply in love with his younger wife, but because I'm your friend and was around John and you more than most, I know it was a man treating you like a precious daughter."

"He was my best friend."

"Am I assuming correctly that Trace doesn't know the true status of your marriage to John?"

"No, he doesn't."

"Are you going to tell him?"

"It's complicated."

"And Nicky?"

"What about Nicky?" she said cautiously.

"Diana, last week when we were in your office and Trace came in, I realized he kept reminding me of someone, but I couldn't put my finger on it. While the two of you talked, it finally hit. He reminded me so much of Nicky. Then I looked for the picture of him, the one you always keep on your desk; it was conspicuously absent, which was strange because you are so proud of that picture. Remember, it was the picture you snapped of Nicky when he lost his first baby tooth, and you cried because you realized he was growing up fast. I couldn't understand why you would remove the picture, but then it dawned on me. You didn't want Trace to see it. Otherwise, why would you remove a picture of your son from your office?"

"You know the answer." Pausing, she took a deep, tired breath. "It's a secret no one knew except John. Not even my parents."

"Trace is Nicky's father."

Diana didn't hesitate. She was tired of holding on to the secret. She needed to share it with someone. "Yes, he is. I was pregnant with Nicky when John and I got married. He suggested the marriage so Nicky would be legitimate. I didn't want my baby to be born a bastard."

"Oh, Diana," Susan offered sadly.

"I was scared and angry. I just didn't know what to do. My parents raised me to be a good girl, and being with Trace made me go against everything my parents instilled in me. I practically lived at his penthouse. I had a key and could come and go as I pleased. If my parents had known what type of life I was living, it would've hurt them."

"I'm sure they weren't so naïve they didn't know what being with a man like Trace entailed. The man is a billionaire and associates with people we only read about in magazines. I think your parents knew but respected your privacy and judgment."

"Still, I can't bring myself to tell Trace or my parents about Nicky." Diana was placid as she thought about sharing this last bit with Susan. "Trace wants more than I'm willing to give."

"Diana, it's obvious to me that you love the man. You need to trust your instincts. You need to tell him about Nicky…and do it soon. Believe me, they will know, if anyone sees Nicky and Trace together. Nicky is an exact replica of him."

"I know." She looked for disappointment in Susan's eyes and found none. "I've created a mess."

"You have time to straighten it out."

"Thank you, Susan, you're…"

"Mommy!"

Diana spun around, shocked to see Nicky running full steam toward her. Close behind were Diana's parents, Estelle and Russell Hamilton. Nicky threw his little arms around her legs. She lifted him into her arms, squeezing him tight as she rained kisses over his soft, round face. She looked over his shoulders at her parents. "Whaa…what are you doing here?" Anxiety and fear ran through her body. She couldn't let Trace see Nicky. "Why didn't you tell me you were coming?"

Without answering, Russell Hamilton engulfed his daughter and grandson in a bear hug and kissed

Diana's temple. Estelle was grinning. "We wanted to surprise you."

"I thought you said Dad had to finish a project and it…"

"He finished early. Can you believe it? It's the first time your father completed a project with time to spare," Estelle said.

"You didn't have to drive all this way. I could've come to Charleston."

"We know that, baby girl, but we wanted to come for the big shindig," her father said. "Plus, as of this morning, we are officially on vacation."

Estelle gave Diana a kiss on the cheek and turned to Susan, smiling and embracing her. "Hi, Susan. It's so nice to see you again."

Susan gave the petite woman a kiss on the cheek and then moved to Russell Hamilton and gave him a hug. "How are you, Mr. Hamilton?"

"I'm good," Russell said as he returned her hug, his other arm still around Diana.

"Susan, have you lost weight?" Estelle asked surveying Susan thoroughly as a mother would inspect her child. "Looks like you could stand to gain a few pounds."

Laughing, Susan said, "No, I haven't. But I'm sure I'll gain pounds today. Did you see the spread out there on the lawn?"

"Indeed we did. Russell grabbed a hot dog and gobbled it up before we even reached the door of the house."

Sheepishly, Russell glanced at his wife. "Ah, Estelle, you know how I love hot dogs, and you only allow me one every couple of months."

"Russell Hamilton, if I didn't monitor your cholesterol level it would soar sky-high."

"Dad, are you still sneaking hot dogs and buffalo wings?"

"Now, baby girl, don't you go and gang up on me with your mother and give away all my secrets."

Tired of the grown-ups' interchange, Nicky squirmed in his mother's arms; Susan gave Nicky a noisy kiss that made him squirm even more. "How's my boyfriend doing?"

"Auntie Susan, I'm not your boyfriend," he said seriously.

With a sad face, Susan poked out her lips. "Oh, I see. Have I been replaced with someone else?"

"Don't be sad, Auntie Susan."

Laughing, Diana placed Nicky on his feet. Russell smiled and ruffled Nicky's dark curls.

"I'm gonna leave so you ladies can have your woman talk. I'll drive down to the cottage and visit with Henderson."

Henderson had worked for the Pisano family for over thirty years. After Diana married John Pisano, the Hamiltons had come to visit and Russell Hamil-ton discovered that the Henderson Diana so lovingly talked about was his old army buddy who he hadn't seen since they came back from Vietnam. Henderson, who was in semi-retirement and still liked to chauffer, lived in one of the estate cottages.

"Dad, you just got here," Diana exclaimed. "Let me fix you a plate."

"Baby girl, we're not here for you to entertain us. We came to bring Nicky home and to see you. Any-way, there's plenty of food outside, I'll grab a couple plates on my way for Henderson and myself. The food will be his consolation prize after I whip him in our chess rematch. I have a new strategy." He rubbed his hands together with glee.

Hiding a smile, Estelle gave her husband a kiss. "Honey, you've been trying out this strategy on Hen-derson for years and it hasn't worked. I don't think it'll work now."

"Have faith in your man." He gave her hug, winked at the others, and walked out the door whistling a hap-py tune.

Diana felt Nicky tugging at her dress. "Mommy, I'm hungry," he said, looking up at her with wide eyes.

"It never ceases to amaze me how that little boy can eat so much," Estelle said, smiling. "Just two hours ago, we stopped at his favorite place for a meal of chicken nuggets and fries."

"Mama, you didn't," Diana said mockingly, grabbing her chest.

"Desperate times call for desperate measures. When you have a cranky child who wants to eat now… you give them a little something to tide them over."

Laughing, Susan captured Nicky's hand. "I'll take him to get something to eat. You stay and catch up with your mother. I'll keep him occupied." Susan shot Diana a knowing look.

"Thank you." Diana gave a sigh of relief and mouthed a silent, special thank you at Susan.

"It's no problem at all." Susan wrapped Nicky in a loving hug. "Come on, buddy, you and I are going to raid the food table."

Hands clasped together, they left the room. Diana glanced at her mother, who was watching her with a frown.

"What?"

"You seem anxious," Estelle said as she took the seat at the island counter vacated by Susan. Diana sat across from her.

She remembered Trace was out on the lawn and might come into the house any minute. It made her nervous and jittery. "I'm just a little tired."

"Did you finish the assignment on time?"

"Uh…ah…what assignment? Oh, yes, I did." She massaged the tension in her temples. She had just lied to her mother again. The hole was getting deeper.

"Diana, what's wrong with you? You look exhausted. You're tense. I know you planned the party but you are used to doing this type of thing."

Diana took a nervous deep breath. "Mama, I have to tell you something."

"Well, whatever it is, it can't…" They both turned, hearing a noise behind them. Trace stood in the doorway with his cousin and best friend, Dominic Mello, a knowing grin on his face. He looked like a man who'd found a pot of gold.

Diana's heart lurched in her chest. She fixed her eyes on Trace and then glanced at the man walking beside him. She pasted a smile on her face. "Hi, Dominic, it's good to see you. You didn't let me know you were coming, but I'm glad you did." She embraced him.

Dominic Mello, a tall, dark-haired man with midnight eyes, was a gorgeous vision to behold. Never married, and with no intention of taking that route, he was never short of women on his arm or, if rumor be correct, in his bed.

He engulfed Diana in a bear hug, sweeping her off her feet and swinging her up in his arms. He gave her a firm kiss on the lips that put a dark frown on Trace's face.

"Put her down and step away, Dominic." The cold and hard timbre of Trace's voice curled around her soul.

"Hold your jets, cousin. I was only greeting the little lady." Dominic placed Diana on her feet.

Trace grimaced and moved to Diana's side, sliding his arm around her waist. "I don't like your type of greeting."

Dominic laughed. "Whew, I was only saying hello."

"Again, I'm telling you I didn't like it," Trace said coldly.

Diana examined Trace. She was surprised. She had never seen him act this way. What in the world had gotten into him? He ought to know Dominic was harmless.

"Stop needling him, Dominic," Diana said.

Dominic laughed. "Oh, how I like doing it." He slapped Trace on the back. "No worries, cousin, no one is going to take your lady from you."

"That's for sure." Trace's voice was hard and decisive.

Dominic was friendly and very Italian. He always greeted her with a kiss, but this time she thought it was a little too much. It was his way of getting a rise out of Trace. A frown marred Trace's face. He looked dangerous and unapproachable.

Walking between the two men, Estelle extended her hand and introduced herself. "Hello. I'm Estelle, Diana's mother."

Dominic turned on his full charm. "Well, well, another extremely beautiful lady. It certainly runs in the family." Taking her hand, Dominic brought it to his lips and placed a gallant kiss on her hand. Her mother actually giggled. Diana looked to make sure it was coming from her mother. Dominic's charm affected all women, no matter the age group, and it seemed her mother wasn't immune.

Rolling her eyes, Diana shot Dominic a stern look. The kiss he'd given her had gotten a rise out of Trace. What surprised her was that Trace had fallen for it. She gave Trace a look that indicated she would deal with him later. His blue gaze stared back in a way that was both territorial and unsettling, publicly staking his claim. She made a concentrated effort not to blush at his bold look.

Trace moved to greet her mother. "Hello, Mrs. Hamilton, it's been a long time. It's nice to see you again," he said as he extended his hand. Estelle took his hand and pulled him into a hug. It surprised Diana to see Trace let her mother enclose him in a firm hug. For a moment, he looked shocked and unbalanced.

"It's good to see you again also, Trace. And remember, it's Estelle, not Mrs. Hamilton."

He cleared his throat. "Thank you, Estelle. I hope you didn't come all this way by yourself."

"No, I didn't. Russell left us to chit-chat. He went to the cottage to play chess with Henderson."

"Good. I'm glad you could make it to the barbecue."

"Me, too, but we aren't staying long. We're heading to Savannah."

"Oh, do you have family there?"

"No, we're vacationing."

Dominic glanced at his watch. "If you'll excuse me, I need to get going."

"You're leaving so soon?" Diana glanced at Dominic and then at Trace. "You just arrived."

"Thank you, little one." He took hold of her hands, but didn't move in too close. "I need to be in Rome tomorrow morning. I flew in from New York a couple of hours ago to go over the Sydney contracts with Trace."

Diana's eyes widened. "Sydney? I thought that was on the back burner until 2013."

"Still is, but we're starting the negotiation process," Dominic said.

"And you still need to eat. Stay and eat with—"

"Diana, we need to finish our business so Dominic can leave," Trace said coolly.

"Trace," Diana murmured in a stern voice.

Dominic laughed. "Thank you, Diana. I'll grab something before I go."

"Are you ready to go over the contracts now?" Trace inquired.

"Trace, you're really possessive of your woman. No need. Like I said before, she already belongs to you."

Diana frowned. "Excuse me, gentlemen, I'm in the room and no one owns me."

Smiling, Dominic kissed her cheek. "If you say so, little one." Turning to Estelle, he took her hand again. "It was a pleasure meeting you, Estelle. Hopefully we'll meet again soon."

"It's been a pleasure for me also. You're definitely a charmer, Dominic. It's nice to see it in a young man. Nowadays, there's little chivalry seen in the younger generation."

"Why, thank you, lovely lady."

"Are you finished, Dominic, or do I need to take a seat while you continue?"

Dominic chuckled. "All right, I'm coming. I had to say my goodbyes."

Trace grunted and turned to Diana's mother. "Dominic and I have some business to discuss before he leaves. Please stay a while. I would love for us to chat." Trace threw her a rare, genuine smile.

Estelle gave Trace a warm smile. "I would like that very much."

"Good." He gave Diana another kiss and they moved toward the door leading onto the terrace but stopped at the sound of high-pitched squeals. Nicky made a bee line for his mother, stopping when he saw the strange men in the kitchen. At his mother's side, he stared upward.

Diana froze; the moment she dreaded was here. She had hoped Susan would keep Nicky occupied. In the midst of talking to Trace and Dominic, she'd forgotten Nicky was home. Hoping she could avoid this moment was only wishful thinking. Time had run out.

"Diana?" Trace looked at her with a question in his eyes. Everything stilled. Confusion marred his features as he walked toward her and Nicky.

"Aren't you going to introduce me to your son?"

Chapter 15

Trace closed the distance between the boy and him. He went still when he saw this child was an exact replica of himself. His eyes, although they were light brown, had the shape and a tinge of violet that was a dead giveaway to Montgomery parentage. He would've known the Montgomery facial features anywhere; the straight, aristocratic nose, the chin with a dimple, the tilt of the head. All were reminiscent of the way he'd looked as a child. He didn't breathe. Time stood still. This child was beautiful…this child created was his.

Trace was amazed at the how the little boy stood perfectly still as he approached. He didn't cringe or drop his gaze, but neither did he let go of his mother's hand. He regarded Trace with wide-eyed, unblinking solemnity, weighing him up with the innocence of youth, until suddenly a smile curved his small mouth.

"Hello, I'm Nicky." Unbidden, a small hand extended in formal greeting. With great care Trace enfolded it within his own.

"I'm Trace," he husked out. He couldn't keep the unevenness from his voice.

His emotions were conflicting. He felt bewilderment, betrayal, and a fierce anger at the woman he loved. He stood there fighting to keep his anger from boiling over. He didn't want to frighten the child. He continued to look at the boy and his heart turned over with joy. He felt Diana covertly watching him, but he ignored her. He would deal with her and her treachery later. For now, his concentration was on the little boy who stood before him.

There was a part of him that wanted to encapsulate the moment for safe-keeping. He had a son. A boy that was undeniably his.

"Mommy?" Nicky said, his voice uncertain. Trace realized his thorough scrutiny was making Nicky uncomfortable, yet he couldn't take his eyes off his son.

Estelle stepped forward. "Why don't I take Nicky outside while—"

"No!" Trace said in a hard, cold voice.

Nicky moved closer to his mother. "How dare you?" Diane snapped. "You're frightening him."

Trace noticed the quiver of the little boy's mouth and fought for control. "Let him stay," he said quietly.

"Trace," Dominic put a hand on his shoulder. "Maybe you should let the boy go."

"Why? So she can continue the charade?"

"Trace…" Dominic scolded. "Let's not do this here."

Trace ignored Dominic and inquired with a forced calm, "How old is he?" He glared at Diana, waiting for the truth. Would she lie to his face? Before she could answer, Nicky held up both hands.

"I'm four," Nicky said, one hand showing four fingers sticking up while he held his thumb down with his other hand. "I'll be five when it gets cold outside." He let another four fingers escape on his other hand and stand to attention to indicate the months. Confused, Trace asked, "When is your birthday?"

Smiling, Nicky was happy to offer the answer. "October first. Mommy said I was the gift that made her heart warm again. I'm better than ice cream," he said. A wide smile broke out on his face. Trace calculated the months from the time she left him to when she married John. He watched the color drain from her face. He couldn't tear his gaze from her. The woman he was willing to forgive for everything—the woman who'd dealt a crippling blow to his heart—the mother of his son.

His gaze bored into hers. "Diana." His voice was deadly quiet. "You have a lot to explain."

"Trace, I don't think this is the time—" Dominic said.

"Why not? Everyone here can see the truth."

"I'm going to take Nicky outside," Estelle said hurriedly and took Nicky gently by the hand. "Nicky doesn't need to be in the midst of this."

"Mama…"

Estelle looked sadly at her daughter. "This is something that needs to be discussed between you and Trace."

"I'm sorry, Mama."

"So am I, Diana." She led Nicky out of the door.

Susan went to her friend, put her arm around her shoulders, and gave her a squeeze. "If you need me, I'll be outside…but not far." She frowned at Trace and left.

Dominic touched Trace's shoulder again. "Trace, I'll wait for you in the study." Trace still stood in stony silence. Dominic continued, "Look, I know what you must think, but let Diana explain before jumping to conclusions." Trace didn't answer and Dominic left the room.

To keep from reaching out to her, Trace crossed his arms. She stood in front of the window with her back to him. He watched as her slender hand waved at someone outside. Her sundress swirled at her ankles. For one traitorous moment, Trace remembered their mind-blowing lovemaking. He grimaced at the thought.

Was it only a few hours ago they'd lost themselves in each other? He had murmured words of pleasure in her ear as they reached the pinnacle of release together. In the past few weeks, he couldn't get enough of her and now… he could barely look at her. What had he done to make her hate him so much that she would deny him his own flesh and blood?

Trace fought the urge to shake her. He was afraid he would've if she'd been within reach. He shook his head. She was the woman whom he had loved more than his own life. What went wrong? How did they end up at this place of pain and distrust? He wasn't looking for love or a relationship when he saw her in his uncle's office that warm spring day almost seven years ago, he mused. He recalled the moment she'd turned her dark brown accusing eyes on him for interrupting the meeting she was having with John. He had been entranced from that moment but unprepared for the instantaneous physical chemistry.

It was six months before she would agree to have dinner with him. Even then, it hadn't been easy; it had taken another month to get her to agree to a second dinner…and the rest was history. In all of their time together, one entire year, it had never entered his mind she could be so devious and heartless. The woman he had known was one of the most loving, giving people he knew. Her family was the epitome of what a loving and caring family was really like. She had had the childhood he'd never had, two parents who loved each other and their children. He'd wanted that with her and had followed his heart. He had been such a fool, and was again.

"Diana." She turned to face him. "I want answers and I want them now."

"I know. We need to talk, but let's do it somewhere private."

He walked to the intercom. "Cook, Mrs. Pisano and I are using the kitchen. Please close the outer doors and allow no one through until I notify you."

"Trace! How dare you? I can imagine what she must be thinking."

"I don't give a damn what anyone is thinking," he spit out. "I want the truth. Is the boy my son?"

"Nicky is my son," she said protectively. He had to admit Diana was a strong opponent. She never would back down from a fight. Now she was in the mother of all fights, for her child. He needed to tread carefully to get what he wanted.

"Is this the game you want to play?"

"No one can play the game better than you, Trace."

"What the hell are you talking about? You're the liar, and yet you act the injured party!"

"I don't know what you are talking about. I'll not stand for your abuse."

An eyebrow lifted. "After what I saw, you have the audacity to be indignant?" He walked toward her, his voice brittle, and his eyes grew angrier with every step. "The boy is my son. I saw it the moment I laid eyes on him. Every damn person in the room saw it. And now you stand before me as if you have done nothing wrong."

"I haven't." She lifted a hand and smoothed it over her hair in an unconscious gesture. "And I'm finished with this conversation."

"Like hell you are! You refuse to admit what I already know?"

"There is nothing to admit."

"I want to hear you say he's my son."

She squared her shoulders and looked him in the eye. "He is my son. Not yours."

He went very still. "Tread lightly, Diana. Lying will make you lose more than you think."

"Go to hell."

One eyebrow lifted in a gesture of determined cynicism. "You're going to wish you were there before I'm through."

"I've already been there." She had the gall to look at him as if she hated him. What gave her the right?

The atmosphere between them threatened to explode.

"You think you know hell?" Trace's voice was clipped. "I beg to differ. You kept my son from me." His expression didn't change. "This is not a topic for discussion. I want him, and I intend to have him."

"My son doesn't know you."

"Whose fault is that?"

Consternation filled her eyes. She was a good mother, by the looks of it. She wouldn't put her son through a fight. It still didn't change what she'd done. He had her where he wanted her, in his control.

"He isn't one of your acquisitions, Trace."

"Nothing you can say is going to sway me."

"Listen to yourself. You act as if he is a toy or a piece of meat. He's my son. Not some prize where you throw the dice to see who has the winning hand."

"Damn you, I'm not a monster."

"Well, stop acting like one."

He breathed deeply, trying to reel in his anger.

"You knew you were pregnant when you married John. Why didn't you tell me?"

"Why would I? It was my problem."

"Problem? Is that how you saw it? As a problem to get rid of?"

"No! I never once thought of aborting my child."

"Good. At least I can be thankful for that," he said with sarcasm.

"You have no right to judge me."

He gave a hard laugh. "Not judge you? You made the decision to keep my son from me—his father—and I'm not to judge you? I have missed four years of his life and I'm supposed to be glad about that?"

"I made the right decision about my child and myself."

"Really? That's something you'll never know for certain. However, I'll tell you this. I will not miss another four years of his life."

"What do you mean?

"I don't think I have to spell it out for you."

"You have no proof Nicky is your son."

"Then I'll get it." He pulled the BlackBerry from his waist and snapped it open. "I'll have a private lab here within the hour to get samples for a paternity test." A muscle bunched at his jaw. "This is no game, Diana. I can verify what I know to be true."

"No." Her voice was terse.

"You refuse to tell me what I already know?"

"I have already told you what you needed to know."

"When I file for joint custody, or perhaps for full custody, believe me, it'll get ugly. The fact that you were pregnant with my child and didn't tell me, not giving me the chance to be a father, won't sit well with the courts. You knowingly married another man—my uncle—a man richer than me at the time. And to top it off, he was older than your own father. What does that make you look like, Diana? A gold-digger or worse—"

"You son of a bitch," she spewed.

Trace's eyebrows lifted in a gesture of mockery. "Is that the best you can do, Diana?"

"I'll not have you frighten my son," Diana insisted. "You're nothing but a stranger to him."

"Damn you to hell." His voice was angry, his features a hard mask. "What kind of man do you think I am?"

"I have no idea."

"You don't know?" he said in harsh tones. She remained silent. "I intend to get to know him, spend time with him so when we tell him I'm his father the transition will be smooth. The boy will know I'm his father, Diana." His pause was almost imperceptible. "The sooner the better."

She momentarily closed her eyes. "You're a ruthless bastard," she said.

"So what else is new?

"You may have dona…"

"Oh, so you admit that Nicky is mine."

"No, I do not. Nicky is mine. I chose to carry him, give birth to him. He's my life." Her eyes blazed with unshed tears. "John and I were the ones who nurtured and loved him."

His eyes narrowed and his mouth tightened. "You dare bring John's name up when you denied me the opportunity to be there?"

"We were finished."

"You ran away like a little girl."

"You're really full of yourself. You think I should've stayed and shared you with other women? I had more respect for myself. In the end you got what you wanted."

"We were in a relationship."

"A lot of difference that made to you."

"What the hell does that mean? I gave you more than I ever gave any woman," he shouted, watching the conflicting emotions run across her expressive features.

"I guess I'm one lucky woman," she sneered.

"Unlike you, I'm not going to resort to sarcasm. There is a more pressing matter to be resolved."

Her features became strained. "What?"

"I've told you. I want my son."

"He is not yours."

Trace continued as if she hadn't spoken. "I want him living in my house. I want to see him each day."

"No."

His mouth tightened. "This is not negotiable."

"No," she said firmly.

He continued speaking as if she never spoke. "I'm moving into Raven's Nest permanently. You can either stay or move out. I frankly don't give a damn what you do. But it'll be my face my son sees in the morning and at night when he closes his eyes."

"I won't continue with this while my parents and the employees are here. You seem to have forgotten there's a party going on out on the lawn," Diana said.

He stared at her for a long moment. "I haven't forgotten." His voice became dangerously quiet. "Don't you dare think about running this time. And don't underestimate me, Diana. I would find you and I would get him back."

"Trace." A pulse beat fast at the base of her throat, a visible sign of her inner turmoil.

Trace regarded her solemnly, noting the slight redness of her eyes, the faint shadows beneath, and her tight features. He knew she hadn't gotten much sleep last night, the same as he, and there was a certain satisfaction to be had in that. It had been a beautiful night, but it was over. And he wouldn't think of it; he needed to remember how devious she could be. These last few weeks had been a game, her plan to keep him in the dark so he would never know his son.

"You want to spend time with Nicky...." She hesitated.

"You're admitting I'm Nicky's father."

A red flush stained her already tightened features. "You can't have my son."

"The truth evades your lips, Diana. Why aren't I surprised?"

"I won't be called a liar."

"The shoe fits very tightly, Diana."

"You're one certified bastard."

"Thank you," he said with sarcasm.

"I'll do whatever it takes to protect Nicky. And I won't let you run roughshod over me."

"Ah...I guess that makes it right."

"I see you aren't going to be rational."

"Rational! I'm being as rational as I can be when I feel like wringing your neck."

"I did what I had to do."

"You stole my son from me. You didn't give me the chance to be his father. You chose another man to take my place and I'm to understand the logic of it? Excuse me if I don't get it."

Diana rubbed her temples. "I'm done here."

"You're right. I don't want to be in the same room with you right now."

"I'm glad we're in agreement."

"Don't leave the estate Diana. We'll finish this later," he warned.

"Am I supposed to take that as a warning or a threat?"

"Take it any way you want," he jeered.

"I'll not run from this." She shot him a defiant look. "Unlike some people, when I make a promise, I keep it." She brushed past him and walked out.

Chapter 16

Diana found her mother sitting quietly under a tree watching Nicky play ball with some of the other kids. She grabbed a fold-up chair from one of the tents, placed it alongside her mother, and sat. For a while neither of them spoke, absently watching the people mingling and laughing. It had turned out to be a beautiful day.

"Say something, Mama," Diana finally said.

He mother gave a tired sigh. "What do you want me to say, Diana?"

She shrugged. "I don't know."

Estelle looked her, incredulous. "You don't know? I taught you morals, ethics, and most of all, I taught you not to lie. I'm very disappointed in you."

Diana cringed with embarrassment and shame. The pain and disappointment she heard in her mother's voice rendered her helpless. She hadn't set out to deliberately hurt anyone. But she'd succeeded in one afternoon to do just that.

"Mama..." she groaned as the repercussions of her actions consumed her.

"I don't understand, Diana, why you had to lie to me and your father."

THE HEART KNOWS

"Mama, I never lied to you and Dad."

"Did you not lead us to believe that John was Nicky's father?"

"Well, yes, but—"

"There's no but to it. You deliberately led us to believe John was Nicky's father, and that is something I don't understand. We're your parents, and you couldn't tell us the truth?"

"In the beginning I wanted to tell you many times, but I didn't know how. You and Dad had brought me up to be a good girl, to wait until marriage for sex, and I hadn't. I was unmarried and pregnant. I couldn't face the disappointment I would see in your faces."

"Did you think your father and I were so naïve and old fashioned that we didn't know you and Trace were lovers?"

Diana felt herself blush.

"Your father and I were once young. We know how hard it is to keep your hormones in check when you are physically attracted to someone. It's even harder when you are in love. Believe me, I know."

"You never said anything to me."

"Honey, it was so obvious. When you and Trace came to visit you two could barely keep your hands off each other. The sly heated looks you gave each other when you thought no one was looking were enough to start a fire."

"I didn't mean to hurt either of you."

196

"What hurts is that you didn't come to us, your own parents, about what you were going through. We're your parents, not your judges."

"I know that. I felt a fool to be caught in a predicament that other girls had found themselves in so many times."

"No one is perfect. It happens. I asked you five years ago, but you never gave me an answer. What happened between you and Trace?"

"It's complicated."

"Love sometimes can be."

"I did love him."

"And you still do," Estelle insisted firmly.

Diana dropped her head. "So much has happened."

"Love just doesn't turn on and off, Diana."

She sighed and looked at her mother. "I thought I was over him."

"And you're not. It's not surprising. What was between the two of you was very strong."

"I used to think so." She took a deep breath. "Trace and I broke up because he was seeing someone else."

"What?"

"You seem surprised."

"I am." Estelle frowned. "Trace seemed so in love with you. I never thought he would be unfaithful. There must be more to it."

"You don't believe me."

"I didn't say I didn't believe you."

"I wasn't surprised. I knew it wouldn't last."

"Why did you think that?"

"Mama, I'm a black woman and I come from a middle-class family."

Estelle frowned. "Diana, I'm surprised at you. You're a bright, beautiful, and strong young woman. We taught you better than that. I don't believe it mattered to Trace you were black."

"It was an issue with Crispina," she retorted.

Her mother rolled her eyes and sucked her teeth. "Who cares what Crispina thinks? That woman has issues with everyone who crosses her path. She's just a miserable woman."

Diana smiled at her mother's assessment of Trace's mother. "I have never let Crispina's attitude bother me."

"Good. Then don't." Estelle reached over and patted her hand. "Remember, you're made of strong Hamilton genes."

Diana was quiet for a moment. She had to give her mother an explanation for her actions. "You know, John tried many times to get me to tell Trace the truth."

"John was right. You should have. How did you end up married to John? Your father and I were shocked when you told us you were marrying Trace's uncle. When we initially met John, at Pisano's, we were introduced to him as your boss and Trace's uncle and the next thing we knew you were marrying him."

"After I told him I was pregnant and I had no intention of telling Trace, John offered me a marriage of convenience. He wanted my baby to grow up a Pisano. He said no Pisano ever was born out of wedlock, and there wouldn't be one then."

"He was a good man. Anyone seeing him and Nicky together knew how much he loved him."

"Yes, he did love Nicky. He protected me, Mama. He wanted there to be proof if anyone ever questioned if Nicky was a Pisano by blood."

"How did he get a DNA sample from Trace?"

"It's company policy. Every year the members of the board of directors must have a physical. Trace would get his when he went to New York for the annual board meeting. John asked his personal physician to do a DNA test."

"Isn't that illegal to do without his knowledge?"

"It is. But Trace had signed the form for the required tests. If he had read the form he would have seen one of the tests was for DNA screening."

"Oh, boy. This gets worse and worse. You need to tell Trace."

"I can't tell Trace. I don't want to give him actual proof Nicky is his son. He doesn't know that John and I had a marriage of convenience."

"Oh, Diana, you need to stop this. Trace doesn't need proof. Nicky is his spitting image. Haven't you covered up enough?"

"I made mistakes. But I won't lose my son because of them."

"You aren't going to lose Nicky," Estelle said calmly.

"Trace wants Nicky."

"He should be given the chance to get to know his son."

Diana frowned at her mother. "Are you taking his side in this?"

"Listen to yourself. There are no sides. You and Trace need to think about what is best for Nicky. You need to resolve your issues, and do it soon."

Wearily, Diana rubbed her hands on the fabric on her dress, wrinkling the delicate fabric. "I know." Lifting tired shoulders, she brought her hands to her temples and tried to massage away the tension intensified by a slight headache. "Will you tell Daddy what happened?"

"No. It is up to you to tell him."

"I can't, Mama. I don't want to see his disappointment."

"No matter what you do or say, you are his daughter. He loves you and nothing is ever going to change that."

"I hope you're right." She wrapped her arms around her mother and laid her head on her shoulder for comfort. Everything was spinning out of control. She was scared she would lose the most precious thing in her life...her son.

⚓⚓

Trace stood at the window and watched Diana and her mother sitting under a large tree with its leaves hanging low. Estelle used her hand to wipe tears from Diana's face. What were they talking about? Was Diana telling her mother more lies to make herself look innocent? How appropriate to be crying under the weeping willow tree, he thought with a sardonic twist to his mouth. His gaze moved from them, searching the grounds, finally landing on his son playing not too far from Diana and her mother. A breath caught in his throat as he looked at Nicky. He couldn't explain the new feeling in his heart, but it felt good.

Dominic picked up the envelope on the edge of the desk. "Are you going to open the letter?" Dominic inquired. He turned it over in hands.

"No. I'm not," Trace answered without turning around.

"Why not? It's in John's handwriting and it's addressed to you. "

"I know that."

"I'm sure John—"

"John's lawyer gave it to me at the reading of the will. As you can see, it's marked personal and confidential," he added with emphasis.

"Okay, I was just asking."

"Don't ask."

"Since your mind isn't on business and you haven't opened the envelope, do you want to talk about it?" Dominic asked.

"No," Trace said in a hard voice, still looking out the window.

"I know when you're in this mood you become even more stubborn than you already are," Dominic proclaimed. He left the unopened envelope on the desk, stacked the papers in front of him, and placed them in the wall safe. After closing the safe, he secured the lock, strode to the bar in the room, and fixed two drinks. He handed one to Trace. Absently, Trace held the drink, continuing to stare at the scene under the tree. The boy ran to his mother. His chest tightened as he watched his son wrap his arms around his mother's legs, leaning his head in her lap. Diana lovingly smoothed Nicky's hair from his forehead. Not one to stay still long, Nicky raised his head, laughed at something his mother said, and ran off again to play. It was obvious Diana was enchanted with their son, but he could have been also if he had been given the chance. He had missed so much, but he wouldn't miss the remaining years of his son's life. Why didn't she think he deserved to know his son? The sudden pain in his heart caught him unaware. It hurt.

"Trace, did you and Diana talk?"

"If you want to call it talking." Trace moved from the window and turned to look at his cousin. "I plan to move into the mansion permanently." He was quiet for a moment and then said, "Even though I know he is mine, I'm going to arrange the appropriate test to make sure."

"You don't need to do that."

Trace swirled the brown liquid in his glass and took a long swallow. "It's necessary. I don't want any misgivings or questions about the boy's paternity."

"Why do you keep calling him the boy? He does have a name."

"I know that."

"Then why don't you use it?"

"Dammit, Dominic, I just learned about him."

"Yes, but I know you, Trace. You don't want to use his name because it keeps you from feeling. You need to fully acknowledge what Diana did."

"I don't want to talk about it."

"Trace, Diana made a mistake...."

"A mistake! You call dumping me when she knew she was pregnant, marrying my uncle, and keeping me ignorant of the fact I had a son a mistake? I don't. I call it a cover-up. She knew what the hell she was doing.

She wanted a richer man and she got him when she married John."

"I don't believe it of Diana. There must be more to—"

"Hell, Dominic. Don't defend her to me. I gave her a chance to tell me her side of the story. And do you know what she said? She said she had nothing to be sorry for."

"Well, I don't believe she did what she did without a reason. It's not like Diana. She's not a malicious person."

"She gave me some crap about not sticking around because she didn't want to share me with other women. I asked her outright if Nicky was mine. She said he was hers and not mine." He cringed, remembering how it hurt to hear her say the words.

"She was trying to protect herself and her son." Dominic gave off a nervous chuckle. "Did she have cause to believe she was sharing you?"

Exasperated, Trace gave his cousin a hard look. "Dominic, you were around when Diana and I were together. Did I act like a man who was cheating? She was what I wanted. I never thought I would to go the commitment route until I met her. I cared deeply about her."

Dominic took a deep breath and smiled. "Well, I'm surprised to hear you finally admit it. Everyone who really knew you saw that you were in love with her. But more importantly, did you ever tell Diana you loved her?"

"I never loved her," he lied.

"Keep lying to yourself, Trace. Maybe one day you'll believe the lie. But you can't lie to me."

Giving Dominic a stare that could kill, he strolled to the desk that Dominic had previously occupied, set the unfinished drink on the smooth surface and slid his hands into the pockets of his slacks. "She knew how I felt."

"I see. So Diana was supposed to read your mind?"

"I'm finished talking about this. After I receive the documented results that Diana's son is mine, I'll begin court proceedings to get custody of him."

Puzzled, Dominic asked, "Custody?"

"That's right, custody."

"If you do that you'll regret it for the rest of your life."

"Really? I don't have anything to lose."

"What about your son? How do you think he'll feel once he understands how he came to be with you knowing that you took him away from his mother? He'll hate you."

"That's a chance I'm willing to take."

Dominic ran his hand down his face. "You need to calm down and think about this."

"I have thought about it."

"No, you haven't. You need to talk to Diana again and get this straightened out. I believe it can be resolved. No matter how much you deny it, Trace, you love her."

"Love has nothing to do with this. This is about justice."

"No, it's about revenge. You want to hurt her for lying and keeping your son from you, but most of all you want to hurt her for marrying John."

Trace stiffened. "Her marriage has nothing to do with this."

"The hell it doesn't. If Diana hadn't been married and you found out about Nicky, I believe you would've been more forgiving. The fact she turned to another man is eating at you." Dominic paused before continuing. "I can understand some of what you're feeling, but don't hurt her through your son. It'll be a wound that will never heal. She'll never forgive you."

"Do you think I give a damn?"

"Yes, I do. Diana is the reason you've never let another woman get close to you. I remember how you were once she left you. And when she married John, you became more ruthless and cold-hearted. It was as if you weren't human. You didn't feel anything about anyone, nor care about the business, not even yourself. In the last five years, you've taken over companies, not because Montgomery needed them, but to release the pent-up anger and pain you've carried since Diana left you."

Trace ignored Dominic's assessment of his feelings about Diana. "I'm not a mealy-mouthed businessman. You know that, Dominic. When I set out to take over a business, I do it."

"No matter who or what gets destroyed?"

"It comes with the territory."

"Why don't you take Diana away from Asheville?" Trace's face hardened. Dominic rushed on. "Someplace where the two of you can talk and come to terms about your relationship."

"How is this supposed to make a difference?"

"Raven's Nest and this town hold good and bad memories for the both of you, but right now all the focus is on the bad."

"Knowing she bedded and shared this house with John has been a bitter pill to swallow," he said crudely. "But I had to live here to honor the terms of the will, and I got past it."

Dominic looked at him with doubt. "Did you, really? I don't believe you did. Reliving the past will never give you a future with Diana."

Trace ran a careless hand through his dark hair. "I don't want, nor do I plan, a future with Diana. All I want is my son."

"You need to listen to yourself, because you'll never have a chance with your son without Diana."

"You don't know what the hell you're talking about."

"Trace, hear me out. Diana isn't going to let you just take her son. She'll fight you tooth and nail."

"Let the fight begin. I don't care how long it takes, I'll crush her."

Dominic shook his head. "Do you hear yourself? I can't believe what I'm hearing. You are talking about crushing her. Hell, Trace, she's the mother of your son, not a damned business deal!"

Trace's eyes bored into Dominic's without flinching and he remained silent. Dominic tried again to get him to see reason.

"Trace, you are letting your anger rule. John left you in charge of taking care of Diana and Nicky, not to hurt them. He wouldn't like what you're doing."

"I've made my decision."

"Once you have rationally thought about it, I know you'll come to a conclusion that will benefit all parties involved."

Trace frowned. "I've made my decision, and nothing is going to sway me from it."

Dominic set down his drink. "At least don't put your son through a paternity test. I believe John knew and accepted Nicky as yours; you should, at least, be as honorable and do the same. No matter what Diana says, I don't doubt he's your son. Anyone looking at him can tell he is a Montgomery." He touched his cousin on the back. "Please think about what I have said."

Trace remained stoic.

"It's time for me to be going. My pilot is probably wondering what happened to me. We were supposed to take off two hours ago."

"Do you need a ride to the airport?"

"No, I'm fine. My driver waited for me. I'm flying to Rome tonight, then Paris in two days, and then on to Barcelona next week. You know how to reach me if you need me."

"I won't need you," Trace said in a flat tone.

"I hope to God that isn't true. Call me before you do anything irrational."

"I don't have an irrational bone in my body."

Dominic let a small smile slip. "I say otherwise." Clapping Trace on the back once again, he moved to the door and opened it. He hesitated and glanced back at Trace.

"Trace, remember how much you loved Diana. I don't believe there was any malice in her intentions. Will you at least promise to give it some thought?"

"You ask a lot. I'll think about it, but I won't change my mind."

Dominic opened his mouth and then closed it. He shook his head and walked out the door.

Chapter 17

Diana opened the French doors into the great room. Her parents and Susan were gathered there. The conversation stopped when they saw her. She didn't comment on that fact, but instead glanced around the room. She and Trace had stood stiffly beside each other as they thanked each person for attending the picnic. They didn't say a word to each other. When the last guest left, they'd turned and went their separate ways.

"Where's Nicky?" she snapped.

Her mother tilted her head at her tone. "Rosa called Luca to tell her Nicky was back. She arrived about an hour ago," Estelle said.

A dark frown creased Diana's brow. "I know Luca is his nanny, but I can take care of him while she finishes her vacation. Rosa didn't need to call her. I'm tired of people thinking I'm helpless and can't make a decision." There was heavy silence while she stalked to a chair and sat. Her mother was the first to speak.

"What's wrong with you, Diana?"

"There's nothing wrong with me."

Russell Hamilton moved to the chair nearest to Diana's and took her small hand in his large one. "Honey, no one is saying you're incapable of making a decision or that you are helpless. No one doubts your mothering skills. You're a very good mother." He paused. "We taught you manners. You don't enter a room in a disrespectful manner or with attitude. Now what's all this about?"

Diana glanced at her mother. "You mean Mama hasn't told you?"

Puzzled, Russell looked at his wife and then back at his daughter. "Told me what?"

"Diana, I told you I wouldn't tell your father. It's up to you to do so."

"Will someone tell me what's going on?

Standing, Diana removed her hand. Not wanting to see the pain in his face, she paced while she talked.

"Five years ago I made a decision. Today it came back to haunt me."

Confusion clouded her father's eyes. Knowing there was no better way to say it, Diana took a deep breath. "When I married John, I was pregnant with Trace's child—and I knew it." She paused. "I never told Trace about Nicky."

"What?"

"Instead of informing Trace of my pregnancy, I went to John for help."

"I don't understand this. John married you knowing you were carrying Trace's child?"

"Yes, he did. Trace and I had broken up. I was scared. I didn't know where to turn. Since I refused to tell Trace about the pregnancy, John suggested we get married."

Russell frowned. Ignoring the first revelation, his frown grew fierce. "What the hell do you mean you were scared and didn't know where to turn?"

"John—"

"No, Estelle, I want our daughter to answer the question. When have we ever been the type of parents whose children can't come to us when they're in trouble?"

"Daddy—"

"No, you listen. Not only did you not come to us, but you married one man while pregnant with another's child. I don't understand it, nor do I condone it."

"Daddy, when I left Trace I didn't know I was pregnant, at least I didn't know for sure. I had been feeling nauseous a few weeks before the breakup but attributed it to stress. At the time, I was the lead marketing rep at Pisano; I was working on my first big project and I wanted to do well. I thought my nerves were causing the nausea."

"It doesn't excuse your actions, Diana. You should've come to your mother and me." Her father shook his head in disbelief. "With the childhood Trace had, what made you think he wouldn't want to know his own child? The man was shuttled between his father, mother, and uncle all of his childhood and you denied him his child."

"I might have made a mistake keeping Nicky from Trace."

"You *did* make a mistake. Now what are you going to do about it?"

"Trace and I will come to some sort of agreement."

"Does Nicky know Trace is his father?"

"No."

"My God, Diana!"

Touching his arm, Estelle got his attention. "Russell, you need to calm down."

"I'm calm, Estelle." He gave Diana a long, hard look. "People make mistakes, but you went against everything we taught you. It makes me feel I failed somewhere down the line because you turned to your boss and not us."

Tears swelled up in Diana's eyes. She ached at the hurt she had caused them. Never had she wanted to see pain on their faces. It tore at her that she was the cause of it. She needed to make them see that her decision had nothing to do with them. Her insecurity in the relationship with Trace had been the catalyst.

"I'm sorry I have hurt you. It wasn't my intention. John was not only my employer, he was also my friend. I was so ashamed. I'd let you both down. By marrying John, I wanted to make everything right."

"Your father and I do understand." Estelle gave her husband's arm a gentle squeeze. "Don't we?"

Russell was silent for a long moment. "I still can't believe you kept Nicky away from Trace, and that John agreed to it."

"John only agreed because I threatened to leave North Carolina. He didn't want that for my baby or me. You know how John was about family."

Russell frowned. "And you don't know how *we* feel about family?

"Russell!" Estelle tilted her head and shot him a stern look.

"Diana, we never questioned your marriage to John, although your mother and I were surprised you married a man you only had introduced to us as your boss. We couldn't understand how you could go from one man to another, especially with them being related. However, we had raised you right and prayed you knew what you were doing." He paused. "Was your marriage the reason for the rift in John's and Trace's relationship?"

"Yes," she said softly.

"Didn't you stop and think what your marriage would do to the relationship between Trace and John? My God, they were more like father and son than uncle and nephew."

"No, I didn't think."

"You're right, Diana. You didn't think," her father said in a stern disapproving voice.

"Russell, I believe you've said enough for one evening. It's getting late and we need to get on the road," Estelle said.

"You don't have to leave. You can stay the night and leave in the morning," Diana offered.

"No. It's best if you and Trace have some time alone. You don't need a third party involved," Diana's mother said.

"Estelle, we still haven't settled anything."

"Dear, it's not for us to settle. It's for Trace and Diana to do the settling."

"But I don't understand—"

"Russell Hamilton, it's none of our business," she said sternly.

He relented. "Yes, dear."

"Now kiss your daughter goodbye." Russell obliged and engulfed Diana in a large hug. Her mother stretched out her arms and Diana went into them and rested her head on her mother's shoulder.

"Diana, we love you. We're here for you," her mother said with a smile.

"I know."

Her mother paused. "Diana, we can take Nicky with us."

Remembering Trace's threat, she said, "No, Mama, it's best if he stays here. Trace and Nicky need to get to know each other."

"Okay. Please call us—"

"I'll be fine."

Susan, who sat quietly during the exchange, walked over and gave each parent a hug. With a last look at Diana, Estelle said, "We'll call when we get to Savannah." Grabbing Russell by the hand, she ushered him out the door. "Come on, Russell."

After they left, Susan gave Diana a hug. "You okay?"

Nodding, Diana moved out of Susan's embrace. She ran her hands through her hair and pinched the end of her nose to keep the tears at bay. "I have never seen my father so angry. Not even when I was five and used his Sunday church shoes as boats in the bathtub." She gave a small smile at the memory.

"Diana, your father loves you. He just needs time. I'm sure he'll come around."

"Eventually. I hope he'll understand what I did. The hurt in his eyes wounded me more than his anger. I have never disappointed him before."

Susan took both of her hands and said, "Diana, you are not infallible. We disappoint people, but life moves on. Your parents didn't put you on a pedestal. I think you did that yourself. You wanted to be perfect for them and it didn't work."

Diana sighed and sat on the loveseat. "Maybe you're right. I always wanted them to be proud of me."

"They are. They accept and love you, faults and all."

"I guess you're right."

"I know I'm right. You're a perfectionist. And you're too hard on yourself."

"You think so?"

Susan smiled. "In all the years you have known me, I haven't been anything less than frank."

"True, but you're also my best friend. I expect a little warmth," Diana said with a slight laugh.

"No matter what, I'll always tell you the truth. Was the lie worth it? Trace lost his uncle. Your marriage destroyed their relationship."

"At the time I didn't think about what it would cost John, and I certainly wasn't thinking about Trace's feelings."

"I do understand." Susan stopped as if she wanted to say more.

"Do I hear a *but* in there somewhere?"

"No, I'm making a point. You made a *big* mistake not telling Trace about Nicky."

Cringing, Diana frowned. "A *big* mistake? You don't pull any punches, do you, Susan? Nicky and I had a good life with John."

Susan sighed. "You did have a good life with John. But you could've had so much more." It hurt to hear the words coming from Susan.

"Your decision affected all of your lives. There's so much anger between you and Trace, Nicky doesn't know his biological father, and John and Trace never reconciled. Now they never will."

"I know what it took for me to make the decision I made. It wasn't easy. I didn't want my baby to be born without a father—I wanted to be safe."

"Honey, being safe is an important factor to a woman, but it can't be the only motivation for marriage." Susan gave her a gentle smile. "Promise you'll at least think about what I said."

"I will."

Susan glanced at her watch. "It's getting late." Giving Diana another hug, she stepped back. "Are you okay?"

Diana took a deep breath and raised a shaky hand to pull her hair behind her ear. "I'm fine." Clearing her throat, she said, "Thanks, Susan, for being honest."

"You're welcome."

Smiling slightly, Diana slipped her hands in the pockets of her sundress. "Drive safe."

"I will," Susan reassured her and walked to where her purse lay. "Diana, everything will work itself out."

"I hope so. You know what's funny, Susan? If I had it to do all over again, I would make the same decision."

"Really? Why?"

Diana shrugged and moved to the large windows and looked out over the semi-dark lawn. The workers had removed all the tents and the tables. Everything was back to normal. Would her life ever be normal again? She turned back to Susan and sighed. "I trusted John."

"And you didn't trust Trace," Susan commented matter-of-factly.

She crossed her arms tightly, trying to understand the complexity of her relationship with Trace. "I was always waiting for the other shoe to drop," she said sadly. "I knew I wasn't in his league and that someday he would want out of the relationship." She drew a deep breath. "I just didn't know it would come sooner rather than later. I guess I always protected a little bit of my heart. I didn't envision the devastating pain when it was over."

"Diana, you left Trace, not the other way around."

"I left before he left me," she argued. "It was bound to happen."

"That's something you'll never know for sure."

"But I do," she stressed.

"My friend, I see nothing is going to change your mind. I believe you need to think about why Trace

stayed in the relationship. If you take the time to ana-
lyze it, you may be surprised at what you find."

Puzzled, Diana said, "What's that supposed to
mean?"

"Nothing." A mischievous grin played on her
mouth.

"I hate when you go mysterious on me."

"Yeah, I know." Susan grabbed her Gucci purse off
the ottoman and walked to the door. Diana followed
closely behind. "I'm really leaving this time."

"Why don't you spend the night?" Diana said as
Susan opened the door.

"Oh, no, you don't," Susan said and laughed.
"You're not going to use me as a buffer. I have chores
I have been putting off for a month. I promised myself
I would try and at least finish some of them before the
weekend is over. Besides, the two of you have a lot to
discuss. I'll talk to you tomorrow." Susan waved and
ran down the steps. Diana closed the door and leaned
against it.

Diana didn't have any illusions when it came to
Trace. What they'd been these past few weeks were
two consenting adults engaging in nothing but sex.
She didn't want to think that it may have been something deeper. Unfortunately, forgetting about Trace
was much harder than she thought.

Chapter 18

Trace leaned in the doorway of the bedroom watching the tiny miracle breathe evenly in sleep. He couldn't bear to remove his eyes from his son. *My son*, he thought—the words resonated through his brain and then bounced into his heart. He caught his breath upon impact.

The soccer-themed night lamp on the table beside the bed highlighted his small features. He sprawled on his side, the duvet kicked to the floor, a hand stuck in the opening of the pillowcase. Trace's lips lifted upward at the familiar scene. They were identical not only in looks, but also sleeping mannerisms. How was Nicky going to feel about a stranger claiming to be his father? He didn't want to confuse him. John had been the only father he knew.

Diana entered the room from Nicky's bathroom. Unaware of his presence, Diana smoothed the light-weight comforter over his son. A light scent of jasmine permeated the room. He'd always enjoyed her scent. He silently cursed. He didn't want to enjoy anything about her. The feelings of betrayal and anger surged through him once again.

Trace's solemn eyes followed her every move. She clicked off the lamp, leaving on a small night lamp in the socket above Nicky's head. It cast a warm glow into the room. She brushed a hand across Nicky's curly head and then kissed him. Shock flared in her eyes when Trace moved from the door. She hurried past him without speaking. He caught up with her at the door of her bedroom.

"We need to talk," he said in a rough voice.

Diana stepped back. "I'm tired. It'll have to wait until morning."

He opened the door and moved aside, waiting for her to enter. She didn't move.

"Your bedroom or mine? Look, Diana, we have a lot to discuss, and it's going to be tonight. The best place not to be heard or disturbed is either your suite or mine."

She didn't want to argue in the hallway where Rosa or one of the other live-in servants could hear. Plus, she didn't want Nicky to wake up. She gave Trace a furious look, then stepped through the doorway to her sitting room. The door closed behind him with a soft click.

She passed her bedroom. The massive door stood open in invitation. She refused to look at the bed where they had enjoyed making love. However, she couldn't stop the rush of blood to her face and the hot shiver racing through her body. Trace had been her first and only lover. Her body knew his so well. As much as she hated to admit it, she still craved him. Closing her mind to her rampant thoughts, she kept walking and he followed close behind. She stopped and faced him. His hands rested loosely on his hips and a menacing and dangerous look was on his face. A chill slithered down her spine. What was she thinking, letting him come in her bedroom? Trace was angry with her—no, he was beyond anger, he was furious. She squirmed under his accusing glare.

"I want to know why."

"I—"

He snapped at her. "I don't want to hear any lies, just the truth."

She bit back an odious remark. "Our relationship wasn't a permanent commitment. You would've wanted out sooner or later." She paused. "I never thought it would matter to you."

His jaw clenched. "You didn't think it would matter?" Trace stared at her. "A child I helped to create. A child I could lo…" He took a deep breath. "You didn't think I would want my own child, Diana? I thought you knew me. What gave you the idea I wouldn't want my own child?"

She didn't want to face the hostility in his eyes so she moved to the large bay window. Her heart felt as dark and empty as the darkness that shrouded the south lawn. In the daylight the beauty of the south lawn usually brought such serene peace. Shouldn't she be able to feel the peace at night? But all she felt was turmoil. Taking a deep breath, she briefly closed her eyes, willing the moment to be over. She turned around and clasped her hands, fighting for control.

"Trace, you were never a one-woman man." She watched his mouth tighten. "When I met you seven years ago, you had never had a relationship longer than a month or two."

"And your point?"

How could she explain her fears and insecurities about their relationship? Years ago, when they started dating, she had tried to talk about it, but he'd shrugged it off. He wouldn't listen to her when she tried to explain her fears, just assured her everything would be fine.

"I'm waiting, Diana."

She stretched her hand toward the sofa. "Why don't you sit down?"

He didn't move. "You're stalling."

He was being difficult. Her legs felt weak and she wanted to sit. However, she would be damned if she would have him towering over her. She wrapped her arms around her waist and tried not fidget or pace. He watched her every move. Her nails dug into her arms, causing pain. She relaxed her hands.

"We discussed a lot during our time together, but children weren't a topic we ever broached. I knew there would come a time when my time with you would be over."

For a moment, she thought she saw hurt flash in his eyes, but she must have been mistaken.

"So you were determined to get out before the ship sank."

"I never—"

"So, based on my past relationships, you decided I wasn't worthy of knowing my own child?"

"It was the only choice I saw at the time."

He moved toward her, anger in every step. "The time for you to make decisions without my input is over."

She stepped back in confusion. "I don't understand."

"From now on, all plans concerning my son—"

"My son," she said heatedly.

"…will be discussed together."

She fought to remain calm. "Now wait one minute. I'm his mother."

"And what am I? You decided I wasn't fit to be a father. I want my son."

"You'll never take him from me!"

"How are you going to stop me?" His voice held steely purpose.

"Damn you to hell! I won't let you do this."

"Really? Well, I wanted to do this right, but your treachery has changed everything. We're getting married. It's the only way I can see Nicky full time. Unfortunately, I have to add you to the mix to keep Nicky happy and balanced. It won't be the *perfect marriage* you had with John." His eyelids lowered slightly so that they looked sleepy. "You'll warm my bed until I decide otherwise."

"You've have lost your damn mind." Shock and anger vibrated in her tone.

"I'll not be separated from him another day. I'll be a father to him and he'll carry my name."

She laughed cruelly. "Trace, I'll never marry you."

"Really? Then I have no other choice but to take you to court."

"No court in the land would give you custody of my son."

"You want to take the chance?"

Unshed angry tears formed in her eyes.

"I didn't think so." Trace gave her a snide grin.

"You're a cruel and heartless bastard."

"Tell me something I don't know."

Trying hard to stop the runaway roller coaster of a ride, she worked to stay calm and get him to see reason. "Trace, being a parent isn't easy. It's not something you pick up one day, and when you're tired, give it up the next."

He laughed without humor. "You never cease to amaze me."

She tried another tactic. "Let's try to be rational."

"Smooth talk? You can save it. I've seen how devious you can be."

"You have the nerve to talk about me being devious after what you did?" she shot back.

"This is the second time you've referred to something I did. Stop talking in riddles. If you have something to say, just say it."

She was furious, so much so she wanted to scream. The anger boiled over. "You're a piece of work. You have the balls to stand before me as if you're innocent."

"What the hell are you talking about? I'm not the one that lied."

"You did that and more!"

"When have I ever lied to you?

Shaking with rage, she wouldn't give him the satisfaction of knowing how his infidelity had ripped her apart. "I'm finished talking."

He ran his hand through his hair, causing it to stand to attention. "Damn, Diana. You're good at turning the tables. You're the guilty party here, not me. You're the one who stole my son from me."

"How could I steal him when he never belonged to you?"

"You cut deep, Diana."

"You did worse."

"Name it," he taunted.

Ignoring him, she stood trembling with anger. "You would like to have me crawl, but I won't give you the satisfaction." He'd never known that his treachery had brought her to the brink of a complete nervous breakdown. If she hadn't realized she was pregnant, she might have gone over the edge. Thinking about it now shot a shiver down her spine. Knowing she was carrying a small life had helped her to think of something other than what Trace had done to her. He'd almost destroyed her. She wouldn't give him the chance to do it again.

"We'll be married within one week."

"A marriage between us would be a war zone."

"It'll be a real marriage."

"I'll not sleep with you."

"We'll be doing more than sleeping. There'll be no disharmony in front of our son. I'm sure we are adult enough to handle disagreements in private."

She sneered. "Is this what you call it a *disagreement*?"

"Don't be snide, Diana. It's not becoming."

"You can go to hell. Before this is over, you'll wish you never forced me into this."

He swept a hot look up and down her body. "Hmmm...your claws are showing. I believe I like it."

Quick sparks of fire spread through her body. She hated herself for it. She didn't want to feel anything for this man.

"We'll tell him I'm his father before we get married. I'll have my lawyer contact Martin to work out the arrangements."

"I don't want your money."

"You've already married once for money, why not again? I would certainly leave you more than John did."

She remained silent. He could think whatever he wanted about her. She wouldn't explain herself to him.

"The contract will be in Nicky's best interests."

"Trace, you need to stop this madness."

"Why? I'm enjoying myself."

"Can't you see this isn't good for Nicky?"

"I'll protect him."

The defensive mother rose up in her. "No matter what you propose, Nicky doesn't know you. It'll seem strange for you to appear suddenly in his life. He'll be confused if I tell him John wasn't his father."

"And whose fault is that?" he said angrily. "Given time, he'll accept me as his father. I'll no longer be denied. The legal system is purported to be fair. If we're unable to reach an amicable decision, a judge will review our respective cases." He paused. "Given the facts, do you doubt any judge will deny me my son at least half of the time?"

"Are you threatening me?"

"I'm not threatening you, Diana. I've told you exactly what I'm going do."

"Is there anything else?" she asked sarcastically.

"Yes, there is. After we're married I plan to take Nicky to Europe. Does he have a current passport?"

"What?" Her head snapped up.

"You're beginning to sound like a parrot, Diana. I'm taking Nicky to see his great-grandmother."

"I didn't know you had a grandmother."

"You didn't stick around long enough to find out." Sighing, he ran his hand over his face. "My paternal grandparents were divorced when my father was two years old. My grandfather got custody of my father."

She was surprised at this new revelation and stared at him in amazement. "Why do I get the feeling there's more to it than you're telling me?"

"There's nothing more for you to know."

"I see."

Evidently, he kept a part of his life from her when they were dating. Even now he still didn't want her to know more about him than he was willing to tell.

"You obviously have not considered," Trace interjected, "that Nicky isn't only a Pisano, but he is a Montgomery as well. Nicky must be established as a legitimate heir of the Montgomery line."

Her chin tilted. "For this, you're willing to marry me and doom us to a life of misery?"

"I'll do whatever it takes to ensure my son gets everything he's entitled to. He's my only heir. A considerable fortune is involved."

This was sufficient to put Nicky on the list as one of the richest little kids in the world, and in imminent danger from every kidnapper out there. She shuddered at the thought.

"No," she said, her voice filled with fear.

"He'll be protected."

Again she said, "No."

"It's his right to be a Montgomery heir."

Diana reached out a hand to touch his arm but pulled back when she saw the coldness in his eyes. "Please don't do this. I don't want him in danger."

"He became a target when you decided he would become a Pisano. Now to the world he'll be known also as the heir to the Montgomery fortune. Don't think I won't use everything in my power to protect my son. He'll be safe."

"You can't make that promise."

He gave her a bold stare. "I guarantee it with my life," he said with unflinching certainty.

"It's too much, Trace. He'll never be sure of being liked for himself. He'll live in a gilded cage, guarded and protected. I want him to have a normal childhood, not be a prisoner behind electronic gates."

Trace walked to the bay windows she had abandoned. Heavy darkness now shrouded the grounds.

"He already has a bodyguard, just as I do." He turned from the window, his face a cold mask. He had changed into a black silk shirt and black linen pants.

The look completed the dark, brooding, and danger- ous persona. "Wealth brings risks. It's something one learns to live with."

"I don't want him to learn to live with it, especially at such a young age." Fear glided down her spine. Ev- erything was spinning out of her control. "When did you get him a bodyguard?"

"I made calls as soon as I learned of his existence."

"You've told people."

"No, I have told no one. I know how to make things happen with discretion. By the end of next week, the world will know he is my son. After our wedding, I don't think it's something you can keep hidden. If the paparazzi photograph Nicky and me together, they'll see there's no question he's mine."

The mere thought of being married to him esca- lated her nervous tension and sent her mind spiraling with great fear of being consumed by the inevitable. She had always loved Trace and dreamt about being his wife. But she didn't want it like this. There was too much anger and distrust between them. She tried again to make him see reason.

"Trace, please—"

As if she hadn't spoken, he continued, "Together we'll tell Nicky."

Diana gave a laugh of disbelief. "You haven't been listening."

He remained silent.

Desperation gripped her. "Trace, I need to—"

"The time for talking is over, Diana."

"What do you get out of this? You don't need to marry me to be in Nicky's life. There must be a catch."

"I won't be a weekend father. And he won't be called a bastard."

Diana flinched. "He isn't—"

"Once the world finds out you were pregnant with my child and not John's, tongues will wag. But no one will dare to speak ill to me or mine." His anger was controlled, his voice too mild, too neutral.

"Now I know why people call you the destroyer. You go for the jugular. You don't maim your prey, but kill it. I have reason to be wary of your motives."

"Really? I never gave you reason to doubt me. I've just told you exactly what I want."

"I haven't agreed."

"But you will," he insisted with cold confidence.

Diana decided not to acknowledge what he was saying. "Before I'll agree to anything," she said with calm determination, "I'll choose when Nicky will be told. He needs to be able to understand what I'm telling him. I'm sure you want Nicky to come to like you."

His expression didn't change. "Perhaps you will offer some sort of explanation on how you denied him his biological father."

"Your sarcasm doesn't sway my decision."

"Those are your terms?" His voice turned placid.

"Yes." She watched him with suspicion.

"All right, I'll let you handle it. I want him told be-fore the wedding—one week. I won't compromise on that.

She'd expected Trace to argue her terms, even dismiss them out of hand. Why hadn't he? She knew there had to be an underlying reason for him to be so agreeable. Trace Montgomery never conceded unless there was something in it for him.

Diana was tempted to try to introduce further de-laying tactics, just to see how far she could go, but such an action might invent problems she wouldn't be able to solve. She didn't have a retaliatory nature, and it was pointless for her to try to create one. She had set the boundaries, but she knew Trace wouldn't bend on the marriage in one week. She needed more time, but she didn't know how to get it.

Nicky did have a valid passport, and it would re-main with her. She didn't trust Trace not to take her son from her permanently.

Without further word, he retraced his steps to the door. He stared at her for a long moment. "I expect you to start weaving me into my son's life tomorrow." He opened the door and was gone.

She let out the breath she had been holding. She walked blindly to the sanctuary of her bedroom and sat wearily on the large ottoman at the foot of the chaise lounge.

Shutting her eyes tightly, she clamped her fists and hung her head. If she ran, where could she go? Maybe to her old college roommate in Pittsburgh? But if she did and he found her, there would be hell to pay. She didn't want to risk him taking her to court.

She'd secretly kept track of Trace through the years. She'd told herself that it was out of curiosity, not a need to know about his life and how he was coping. John had always wanted her to tell Trace about Nicky, and now his wish had come true, although she didn't think he could've envisioned the uphcaval, the angry and painful words that would transpire between them. Nevertheless, Nicky would get to know his father.

Tears swelled in her eyes and slowly ran down her cheeks; she bit her lip to keep from succumbing to the wrenching agony in her heart. She stood and walked unsteadily to the bed and curled up in a fetal position. The tears refused to stop. She cried for loving Trace, and losing him a second time, for the pain she'd felt at finding Lisa Davenport in Trace's bed, and she cried tears for the severing of John and Trace's relationship. It was because of her that the father and son bond they so lovingly shared was broken and never repaired. Finally, the tears slowed and, sometime during the darkest part of night, shc fcll into a restless sleep.

Chapter 19

Diana opened her eyes to complete silence and sat up in the bed. The digital clock on the nightstand indicated she had slept for hours, but she felt as if she'd only had a catnap. Diana gingerly touched her eyes, feeling the puffiness. The tears had finally found a resting place on her cheeks. Deciding to get a start on the day before Nicky woke; she swung her legs to the side of the bed. A twinge in her neck caused her to lift a hand to massage the knot of tension. Troubled thoughts went back to the events of last evening and a knot formed in her stomach. She jumped when the phone on the nightstand rang. It was her personal line. She reached for the phone.

"Good morning." Susan's slightly accented voice sounded happy. "I see you made it through the night alive."

"Funny, Susan. Real funny," she said, hoping Trace had left the house and she wouldn't have to face him.

"Did you come to any conclusions?" she asked.

"Not really," she hedged.

"Diana, remember who you are talking you to," sighed Susan. "I'm not your enemy."

"I know," Diana mumbled. "I'm sorry."

"Well, tell me what happened."

"Trace was out for blood." As soon as the words were out of her mouth, Diana wished she could retract them.

"Whoa, it sounds as if things went from bad to worse."

"You can say that." Diana continued massaging the tension that had grown into a deep ache. She wished she could end the conversation with her friend but knew how persistent Susan could be, so she added, "A lot was discussed."

"What happened?"

"We're getting married." It was best to get the news out and let Susan draw her own conclusions.

There was long silence. Diana wondered if Susan had hung up. Then Susan squealed, "Did you say *married*?" She was now screaming with joy. "You're getting married? I knew you guys would finally realize how much you love each other."

Diana closed her eyes and groaned silently. "Don't go there, Susan. We're only getting married because of Nicky. Trace wants to be a full-time father."

Diana didn't tell Susan the whole horrible truth. She was afraid to utter the words. Just thinking about her son being shuttled back and forth between her and Trace made her heart pound alarmingly. If marrying Trace prevented that from happening, then she'd do whatever it took.

"Hmm. If you say so. I believe this is an act of God."

"Earth to Susan. God has nothing to do with this. You must have a screw loose, and it needs to be tightened."

"I don't care what you say. I believe it was destined to happen. When is the wedding?"

"In a week."

"Wow. That's fast. We have a lot to do."

"It's not going to be that type of wedding. I don't need flowers, a cake, or —"

"Are you kidding? You certainly do need those things, and I'll take care of everything," Susan said. "Of course, I'll be your maid of honor."

Diana couldn't help laughing at Susan's enthusiasm. "You're such a hopeless romantic. Thank you for being my friend. I really love you, girl," Diana whispered, feeling weepy and strangely happy.

"Don't mention it. I love you, too," Susan replied in a choked voice. "I got to go. I have a lot of planning to do." Susan hung up.

Diana rubbed the tension in her neck, again determined to keep Trace in the far section of her the mind. Standing, she discarded the short nightgown and headed to the shower.

She dressed in white jeans and a red cotton blouse, slipped her feet into a pair of soft leather sandals, and glanced at her slim gold wristwatch. She was late. Nicky would probably be awake. She was surprised she hadn't seen or heard him. She hurriedly applied minimal makeup, ran a brush through her hair, and twisted it into a messy knot. She looked at the finished product. Her eyes were puffy, but, other than that, she was ready to start the day.

Shaking off the melancholy feeling, she moved toward Nicky's room with slow steps. She had to get a grip or Nicky would certainly notice her mood.

She pasted a smile on her face and threw open the door. The room was empty. Thinking Luca must have Nicky with her, she headed to the kitchen. It was Nicky's favorite place besides his playroom. She stopped in her tracks at the entrance. Trace and Nicky were sitting at the round table usually reserved for the staff. A glowing Nicky was the center of attention. He was being fussed over by a benevolent Rosa and an attentive Trace. In front of them sat plates of pancakes, glasses of orange juice, and milk. Trace had his normal ration of bacon to complement his meal. They were talking, laughing, and, by the looks of it, enjoying themselves. The housekeeper was the first to notice her. Trace and Nicky at the far end of the kitchen hadn't seen her yet.

"Good morning, Mrs. Pisano. Give me a moment and I'll fix you a white egg omelet," Rosa said as she poured steaming coffee into a cup and handed it to Diana. Rosa produced a tray with a choice of biscuits, croissants, and muffins. Diana shook her head and chose fresh fruit from the sideboard.

"I'm still full from yesterday's barbecue," Diana said with a wry smile. "I'm going to forgo the omelet this morning."

Suddenly Trace looked up and caught her eye. The laughter left his face.

Not to be ignored, Nicky turned to see who had distracted Trace's attention. "Mommy!" he squealed when he saw her.

She hurried to his chair. "Hi, sweetie," she said as she gave him a hug and kiss. Smoothing the curls on his head, she smiled at him and said, "I see Luca beat me to it and helped you dress this morning."

"No, Mommy, Trace helped me," he said with wide-eyed innocence.

"He did?" She stiffened with shock. She wanted to scream at Trace. *How dare he take it upon himself to dress my son?*

Nicky bobbed his head. "He was by my bed when I woke up this morning."

She shot Trace a hard glare. "Really?"

"Uh-huh. He even helped me brush my teeth. See, Mommy?" He showed his teeth for her inspection.

"Well, that was nice of him." She felt a faint tremor of apprehension but struggled to keep her voice calm. Trace sat unmoving during this exchange. "We had chocolate chip pancakes. I told Trace they're my favorite. Trace said they're his favorite, too."

"Honey, remember your manners. You must call him Mr. Trace."

He frowned at her in confusion. "But Mommy, he told me to call him Trace, not mister." He turned his curly head toward Trace for confirmation. "Didn't you?"

He ruffled Nicky's dark curls and smiled. "That's right. Buds call each other by their first names."

"That's right, we're buds." Nicky giggled and gave Trace a high five.

Diana was stunned. Buds! When did this happen? Yesterday he had frightened her son and today they were buds. What had he done to captivate Nicky? This was moving too fast. *Do I want Nicky to like his father?* She refused to answer the question. If she did she would have to look deep, and she wasn't ready to do that.

Trace looked fabulously dark and handsome…and so alarmingly magnetic she feared she wouldn't be able to resist his pull. She didn't want Nicky to be like her and fall victim to his charm.

"Well, if Trace has said it is okay, then you can call him by his first name," she said in a tight voice.

"Mommy, your voice sounds funny," Nicky said.

Clearing her throat she said, "I still have a sleepy voice." Diana didn't look at Trace to gauge his reaction.

Nicky squirmed in his chair, a sign he had to go to the bathroom or he was excited about something. She didn't have to wait long.

"Mommy, Trace said he was taking me on a plane ride today," he shouted with both hands in the air, jumping out of his chair.

"What?" Trace wasn't taking her child anywhere.

"We're going to Golden Bloom."

"No, Nicky, I don't think Trace has the time to take you—"

"But Mommy, Trace said we're all going. I really, really want to go. Please…"

Diana raised her eyes to meet Trace's steady gaze and froze. He'd planned all of this overnight. Golden Bloom was an amusement park in Tennessee. He was declaring war. He'd moved on to persuading her son into accepting him as a friend, then wooed him with the promise of a plane ride to his favorite place on earth, an amusement park.

"All right. But—"

"Yippee! You're the best Mommy in the whole wide world." He threw his arms wide. Knowing she had been conned, she allowed it. She wouldn't be the villain in this. Trace expected her to say no. She refused to be the mean parent while he came out smelling like a rose.

Clever, smooth, and calculating, she thought as she regarded his arrogant stance while Nicky rambled on about the trip. Luca entered the kitchen to retrieve Nicky to help him prepare for the trip. Did the entire household know? He continued to chatter, ordering them to hurry so they could all leave soon. Throughout Nicky's orders, Diana's gaze didn't drop from Trace's face.

"I wanted him get to know me without interference. It needed to be done before the marriage," he announced once Nicky was out of hearing. She remained silent. "Arrangements have already been made for a quiet ceremony."

"Where?"

"The old church on the south property, near the edge of the mountain."

"The church built by your great-grandfather for his wife?"

"Yes. It's been preserved. It was meant to be the place where all Pisano brides would take their vows."

"It seems you've organized everything," she bristled.

Like her, he wore casual jeans and a shirt, the difference being that no matter what he wore, he always looked as if he'd stepped off the pages of *GQ* magazine. Then again, everything about Trace oozed class

243

and money, she mused bleakly. He was a powerful force with his dominating height, undeniable physical attractiveness, and the stunning bone structure that made up his too-handsome face. Naked he could take your breath away, dressed he looked fabulous. Though his outer shell was magnificent, inside he was a sneaky and ruthless predator with his attention concentrated solely on what he wanted.

"Yes, I have," he said without guilt.

Diana folded her arms tight across her slender ribcage. "If this is going to work, I need to have a say," she threatened when he still made no effort to justify what he'd done.

"You had your say five years ago," he countered evenly. "You have made a commitment to me and this marriage."

He was right. He also knew she wouldn't break her word. But it didn't make Diana feel less hostile towards him. "Is that why you made plans with Nicky without my consent?"

He dared to arch a black eyebrow. "Of course." He added a shrug. "I knew you were going to drag your feet telling Nicky I'm his father. I just helped speed up the process. You would have fought me to hell and back. I want to form a relationship with him."

"You're one sneaky bastard," she said through clenched teeth. "It's always about what you wanted and damned the consequences. Did it ever cross the mind that *I* wanted to ease Nicky into getting to know you? "

"Don't pout, Diana." He reached out and urged her forearms apart. "It wouldn't be good to let Nicky see you so uptight."

She barely breathed a gasp of protest before he loosely took her in his arms. "I want my son to be legally bound to me…and I want you."

She laughed without mirth. "What? Last night you couldn't stand the sight of me and now you want me?"

"I haven't forgotten what you did, Diana, but that doesn't stop me from wanting you. For Nicky, you and I need to be a family; we need to move past the anger. I'm willing to do that. I want to start this marriage with a clean slate."

"Just like that. So everything is now fine?"

"No, I'm not saying that. Given time, we can work our way to something solid. We are compatible."

"Sexually."

"I'm not knocking it." His voice deepened. "We could have much, much more."

Diana tried to step out of his arms but he closed the space between their bodies and brought his mouth down onto hers. She was on fire. She felt as if he had branded her. He deepened the kiss. His hands gripped her hips, holding her clamped against him, his tongue exploring her mouth. She bit his tongue.

"You little witch," he gasped, his eyes showing his surprise. He then laughed, but he didn't let her go.

"Next time, ask."

He had the gall to laugh harder. "You want me," he said. "You'll have to be patient. No more sex until you're my wife."

"You're still delusional. I don't want you. The only reason I agreed to marry you is because you threatened to take me to court."

"Oh, so you finally admit out loud you're going to marry me."

She pushed against his shoulders. "You can let go now."

He didn't loosen his hold. His eyes pinned her with a dark blue stare of certainty. "We are getting married."

"This is ridiculous."

"We both know that marriage between us is the best logical solution. Why do you feel the need to fight against it?"

The answer to that was simple. "I'm doing it against my will."

He frowned at her. "You would do anything for our son, including marrying me?"

Diana stared at him. "I would align myself with the person I hate most in the world for my son."

The shock on his face was almost enough to make her take back the words, but Diana didn't. She could feel his contained anger. What did he expect her to say? It was only because of Nicky they were entering into this farce of a marriage. They both knew it, so why pretend it was anything different? She frowned. He was trying, so why couldn't she? She knew the answers; she wanted him to hurt as bad as she hurt.

A sound coming from the hallway warned them Nicky and Luca were returning to the kitchen. Trace cursed as he stepped away from her and pushed his fingers through his hair. The tension was palpable. She tried her best to act normal.

"Mommy! Trace! I've been waiting and waiting for you. I'm ready to go," Nicky said impatiently.

Diana jerked into motion, making for the door on trembling legs. "Well, let's go. The amusement park awaits." She forced a smile.

Nicky shouted to Trace before running out of the kitchen, "Come on!"

"Give me a few minutes to…grab a camera. You and your mother head for the helicopter pad; I'll be right behind you."

"We can cancel the trip if you…"

"Don't," he said, "think I'll cancel this trip. Nicky is looking forward to it. Like you, I won't do anything to hurt or disappoint him. The pilot is waiting."

Moistening her lips, her heart thumping, she heard the tension shadowing her voice. "Trace, you—"

Nicky shouted again for them to come on, forcing whatever she was going to say back down her throat. She walked out of the room without another word.

Chapter 20

They completed the journey to the park in silence. Nicky's excitement was in high gear. He was so impressed with the Sponge Bob ride that he didn't notice Trace's silence or the quiet tension threading through Diana's husky voice.

Trace smiled and laughed with Nicky but ignored Diana. After taking advantage of each ride at least twice, they retreated to a restaurant for dinner. It was a simple dinner and a solemn affair, but Nicky chattered away. After dinner and just before the park closed, they watched the display of fireworks. Diana wanted the night to end so she could curl up in her misery. Her words earlier had created a wide rift in their fragile relationship. She knew she'd implied she hated him, but she was angry and she wanted to hurt him. *Then why can't you tell him that?*

The driver pulled up to the private airstrip outside of Gatlinburg. Due to the lateness of the hour, Diana had assumed they would stay over and fly back in the morning.

"I thought we might spend the night," she said.

"No," he said and stepped out of the car with a sleeping Nicky in his arms. Looking at Nicky with his arms wrapped around Trace's neck caused a sudden lump in Diana's throat. The touching scene filled her with a fresh anxiety. On the plane, he gently laid Nicky on the bed and came to sit beside her on the sofa. Even with her eyes closed, she felt his intense look as she waited for him to speak, but he cupped her cheek and brushed his thumb across her soft, trembling mouth. Her eyes flew open. "What are you doing?" she asked, surprised at the butterfly softness of his touch.

"What does it feel like I'm doing? I'm helping you relax."

"I don't need to relax. I'm already tired."

"Well, go ahead and sleep." He continued to stroke her cheek.

"Don't." She jerked away from his touch.

The next thing Diana knew she was plastered against him. He stared at her mouth for a moment and finally kissed her. It was a possessive and hungry kiss. Just like that, all the bad that had transpired between them disappeared. He explored her mouth with the determined intimacy of a man seeking to claim what was his.

Diana was drowning, but she didn't care. She encouraged him, arching into his body, letting her hand trail under his shirt and through the silky black hairs on his chest.

When he released her mouth, she was weak, her breathing a quick, raspy sound of abandonment.

"I like making up," he said with certitude, sending a rush of heat down her spine. "Do you still hate me now?"

Diana moved out of his arms. "We can't keep doing this. It solves nothing."

"I don't see why not. You want me and I certainly want you. And we're going to be married soon." He claimed her mouth again and then released her. "I can't stand too many more cold showers."

"Really?"

"I haven't touched or wanted another woman since the moment I saw you again. I promise to keep my vows."

She remained quiet.

"Do you doubt me?" Trace gave her a long, unflinching stare.

Could she forget the past? She wanted to. He wanted them to be a family. To have that, she needed to forgive. A shiver ran down the length of her spine. Diana wrenched her eyes away from Trace, wanting to give not just the right answer but an answer that would make the past go away. She wanted him. That she knew for sure, but she didn't want to lose herself in the process.

What if she gave him her heart again and he trampled it? Did she really want to take another chance with him? She swallowed and cut off her painful thoughts and made a decision that would change her life. "No, I believe you'll keep your vows."

Diana heard his breath slowly release. She hadn't realized how important her answer was to him. Genuine relief glinted in his eyes. "We both made mistakes. It's about the present and where we go from here." He inclined his head. "Do you agree?"

"I want to try and make this work," Diana said.

"I do, too. We've both said some hurtful things to each other. For my part, I apologize. I want to be a real father. I want to be able to take Nicky to school, and be there when he comes home. To teach him how to play baseball, pick him up when he scrapes his knee. I need to be the one to tell him its okay for little boys to cry because it makes them stronger. The only way I can do that is for us to be together. It might not be a good basis for marriage, but I know people who have started marriages on less and now have solid unions."

Amazed at Trace's private thoughts, she fought hard to hold back the tears that threatened to escape. The old Trace would've never let anyone see this side of him. He'd personified the strong, silent type. He hadn't been one to give flowery speeches or to say things to appease.

"What did I say to make you cry? I hope there's at least a happy tear there," he said with a crooked smile, trying to lighten the seriousness of the moment. "I don't want you to be unhappy."

The tears clogged her throat to the point where she couldn't speak for a moment. "You're serious?"

"I've never been more serious about anything in my life. All the pain and hurt is in the past. It has no place in our future." He took her face in his hands. "I really want this to work, but I need you to want it also."

"What triggered this new Trace?"

"You did," he responded. "I looked past the harsh words and anger and remembered the Diana I first met, and then I looked at who you are now. You're still furiously loyal to your friends, dedicated to your job, concerned for your employees, and a lioness when it comes to protecting your cub. I saw you hadn't changed that much. I'm willing to take a leap of faith, Diana," he persisted softly. "Will you take it with me?"

Although she wasn't in his arms, they sat close to each other on the sofa. She moved to create space and stood. She couldn't think when he was near her. He also stood and watched as she paced back and forth.

"I'm asking you to marry me—not demanding, but asking," he said quietly.

She stopped pacing and turned toward him. There was no hint of arrogance on his face, no twisted smile on his lips, no sign that he held the winning cards in his hands. Here stood a man she had loved most of her adult life.

"All right," she responded. "I'll marry you."

His response was immediate and gentle. With a graceful movement of his long body, he gathered her in his arms. "Thank you, Diana." He sighed.

She gave him a puzzled look. "Why are you thanking me?"

"I know it isn't easy for you to trust me. But I'm glad you do."

She spent the rest of the weekend in a timeless euphoria. The following week, while Nicky enjoyed being the center of attention, they relaxed together after dinner in the family room. Nicky lay on the floor coloring and drawing pictures while Trace leaned against the sofa with his laptop balanced on his thighs. Diana lay propped against pillows on the sofa reading the latest Mary Higgins Clark novel. Trace had given her a four-carat pear-shaped diamond in a cluster of smaller diamonds set in platinum a couple days ago. She hadn't expected an engagement ring, but Trace had ignored her protests and slid it on her finger.

"Trace, do you want to see my picture?" Nicky asked as he scrambled to his knees. He scooted beside Trace and leaned against the sofa, mimicking Trace's position.

"Of course," he said and set aside his computer. Taking the picture in his hands, he gave Nicky his full attention. "Nice picture. Who are all these people?"

Pointing to each person, Nicky explained, "That's Poppy, Mommy, my daddy, and me." There was a hush in the room. Diana sat up, swung her legs off the sofa, and knelt beside Nicky.

She cleared her throat. "Honey, you mean Poppy, you and me?"

"Mommy, I had to put my daddy in the picture."

"I don't understand," she said, clearly confused.

"Poppy told me one day my daddy would come. I put him in the picture so I wouldn't forget."

"Nicky," she said slowly, "when did Poppy tell you this?"

"On my birthday."

"That was almost a year ago." Shock was evident in her voice. "What else did he say?"

"Poppy said he was taking care of me until my daddy came. He told me he lived far away and built big buildings for people. He said my daddy would come one day soon, but until then we had to keep it a secret. I was going to ask you to help me write him a letter, but Poppy said not to because it might make you sad." His little lip trembled. "I don't want to make you sad, Mommy."

"Oh, honey. I'm not sad...not sad at all." She wrapped her arms around him.

"Since Poppy is gone it's not a secret anymore?" He gave her an innocent look, his beautiful brown eyes wide and searching. "Mommy, can we write my daddy and ask him to come see me?"

That simple question brought Trace out of his shock. All this time his son had been waiting for him. He felt his world shift. Somehow, John had instigated this day. He had divided Raven's Nest between him and Diana knowing it would bring him back to Asheville.

Trace struggled to compose himself and failed. He closed his eyes, fighting back the tears that threatened to escape. He lost the battle. The tears flooded his cheeks unhindered and formed drops at the end of his jaw. His heart released the raw pain that he had hidden so long ago. For once in his life, he didn't want to be strong.

"I'm your father, Nicky. I'm sorry it's taken me so long to come." His voice was strange even to his own ears.

"You're my daddy?" Nicky said, his eyes wide with surprise.

"Yes, I am."

"I prayed you would come."

Trace cleared his throat. "I'm here now."

"Are you going to stay?"

Trace's hands trembled as he gently took Nicky in his arms. "Yes. I'm going to stay. I promise to never leave you."

"I'm glad. Can I call you Daddy?" he asked.

Trace swallowed the lump that had formed in his throat. "It would make me happy for you to call me Daddy." Tears swelled again in his eyes. He cleared his throat. "Your mother and I are getting married. You'll see me every day. Is that okay with you?"

"Yippee! I can't wait to tell Billy my daddy came home."

Trace looked questioningly at Diana.

Diana swallowed and said, "Billy is his best friend. They are in the same class at school."

"I see. Well, you certainly need to tell your friend."

Nicky pushed out of his father's arms. "Where are you going?" Trace inquired.

"I'm going to tell Luca and Rosa."

They watched him run from the room. There was a long silence after his departure. Trace stood and placed the laptop on the table. He moved to the French windows and looked out. He stood there a moment. He wanted to laugh and cry. He hadn't realized until now how nervous he had been. His son had accepted him. He released a deep breath.

"Trace, I didn't know John told Nicky he wasn't his father." Trace remained silent, letting her continue. "John always wanted me to tell you about Nicky."

"John knew Nicky was mine," he stated.

"Yes, he did. When I found out I was pregnant, I went to him asking for help leaving town, or at least a transfer to somewhere where you wouldn't look for me. You were head of acquisitions. The chance of you visiting a small branch was slim. Of course, he knew something was terribly wrong. I finally broke down and told him the story. He begged me to tell you, but I refused. He tried to pressure me. He even threatened to tell you himself. I became angry and told him to forget about helping me, that I would go where no one would find me. In my state, I meant it. He suggested marriage to give the baby legitimacy and to keep me in Asheville."

"Your parents…"

"I couldn't let my parents know. I was practically living with you. They raised me to be different. I had already disappointed them enough."

"You never told me how your parents felt about us."

"Don't get me wrong. They liked you. As long as I was happy, they were happy."

"Why couldn't you tell me you were carrying my child, Diana? You and I had been together an entire year. Help me to understand this," he persisted.

"I was humiliated and hurt."

"Humiliated? Hurt?" he questioned. "I don't understand."

"Don't pretend you don't know what I'm talking about."

"Diana, what the hell is this? You keep talking in riddles."

"Lisa Davenport," Diana shrilled at him.

He looked at her perplexed. "What about Lisa?"

"You were sleeping with her while you and I were lovers."

Chapter 21

"What the hell are you talking about? Is this a joke? If it is, it's a bad one."

"While we were lovers, you were bedding Lisa Davenport."

"Where did you get such an insane idea?" Trace crossed his arms and gave her a pointed stare.

"You were lovers," she insisted.

"The relationship between Lisa and me ended six months before I met you."

"Really? From what I read in the magazines, it looks liked you've renewed your acquaintance."

"We travel in the same circles. I see her at social and charity events. I'm cordial; our families have been friends for years. I'm not going to stop speaking to her because you have some warped idea we're sleeping together."

"I can't believe you're going to continue to lie. After all of this time, you still don't have the decency to tell me the truth."

"I have never lied to you, Diana," he declared without hesitation. "I won't tolerate you calling me liar."

"I don't believe you. Did you sleep with her when were together?"

"No."

"Did you want to go back in the past and start over with her?" she challenged.

"No!" he exclaimed. "What the hell is this, an inquisition?"

She didn't flinch at his tone. A pulse flickered in his jaw, as if he were straining to control his anger. She didn't give a damn. And she refused to let him get away with lying to her face.

"An inquisition? You won't tolerate?" she croaked. "I've endured more than you'll ever know. Your mother wasn't a piece of cake."

"Don't change the subject. My mother has nothing to do with this."

"You're right. This has to do with your inability to commit to a monogamous relationship," she sneered.

"I stayed with you longer than I have ever stayed with any woman. If that isn't commitment, I don't know what the hell is."

She looked at him, defiant and angrier now at his continued persistence of being the wounded one. "Your sheets were far from cold. With Lisa rolling in them, they were burnt to a crisp."

He frowned. "What's this fixation you have with Lisa?"

She swallowed painfully. She thought back to the evening that changed her life.

"I don't have a fixation. I walked into your bedroom and found her in your bed."

"What?"

"The night before you were due back from Rome, I went to the penthouse to plan a surprise homecoming." She laughed cruelly. "I'm the one who received the surprise. Lisa sprawled out naked in your bed."

She watched as hot color stained his jaw line. "I didn't know you had come to the apartment." Seeing the guilt and the conflicting emotions cross his face, she almost choked on her pain.

She shook her head warily. "Apparently you couldn't wait until you finished with me before you started sleeping with her."

"You didn't see what you thought you saw. Yes, Lisa was in my bed, but we didn't sleep together."

She was speechless. The hurt she'd tried to bury rose from its hiding place, strong and powerful. Humiliation flooded Diana when she remembered how she had loved him unconditionally. How her body had burned for him, how for once she had thrown her inhibitions aside and succumbed to sensations that overwhelmed her. And how she'd imagined a future with him. Oh, she could've stayed but he didn't love her. She'd had no doubt if she had told Trace she was pregnant, he would've married her. But she hadn't wanted that.

"Do you think I'm stupid?" She swallowed the lump of pain in her throat. She wouldn't cry in front of him. "Catching the man you're sleeping with screwing another woman isn't something to gloss over," she shouted.

"You didn't catch me in bed with Lisa," he countered.

"Oh, excuse me. It's semantics. You left her in your bed savoring the after effects of your tryst while you took a shower."

"Yes, I was in the shower, but you don't—"

"Understand?" she finished. "I understand more than you give me credit for. Lisa made sure I understood perfectly everything that happened."

"You talked to Lisa?"

"Yes. I did."

"You took her word? You know Lisa can be a bitch. Why didn't you wait to talk to me?"

"You're priceless. I didn't need to talk to you. Lisa filled me in completely. She told me how the two of you ran into each at a function in Rome. You started to reminisce about old times and one thing led to another."

"We did see each other at a party. But I told you that."

"You told me about the party. You didn't tell me Lisa was there."

"It was unimportant."

She laughed regretfully. "Lisa being at the party was important. Evidently, that was where you decided to take her to your bed."

"This conversation is getting ridiculous. I didn't sleep with Lisa."

"Did Lisa fly back with you?"

"Yes, she did. But my mother—"

She interrupted. "Did you bring Lisa to the penthouse?"

"Dammit, Diana. I'll not be interrogated."

"Did you?" she screamed.

"I did not sleep with Lisa in Rome, or any other night. This jealousy you have of Lisa must stop."

She was shocked. "Jealousy?" She was speechless. How dare he think she would waste any emotion on his little hussy?

"Yes, jealousy. I never gave you cause to believe I was cheating on you."

"I'm supposed to believe you after what I saw?"

Trace stiffened. "I have never felt the need to explain myself to anyone, but you're making this extremely difficult. Yes, Lisa flew back with me. Once we landed, she told me she needed to go to her office. Since it was on the way to my place, she asked if I would drop her off. In the limo, she spilled soda on her clothes. I let her come up to the apartment so she could clean the stain before going to her office.

She did that. My driver waited to take her to her office complex."

"I assumed if I asked her your stories would coincide."

"It's not a story. It's the truth."

Diana couldn't say a thing. She was angry at her vulnerability and pathetic weakness with this man. She refused to believe his story.

Trace took a deep breath and exhaled slowly. "Diana, I directed Lisa to one of the guest bathrooms. I told her I had a pressing engagement and I was going to take a quick shower so I could leave. I told her to let herself out when she was finished. When I got out of the shower, she was still there—and in my bed. I was furious. I don't know what gave her the idea I wanted to resume anything with her. She knew the score before we dated. Once I ended it, it was over. I forcefully removed her from the bed. She was angry. She never told me you'd been in the apartment. If I had known you'd been in the apartment, this misunderstanding could've been cleared up. You would've never been hurt."

She was derisive. "Oh, you didn't hurt me, Trace," she lied. "But you did open my eyes to what a callous and thoughtless bastard you are."

He bristled. "You don't believe me?"

"How did Lisa know I was coming to the apartment?"

"What?"

"She wasn't surprised to see me."

"Dammit, Diana. Everyone knew we practically lived together. No one would've been surprised to see you. I'm sure as hell not going to take responsibility for something I didn't do. And calling me names isn't going to change any of it."

The pain she felt was intense. "You're right. It won't change anything. You're a man who makes his own rules no matter who gets hurt. I don't want to keep running into your women and always wondering—I have pretended enough…" She broke off when her voice caught and she desperately blinked back the sting of tears, hating that he might see her pain. She dropped her head and entwined her fingers, trying to gain control of her emotions. She wouldn't let him destroy her. No matter what she felt for him, it was time for her to think about her herself. "You want me to believe you instead of my own eyes?"

"Yes, I do." Trace's tone was urgent. "I want you to believe me."

"I can't keep doing this."

"Keep doing what?"

She lifted her chin. "I can't marry you."

"The hell you won't. You want an excuse. Well, it won't be this. I'm not going to let Lisa's tricks stop us from getting married."

"Surely you don't want to get married now?"

"I'm glad you know what I don't want," he snapped. "I told our son we're getting married. I'll not go back on my word and disappoint him."

"Children are resilient. They bounce back."

"Well, my son will not be one of them. Diana, you made a promise to me and I will not let you break it. My word has always been my bond. If you can't trust it, our marriage will start on shaky ground."

She swallowed hard. How could everything have gone so wrong? Was he telling her the truth about Lisa? According to him, nothing had happened. Did she have the strength to believe him? Dare she trust her heart to him? And if she did could she accept the consequences? Could she overlook Trace being unfaithful? She wasn't sure if she was up to that yet. Her dream was at her fingertips. To be his wife…finally, after all this time.

"I need time to think. I can't—" she said, hoping for a small reprieve.

"No."

Her eyes widened. "But maybe a temp—"

"Once we marry, we will stay married. There's no turning back." A muscle ticked in his cheek. "It's forever, Diana. Remember that."

Her heart thudded inside her chest. "I haven't told my parents about the wedding. Susan is the only one who knows."

"Why?"

266

"I want a civil ceremony." She felt no need to explain further. "I think it's better to tell them later."

"I don't. Still keeping secrets, Diana?"

She lifted her chin and glared at him.

"I'm not going to pressure you. It's your decision. The wedding is in two days. You still have time to notify them. If you have a problem doing it, I can call them for you."

"No, thank you. I don't want to interrupt their vacation. It's not like this is a real marriage."

He looked at her. "One thing is certain; it will be a real marriage."

"I'm not going to argue with you," she insisted stubbornly, knowing she was fighting a losing battle but determined to fight all the same. "I'm doing what I need to make sure my son is happy."

A satisfied look crossed his face, making her even more tense. "That's settled, then." He came toward her.

She was suddenly too aware of how close he was. She quickly stepped back, putting distance between them. Desperately she tried to conjure up reasons why she needed to be unaffected by his touch. None came.

He put his hand on her arm and pulled her toward him.

She could feel the craving for him gnawing beneath the surface of her flesh.

"What do you want, Trace?" she said huskily, unable to stop herself from wanting him. She took a deep breath and inhaled his scent. She savored the smell. It tantalized her senses and made her heart flip in her chest.

His gaze dropped to her mouth. "You."

"No," she said.

"Yes. And we will be married in a church before God and witnesses. There'll be no doubt this is a real marriage."

In the pace of a heartbeat, he molded her mouth to the fullness of his own. Unable to ignore his taste, she let him kiss her and tried not to respond to the heat he generated in the kiss.

He finally broke off the kiss as she watched a pulse beat wildly in his throat, her mind staggered with final acceptance. After everything, good and bad, she still loved this man.

Chapter 22

It was pouring rain when Diana reluctantly crawled out of bed on her wedding day. She looked out the window and grimaced. Although she admitted to herself that she loved Trace, she didn't know if she trusted him. Oh, he wanted her. Of that she had no doubt. But love didn't enter into the equation. It was all about power, control, and sex for him. Could she learn to live with that? Would her love be enough to keep the weak thread of their relationship from breaking? She padded to the sitting room off from her bedroom and saw that Rosa had already brought her a tray with a pot of coffee, toast, and fruit. She decided on a slice of dry toast to help settle her stomach. Because of the stress between her and Trace and her doubts about what happened between him and Lisa, they had come to an uncomfortable truce, each careful of what they said to the other. He was angry that she didn't fully believe him and she was sad that she couldn't. The old feeling of unworthiness rose up in her. She never had been able to understand why he had chosen her out of all the women he could have had. God, how she hated being in a state of uncertainty. She walked back to the bedroom and stood at the window. She nibbled the toast, lost in thought as the rain bounced heavily against the window.

$$\rightsquigarrow$$

Trace stood at the window in his penthouse apartment. He wondered what Diana was doing. Had her night been as sleepless as his? He thought about their last confrontation. He'd told Diana the truth about Lisa being in his bed, but she didn't believe him. At first he hadn't wanted to explain what happened. He'd wanted Diana to accept what he said at face value. He shouldn't have to explain himself. When he had come out of the shower and found Lisa sprawled naked on his bed, Trace had been furious. He wanted to wring her neck. If her family and his weren't friends and business partners, he would've pulled out of the joint venture to build a resort in Sydney, Australia. He hadn't wanted his anger to ruin the deal. And he'd never let his personal feelings overrule his business sense. Learning that Lisa had purposely lied to Diana made him angrier. Lisa loved to play games. He would deal with Lisa, but first he had to smooth things over with Diana. He'd followed Dominic's suggestion and spent the night at the penthouse. He was glad he had. He needed to think, to collect himself. He ran a hand through his hair and stared unseeingly out of the window at the heavy rain. He hadn't planned on pushing Diana into marrying him, but everything seemed to snowball out of his control. Yes, he wanted Diana… more than he thought possible. Hell, who was he kidding? He needed her. When he saw her for the first time after five years, he'd expected to feel detached, but he hadn't. He'd felt anticipation that had gone beyond the mere physical. Damn! He loved Diana. To be honest he'd never stopped loving her. There, he admitted it to himself. Granted he used his son to get her to the altar, but would it be enough to keep her? He wanted them both desperately. He finally held within his grasp what he'd wanted all of his life…Diana and a son. He had what he secretly craved—a real family—his family.

That afternoon, Diana married Trace in a simple ceremony at the small chapel on the grounds of Raven's Nest. Susan was her maid of honor. Nicky, looking cute in his little black suit, stood beside his father as a junior best man. Rosa and Henderson also attended. Having Henderson there made her feel connected to her father.

The only family Trace had in attendance was Dominic, who was his best man. He had flown in from Europe the night before and stayed at the penthouse with Trace. Crispina didn't attend. When Diana had asked Trace about her, he'd gruffly commented she wasn't invited. Not that Diana cared. She was happy she didn't have to look at her face on her wedding day.

As for her parents, she'd decided not to tell them about the wedding until afterward. She didn't want them to ask questions she didn't have the strength to answer. If they did, she was afraid she would break down in tears. It was a blessed relief not to have to put on a brave face in front of everyone, Diana told herself while she dressed. She frowned at Susan as she fluttered around as if the wedding were the event of the year. Good, let her project the happiness she couldn't find.

Dominic had spoken to her briefly the night before, saying she was doing the right thing, which only made Diana more anxious. She had mixed feelings when it came to Trace. One moment was wanted him with everything in her, consequences be damned. Then the next moment the pain his callous actions caused would bring her back to reality.

After the brief ceremony was over, Trace spoke to the minister. Susan stood talking to Rosa and Henderson; Dominic came to stand beside Diana.

She turned to him. "I appreciate you coming, Dominic." She gave him a small smile. She was finding it difficult. Lack of sleep had made her uptight and nervous. To be specific, she was nervous about what was ahead for the night.

He wrapped her in his arms and hugged her tight. "I wouldn't have missed it for anything. Besides, it's the best I can do for my favorite cousin." His eyes scrutinized her. "Are you okay, Diana?"

"Of course. Don't I look okay?"

"To be honest, you look lovely but tired."

"Thank you, my friend."

"You know what I mean. If you allow it, you and Trace can have a happy marriage," he said.

She took a deep breath. Today was her wedding day. She should at least be honest with herself and acknowledge the fact she was where she wanted to be... with Trace. But one thing was for certain—her feelings for Trace were completely out of the realm of her experience. She loved him, but she could never tell him. She didn't want to get hurt. She was in a dilemma. And it didn't stop the pain from increasing.

Since he was a friend to both, Diana thought he wanted to see more than what was there. "Trace and I have some things to sort out," Diana conceded. "And I know it's not going to be easy."

"He loves you, Diana."

Diana stiffened. "What gives you that idea?" He had certainly lost his mind. "We haven't left the church yet for the reception, and I didn't notice that you were drunk when you came in."

Dominic laughed. "No, I haven't had a single drink." He stopped laughing and stared at her unblinkingly. "Trace has always loved you."

Diana frowned. "You're mistaken."

"I don't believe I am." He paused. "No, I'm going to say that without a doubt I know Trace loves you."

"Dominic, I know you want Trace and me to have this fairy tale marriage, but it's not going to happen."

"Trace is a good man."

"But his relationships never last."

"This is different, Diana. You're his wife. You and Nicky are the most important people in the world to him."

Diana dropped her gaze. "I know. But I'm cautious—"

"Please, just give him a chance. Will you promise me that?"

She smiled weakly. "I can only promise to try. I can't promise more than that."

"Okay. That's all I'm asking." He hugged her again and changed the subject.

❧❧

It had stopped raining by the time they went back to the mansion dining room for the reception. The minister left after offering his congratulations and prayers. It was late evening and Nicky was a little restless. Susan was taking him home with her for the night so Diana and Trace could have an uninterrupted wedding night. Trace held Nicky in his lap while he talked to Dominic. Happy to be in his father's arms, Nicky looked at him adoringly.

Finally, Luca came to retrieve him so she could prepare him to leave with Susan. Diana watched the scene unfold before her. Trace lightly kissed Nicky's head, quietly whispering something in his ear. Nicky smiled up at him and hopped off his father's lap. Whatever he said to Nicky put a skip in his step. He left the room without once glancing at his mother. Watching the scene, Diana closed her eyes to cover tears that sprang up without warning. Trace had her son's love and, it seemed, also his devotion.

Though the chef had prepared a scrumptious meal, Diana ate only a spear of asparagus. She was afraid if she tried the delicate shrimp or roasted chicken she wouldn't be able to swallow.

After dinner and wishing them much happiness, Rosa and Henderson excused themselves and went to their private quarters. Diana stood next to Susan beside a small table of assorted desserts and slices of fruit; Diana picked a lemon square, took a nibble and chewed slowly. Her nerves already on edge, she attempted to put something in her stomach to quiet the queasiness.

"You look beautiful, Diana," Susan said. "The ceremony was short and sweet." She looked through the doors to the terrace where Trace and Dominic stood talking. "Trace reminds me so much of my Tony, God rest his soul. Handsome. Gorgeous. Once you get past the wall of detachment that is inherent in strong and powerful men, I believe he will make a wonderful husband."

Sudden despair wrapped around Diana's heart. She wasn't sure Trace would be a good husband; only time would tell. However, she did believe he would be a good father.

"Mercy, your face is ashen," Susan exclaimed. She touched Diana's forehead. "Are you feeling sick? Why don't you go and lie down? I'm sure Trace would understand."

"I'm fine. Just a little tired."

"It's certainly understandable. It has been an exciting day."

Diana appreciated her kindness, but there was so much going on in her mind. Part of her wanted to blurt out everything, but the time wasn't right.

Just then, the men returned. Trace looked magnificent in a dark suit and white shirt. He was talking in low tones to Dominic. By the expression on his face, the conversation was serious. He was so striking that her heart thudded against her ribs.

When he saw her staring at him, he paused briefly. Then his mouth tilted in a sardonic grin.

"I hope you aren't plying my wife with too much alcohol," he said, walking toward them.

Susan gave a light laugh. "Of course not. Only girl talk."

"I have something much better." He grabbed a bottle of champagne and filled four glasses. He handed a glass to each of them.

Despite his relaxed air, those piercing eyes studied her thoughtfully for a moment, giving nothing away.

He held up his glass. "A toast. To my lovely bride."

Somehow she managed to raise her own glass and smile.

Chapter 23

The house was quiet. No words passed between them as they climbed the stairs together. Diana ignored him and purposely kept her eyes focused straight ahead. If she looked at him, she would be lost. She'd always loved looking at his profile, and he looked even more attractive this evening. There was something very potent and powerful about the picture he made, and she felt a tremor inside knowing she was now married to him.

Diana and Trace were now alone. Stalling, she turned toward her bedroom. Before she took a step, Trace reached for her hand. When she stumbled, he caught her in his arms.

"You're going the wrong way," he said with a smile.

"I was going to my room to…"

"Everything you need is in my suite…our suite," he drawled, caressing her cheek with the palm of his hand.

He opened the door and waited for her to precede him. She walked through and noticed a tray of strawberries, chocolates, and champagne resting on a lace doily on an oval table by the sofa. He came up behind her and laid his hands on her shoulders, massaging them gently. She felt a light kiss at the base of her neck.

"We need champagne," he said. He walked to the table and uncorked the bottle. Startled by the popping sound, she watched as he poured champagne into two glasses and then handed her one.

He took a deep swallow; she sipped hers. She lifted her eyes and saw his blue gaze fixed on her.

"You are a very beautiful woman. I'm a lucky man."

She gripped her champagne glass so tightly her hand went numb. She forced her fingers to relax. "Thank you."

He glanced at her hands. She knew he noticed her nervousness.

"Are you worried about Nicky?"

"What? No. Nicky has never spent the night at Susan's, but he'll be fine. He loves spending time with her."

"That's good to hear. I want someone who is trustworthy while we are gone."

"Gone?"

"Yes. We'll be gone for a couple of days."

"You never told me we were going away."

"Every bride expects to go on a honeymoon."

She met his gaze levelly. "I'm not every bride."

"But you are my bride, and we are going on a honeymoon. A short one, but nevertheless, a honeymoon," he stressed.

The thought of a honeymoon, just her and Trace together, caused waves of panic.

"Are you going to tell me where we're going?"

"Rosa has packed your bags and they are already stored on the jet."

He was being deliberately obtuse, which frustrated Diana. "Am I to play twenty questions?" She was aware she was being snappish. There was a strained edge in her voice. Trace regarded her coolly as he drank his champagne, looking relaxed and at ease. She felt angry and unbalanced.

"We are going to my villa in Bermuda."

She lifted her chin. "I guess I should be honored to be Mrs. Trace Montgomery," she said sarcastically, even as she fought conflicting emotions in saying the name.

"Of course."

The answer was so unexpected that her lips twitched as she tried to hold onto her anger. "Your arrogance astounds me."

"Did you expect anything less?" he teased, sounding like the Trace of old. It was a reminder of how they used to be.

"No," she said. "How long will we be gone?"

"A week."

"I can't possibly be gone that long. Nicky just came home."

"I have talked to Nicky and told him we were going on a trip. He's four years old and inquisitive. He wanted to know why he couldn't come. I explained to him that we need to get to know each other. I believe he understood. I promised we would bring him something from the trip. He was very happy about that."

"It seems you took care of everything." She turned from him and looked at the bed. She closed her eyes, not wanting to think about what was next. His arms circled her waist. She wanted to lean back against him, but fought to remain still.

"Why don't you take a shower and get into bed? We'll leave early tomorrow morning. I have some calls to make." He turned her toward him, gave her a long stare, and then planted his mouth on hers. The kiss was deep and promised of more to come. He released her and walked out the room. She didn't know she was holding her breath until she heard the door close and released it.

Diana woke to the early morning sun shining through the bedroom window. She looked at the pillow beside hers and noticed the indentation. Evidently Trace had come to bed, but he hadn't wakened her. The clock on Trace's nightstand said it was only seven o'clock. Diana let out her indrawn breath. Nicky rarely stirred before eight. Then she remembered Nicky had spent the night with Susan. Today she was leaving for her honeymoon…a honeymoon with Trace. Where was he? She threw back the covers and swung her legs to the floor at the same time Trace emerged from the *en suite*. A pair of linen navy slacks hung low on his hips; the button at the top was unfastened. He wore nothing else. A slow smile curved his mouth as he caught her gawking at him.

"Good morning. I was going to let you sleep for another hour." His voice was a husky, intimate drawl as he came and pulled her from the bed. She was powerless to prevent the descent of his head. His mouth covered hers in a slow, evocative kiss.

Diana closed her eyes, trying to hide her conflicting mix of emotions. Trace lifted his mouth fractionally, eyes drifting open. His hand slid the thin straps of her gown off her shoulders. He cupped her breast and teased the tender peak before slipping his hand down to the soft curls at the apex of her thighs.

His touch was gentle as he stroked the sensitive bud, and he absorbed the slight hitch in her breath as he sent her spiraling to climax. She floated with contentment as she descended. The hardness of his erection pressed tight against her hips. She tried to reach for him but her arms were lifeless.

At that moment, as he brushed his lips against each closed eyelid, the past didn't exist. His forehead touched hers in silent communication before he released her.

"Today we begin our honeymoon in earnest." He ran a finger down her neck into the V between her breasts. His gleaming gaze locked with hers. "I'm tempted to start it this minute."

Diana pulled the straps onto her shoulders in a delayed sense of modesty as she turned away from him.

He waited until she reached the door of the *en suite*, and then said quietly, "This marriage *will* be consummated. We leave in one hour."

She didn't answer, for she was unable to find the words for either obedience or argument. She opened the door and walked from the room.

❦

The car came to a smooth halt at the private airfield. Within minutes, they were escorted to plush leather seats in the plane, sitting opposite one another. Diana still felt out of control. She couldn't let her guard down again. Trace was hot and cold. One minute he was angry and the next minute he was acting as if everything was fine between them. She refused to be in the position of watching everything she said, having to control every impulse and word. As they took off, she avoided meeting the dark gaze that rested on her.

❦

Trace took in Diana's averted profile, the way she held herself stiff and upright. Many conflicting emotions ripped through him. He had seen the sadness behind the sheen of tears as they traveled in the car to the airport. The unshed tears had thrown him completely. Why did it have to be this way? Last night when he entered their bedroom, she had been lying on her side, facing away from him. Although he normally slept in the nude, he had slipped on a pair of pajama bottoms and crawled in beside her. He did it more out of protection for her than himself. She was tired and he wanted her to rest. However, it didn't stop him from wanting her desperately. Finally, he couldn't control himself; he had glided up to her back and wrapped his arms around her. She had sighed and snuggled more deeply into him. In sleep, she'd turned to him and he slept peacefully through the night.

His jaw clenched. He had to remember the reason for the marriage. It was so he could be with his son. Diana was just an added bonus. She would not manipulate him. Tears would not move him.

He glanced at her moodily and then stared out the window of the plane at the clouds. She would never know what he felt for her. He wanted to give her time to get used to the idea of their marriage before he consummated the marriage, but he didn't know how long he could lie beside her and not make her his. He would bed her until he got her out of his system and then they could settle down to a polite marriage of convenience. She would have her own interests and he would have his. *Who are you fooling? You know you want more than that with Diana.*

❦

Diana was slightly startled when a gentle hand touched her shoulder. The flight attendant smiled over her. She hadn't realized she had fallen asleep.

"Mrs. Montgomery, we're landing in a few minutes."

Surprised to hear someone calling her that, she frowned momentarily in puzzlement. When she straightened from her cramped position, she was relieved to see that Trace was missing from his seat. She pushed her hands through her tumbled hair and secured it in a knot. She removed the blanket and wondered who had put it over her. The thought that Trace might have done it caused her to frown. She chided herself. More than likely the flight attendant had done it. She looked up when Trace emerged from the cabin in the back. Her cheeks felt hot and her eyes sticky from sleep as he came towards her.

"We're getting ready to land," he said.

She just nodded. She didn't trust herself to speak and diverted her attention to the view outside.

Once they landed, everything happened in a blur. They were out of the plane and, within minutes, sheltered in a luxury four-wheel drive with tinted windows. One bodyguard rode in the front with the driver, the other following in another vehicle with the luggage. She'd always known bodyguards accompanied Trace wherever he went. However, this was the first time that she'd actually seen them. It was unnerving to have these unsmiling but polite men sitting in the car with them.

The hot air caressed Diana's skin like a thin leather glove as she stepped from the vehicle outside Montgomery Villa. Diana sucked in a surprised breath upon seeing Trace's house. She was in awe. It was painted a bright white and complemented by beautiful, colorful flowers surrounding it. It was smaller than she'd imagined; although massive by normal standards, it was unassuming and very intimate. The wide veranda leading up to the front door hinted at the luxury that lay inside. Trees were spaced on the grounds in such a way as to enhance the view of the villa, not detract from it.

The front door opened. A full-bodied figure rushed out and down the steps, her round brown face wreathed in smiles. Diana blinked, surprised, when the woman threw her arms around Trace and gave him a big hug. Trace introduced the woman as Cassie, his long-time housekeeper and friend. Diana extended her hand, but Cassie grabbed her and engulfed her in a big hug.

"Welcome to Bermuda, Mrs. Montgomery."

"Please call me Diana. Mrs. Montgomery is too much of a mouthful."

Cassie chuckled. "Since I call Mr. Montgomery Mr. Trace, I'll call you Ms. Diana. Is that all right?"

"That's fine. Thank you."

"Good. It's settled."

In the entrance hall, Cassie summoned a young maid and asked her to show Diana to the master suite. Diana followed the young girl upstairs. She was tired. She wanted a long bath and a nap. She was in the process of unbuttoning her blouse when Trace appeared at the door, leaning against it nonchalantly.

"Is the room to your liking, Diana?" he asked as he came in. She backed away from the bed, watching him as he walked to another door and opened it. That led to the sitting room. He left it open.

"Yes. It is lovely."

"Good. I'm glad you like it," he said with a crooked smile. "There are no locks on doors between us. You can use the sitting room for your private time. I want you to relax and be comfortable here."

He walked over and stood very close. He reached out a hand and trailed fingers over her collarbone, which was bared. Her breath hitched. The energy crackled between them as his hand went down until his fingers found the slopes of her breast. He watched her intently as he let his hand cup one breast. Her nipple hardened pushed against the palm of his hand.

287

When he took her mouth, she moaned. She couldn't stop herself. She grabbed him, pulling his head closer. Then abruptly his mouth was gone and he removed his hand from her breast and stepped back. Nothing showed that he shared her turmoil.

"Why don't you take a bath? It'll help you relax."

Diana wanted nothing more than to wipe the smugness off his face.

He walked to the door, turning back just as he reached it. "Dinner will be served at eight."

She stood for a long time, waiting for her body to cool down. Her head reeled, her emotions still raw. Finally, she sat on the bed. She must keep in mind the reason for the marriage. She wasn't going to have that fairy tale happily-ever-after with Trace. She needed to keep the promise she made to herself. She wouldn't let him hurt her again.

Chapter 24

"Did you rest?" Trace asked.

"I did," she lied, noting that he looked vibrant and rested. After Cassie had given her a short tour of the downstairs, she'd tried to take a nap but found she was too edgy. Diana had asked Cassie to serve dinner on the terrace and they sat at a beautiful glass table that overlooked the ocean. The sun had gone down and the heat had relented in its fierceness. It was a magical time. The trees swayed in the seductive breeze off the water and the lights shimmered from the houses below.

She had dressed in a white peasant skirt and blouse, added very little makeup, and twisted her hair into a knot atop her head. Flat bronze sandals completed the outfit. She crossed her legs and leaned back in her seat.

"It's really beautiful here."

"Yes. It is."

Their conversation over dinner had been pleasant. Diana didn't want to think what the night held. Granted, Trace hadn't touched her last night. He was waiting for something, but she didn't know what. She was tired of feeling like the hunted. She stood up, her chair scraping against the marble tile.

"I'm really tired. It's been a long day." Her voice sounded forced.

He looked up at her and nodded. Why didn't he say something? she wondered. Diana let out a breath. What did she want him to do, stop her from leaving? She shook her head, disgusted at her thoughts. She went to walk past him and he grabbed her wrist in a loose yet firm grip. Her heart skipped a beat. She looked at him warily, eyes guarded in the dim light of the evening.

His voice was smooth. "Leave the light on. I'll be up soon." Diana removed her hand from his grip and fled.

Trace swallowed the last of his cognac robotically. This evening had been torture, sitting opposite Diana with the sunset bathing her skin and the slight breeze in her hair. It had taken all his strength not to reach out and touch her. He had seen her covertly watching him all through dinner. He wanted her, but he wanted his wife to come to him first. His wife…it was hard to believe they were married. He had started this journey for revenge. It had been born out of the hurt he felt when he lost her. He didn't know where he had gone wrong. She certainly wasn't like any other woman he knew or had known. There was no hunt. It had been easy, like a dance he knew well. With Diana, it had been a complicated waltz. He shook his head abruptly. This woman lied to him and kept his son a secret. He was trying to get past it, but it was difficult. He stood up with brusque movement and went inside, doing his best to shut down wayward thoughts that made him want the impossible with Diana. He wouldn't make love to her until she came to him. He comforted himself with the fact that it wouldn't be long. Their desire for each other was simmering; once it spilled over, there would be no turning back.

❧

Diana woke the following morning with a slight headache. She had been tense lying in the bed waiting for Trace. Exhausted, she'd finally fallen into a restless sleep. Glancing at the night light on his side of the bed, she noticed it was off. The pillow next to hers showed Trace had lain beside her sometime during the night. Again, he hadn't come to bed until she was sleep. She shook her head in confusion. After a quick shower, she dressed in a pair of comfortable shorts and a lightweight knit top. She stuck her feet into a pair of sandals and headed downstairs to the kitchen. Warming trays in the kitchen were full of delectable choices. Because of her nerves at dinner, she hadn't eaten much. This morning she was hungry. She put sausage, eggs, and potatoes on a plate and sat at the table to eat.

Cassie came into the kitchen. "Good morning, Ms. Diana." She gave Diana a wide smile.

"Good morning, Cassie." Diana returned the smile.

"I'm glad to see you're eating. Mr. Trace barely had coffee. I was surprised because he usually eats a full breakfast."

"Is Trace still in the house?" she asked. She wondered if he was avoiding her.

"He went into St. George. I believe he said he would be back this afternoon," Cassie offered.

Diana frowned in confusion. A whole day alone in the villa. She was glad to have this time to herself. Or was she? *You want to be with Trace. You have what you always wanted…to be his wife.*

Cassie threw her a smile. "He asked me not to wake you. He wants you to rest and relax."

"Did he tell you that?" She was curious to hear the answer.

Cassie giggled. "Yes, he did. The man really has it bad for you."

Diana cleared her throat. "Cassie, have you known Trace a long time?"

"Mr. Trace's father gave him the villa for his eighteenth birthday. I came with the purchase." She laughed. "The villa has been in the Montgomery family for about thirty years. I have been here the entire time." Cassie wiped her hands on a towel. "Can I get you something else?"

"No, I'm fine. I'm going to finish my coffee. You go on with whatever you were doing."

After breakfast, she went into the library. She called Susan and had a long one-sided conversation with Nicky. He wanted to tell her all the fun places his Auntie Susan had taken him. She listened and finally told him how much she loved him and that she would be home soon. Finally, he gave the phone back to Susan. "How is everything going?" Susan asked.

"Okay," Diana said.

"Are you enjoying yourself? I had imagined you would be more excited being on a romantic island with the man you love."

"Everything is fine, Susan. It's hot here. I'm trying to adjust to the heat, that's all."

"That's understandable. Trace has called three times to ask about Nicky."

"Really?"

"Yes. He's like any other father, he loves his son," Susan said.

"I believe he does." Diana wasn't surprised he called; however it did make her nervous that he hadn't mentioned the calls to her. She still felt far too vulnerable.

❧

That evening Trace returned to the villa happy that he had managed to stay away all day. He'd intended to come back in the afternoon but changed his mind and instead spent the day traveling to other properties he owned on the island. The word had spread that he was there on his honeymoon. He had caught his overseer looking at him strangely throughout the day. He knew he was wondering why he was with him viewing properties that didn't need his attention when he should be with his new bride. Trace had ignored the question in his eyes.

It was quiet when he entered. The coolness inside soothed his frayed edges. He walked from room to room. There was no sign of Diana or the staff. He finally came across Diana in the library napping on the sofa with a book in her hand. Her breathing was so graceful that it almost hurt to watch. She reminded him of a beautiful swan resting at the edge of a lake, unaware of the danger that lurked. As if she knew she were being watched, she slowly opened her beautiful eyes and blinked when she saw him standing over her. She immediately awoke and sat up. "Oh, I didn't hear you come in."

"You looked peaceful; I wondered if I should wake you."

"I didn't realize I was that tired."

He stepped back to give her space. She stood and moved to the bookshelf.

"Grisham?" He lifted a mocking brow. "I thought you favored Mary Higgins Clark."

"I like them both," she said.

"We're eating out tonight."

"Okay." Anything to avoid being alone with him in the villa would suit her just fine. "We really don't have to eat together. You can go out if you wish. I don't mind staying here."

He ignored her, opened the library door, and walked through, not looking back. "We'll leave in an hour."

The restaurant was French and very quaint. It was set on a hillside overlooking the ocean. It was breathtaking. They'd been treated like royalty since their arrival. Evidently Trace knew the owners. The dinner had been exquisite, the surroundings beautiful. There was a change in their normally stilted conversation. She found herself lowering her guard a little and actually enjoying herself. Laughing, if only briefly, felt good after so many weeks of tension.

The server delivered dessert. Diana took a spoonful of the cherries jubilee and savored the sweetness of the cherries along with the smoothness of the ice cream. She delicately licked the spoon, not wanting to waste one drop. She looked up and noticed Trace intently watching her with a strained look on his face. She put down the spoon and dabbed her lips.

"Are you finished?" he asked, voice rough but controlled.

"Yes. Aren't you going to eat your dessert?"

"I don't want it."

"Okay. Well—"

"Are you ready to go?" He signaled the waiter for the check. He glanced at the check, then pulled out his credit card and handed it to the waiter. The tension was back. They didn't speak as they waited for the server to return. He pocketed his card and came around to her chair to assist her. She reached for her wrap but he retrieved it quickly and placed it around her shoulders, his hands lingering for a moment.

They entered the house in silence. She waited while he set the alarm.

"Why don't you go up? I have a few calls to make," he said dryly.

She looked at him in surprise. "At this hour?"

"It's morning in some parts of the world."

"You're working on our honeymoon?"

"I thought you would be glad for me to be out of your hair."

She lingered for a moment. What was he playing at? How long would he continue to come to bed well after she had fallen asleep? She gave him a look and turned towards the stairs. She could feel his eyes on her as she walked up the long staircase.

As Trace watched her disappear from his sight, he ran an agitated hand over his face. His body had an unfilled ache. He didn't know how long he could continue to deny himself. But he wanted her to make the first move. Why, he wondered? What difference did it really make? He was the one who'd insisted on marriage and the one who had made the ground rules. The rules would be broken tonight. He climbed the stairs in a hurry. He would not deny himself the woman who had haunted him for five years.

He walked into the bedroom as she was coming out of the shower. She stopped when she saw him, shock evident on her face. Her breath came in short pants as he strolled toward her, never losing eye contact. His arms circled her body.

"What are you doing?"

"What do you think I'm doing?"

"Trace, I think—"

"The time for thinking is over. I gave you plenty of time."

"We have too many issues."

"Diana, we're married. We're always going to have issues. We'll learn to discuss them, forgive quickly, and move on."

She blinked. "I'm supposed to forget about Lisa?"

"Nothing happened between Lisa and me. I have told you the truth. But I, on the other hand, will not let your marriage, or the fact you shared John's bed, keep me from you."

She was silent for a long moment. "I never shared John's bed."

"Am I supposed to believe you?"

She stiffened. "I'm telling you the truth. John was my best friend. He was like a father to me, not my lover."

"I am glad to hear it."

"Then why did—"

"Enough talk." He lowered his head and kissed her. Her lips parted and his tongue swept into her mouth, as if it belonged there, brushing aside doubt and objections. The possessiveness of it made her melt into him with a low moan. Part of her was dismayed at how quickly she weakened, and another part celebrated the feel of his lips against hers.

He lifted his mouth and gave her a heated look, then took her hand and led her to the bed. She allowed him to lead her, knowing this was what she wanted. It was meant to be.

She shivered as his fingers lightly caressed her arm, igniting sparks of desire where they touched.

"My wife," he murmured and brought his mouth to hers once more, this time capturing it fully in a deep, penetrating kiss.

She tingled at his touch, every pore in her body recognizing him, acknowledging him. She was lost. As lost as any woman had a right to be when in the arms of the man she'd once loved…still loved.

"Tell me, Diana. Tell me you want me as much as I want you," he said in a rough and strange voice.

She laid her hand across his cheek. "You're mine. I don't share," she whispered. "I have missed this."

His hands slipped to the front of the towel and undid the knot at her breast. The material fell to the carpet and she stood naked before him.

"I need you." His eyes darkened as he took a nipple into his mouth. He sucked hard. She clutched at his shoulders as he moved to the other breast and repeated the rhythm.

He discarded his clothes in quick jerky movements, guided her to the bed, and sank down, drawing her close. His mouth found her core and he teased her lips. She closed her eyes, welcoming his touch, winding her fingers through his hair, holding his head tightly between her hands. She moaned and threw back her head.

Just when she thought she could no longer stand it, when a cry of pleasure was about to burst from her lips, he lay back on the bed with her and slowly stretched her out beside him.

He stroked her hip, her stomach, her neck, and finally her face with light, feathery movements. She felt as if he were creating an imaginary painting. She moaned and buried her face against his throat, savoring his scent and his masculine skin touching hers.

For long moments, they lay there. Then he leaned up on his elbow and slowly traced a fingertip over the top of her breasts, his finger searing everywhere he touched.

"You are perfect for me," he said, his eyes now locked with hers.

She swallowed the emotion lodged in her throat. "Yes," she said, finally giving in to what she had craved for so long.

He reached over to his bedside table and took a condom out of the top drawer. "I want you to put it on me." He handed it to her.

She tried to open the small foil package, but her fingers shook. Giving her a satisfied look that said he was glad she was nervous, he ripped it open with his teeth and held it out to her.

Swallowing hard, she looked down at him. Fiery warmth ran through her. She reached out and slid her hand around his erection, hearing a groan rise up from his throat, making the breath hitch in her own.

Without warning he muttered, "I can't stand anymore." Then he put his hand over hers and released her fingers from around him. Quickly, he rolled the condom on himself, moved her back against the bed, and then nudged her thighs until she opened herself to him.

He entered her in one thrust. He waited, looking down at her with desire-darkened eyes, the veins in his neck standing out as he held his body above her. He held himself still.

"Now," she said, sliding her legs around his hips and running her palms down his back.

With a groan, he pushed himself powerfully into her wet warmth. Then he kissed her deeply as he moved in and out. She moaned and crawled toward the peak of desire. She tried to wait. She wanted it to last forever. But her body had a mind of its own. She climbed higher and higher, with nothing to hold on to except this man within her. "Trace, please…Trace…I can't hold on."

"Diana, come with me," he rasped, and she gripped him tight in her climax.

❧❧

Trace woke with the scent of the ocean streaming into the open window of the bedroom. It was early morning and he kept his eyes closed as he enjoyed the quiet and inhaled Diana's scent. His body and mind remembered the pleasure of the night. He rolled on his side and reached for her, but his hand found a cool sheet instead of a warm body. His eyes opened. Where was she? He wouldn't let her hide from him. If this marriage was going to work, she needed to meet him halfway. He listened for a sound. Not even the hustle and bustle of Cassie could be heard. No more roller-coaster rides in this relationship. Mason threw back the sheet and walked to bathroom. After quickly brushing his teeth, he threw water on his face and looked for a pair of jeans. He pulled them on and slipped his feet into a pair of flip-flops. He didn't bother with a shirt as he took the stairs two at a time. Trace looked for her in the library, the sunroom and on the veranda. With his irritation growing, he came to the kitchen last. The sun streamed through the open door to the patio. He heard muted voices and the sound of laughter.

He followed the sound and stood stunned at the sight of Diana smiling and laughing with real joy. She was dressed in white shorts and a camisole with tiny straps. Her hair hung loose under the huge straw hat that protected her face from the sun. She and Cassie's heads were together as Cassie showed a book of photos.

Diana saw him standing in the door, a frown on his face, and her smile slipped. He walked over to her and dropped a fierce kiss on her lips. It was a punishing kiss for her daring to leave his bed before he woke. Oblivious to Cassie, Trace deepened the kiss and it turned from punishment to hunger. Finally, he heard Cassie clear her throat and he broke away. A wide grin rested on Cassie's mature brown face.

"Good morning, Cassie," he said.

"A fine morning it is, Mr. Trace," she said, and her smile broke into laughter. "I'm going to leave the two of you alone so you may greet each other properly…again. Breakfast is ready whenever you are." She winked at them and, still laughing, left the patio.

"Cassie is right. I haven't finished greeting you." He took her lips again. He broke off the kiss and muttered, "I needed that." He pulled slightly away and gave her a gentle look.

"Why did you try to escape from me?"

She frowned in confusion. "I woke up early and decided to explore the grounds."

"You could have waited. I would have taken you."

"No need. Remember, you have the invisible bodyguards," she said cheekily. "I felt safe. It's such a beautiful morning. I enjoyed the peace and quiet."

"A bride who seeks peace and quiet on her honeymoon?" He smiled. "I have been remiss in my duties as a husband."

She moved out of his arms.

He frowned. "What's wrong?"

"Nothing."

"Are we going to do this again? Do I need to keep asking you what's wrong a million times before you tell me?"

"Where do we go from here? I won't tolerate infidelity."

"I'll never cheat on you. We are married, Diana. We have a son and I hope to have more children some day with you. There's nothing casual about our marriage."

Surprised, she said, "You never said you wanted more children."

"It's a natural progression. I want our marriage to work. Please give us a chance."

He didn't wait for an answer but took her into his arms, locked his eyes on hers, and kissed her fiercely.

Chapter 25

Trace and Diana spent the next few days oblivious to the outside world. They explored tiny caves, swam in the blue waters, and made passionate love at night. Even sometimes during the day they would sneak off and succumb to their desire. But most of all, they were getting to know each other again. They laughed together so much that Diana sometimes forgot there was ever a problem between them. Since it was her first time on the island, she was like a kid in a candy store when she saw the pink sand on the beach.

Cassie had prepared a picnic lunch for their excursion. They lay on a private stretch of the beach connected to the villa. Trace's profile was relaxed. He apparently hadn't shaved this morning because a five o'clock shadow graced his chiseled jaw, making him appear more handsome and dangerous. She had to look away, feeling a sudden rush of love in her throat. She flipped her sunglasses over her eyes.

"Even though we speak to Nicky two or three times a day," Trace said, "what do you think about us flying home tomorrow?"

Diana just nodded. They had already been in Bermuda a couple of days longer than planned. She missed her son terribly but was glad for the time she'd spent with Trace. They had become closer during their days on the island. It surprised her that Trace understood the need to be physically present for their child. It showed that he took fatherhood seriously. His love for Nicky was evident in his speech when he talked to their son each night. She had misjudged him, and for that she was sorry.

"Did you hear me, Diana?"

"Yes. I do miss Nicky."

"We can always go on another honeymoon, but the next time we'll bring him with us."

Was this his way of saying he was already tired of her? *Stop it, Diana.* He had told her they would be away for a week, but he was the one who'd suggested they prolong the trip.

Diana was glad for the sunglasses so Trace couldn't see the confusion in her eyes. She popped a grape in her mouth and grabbed the cheese and bread, avoiding his gaze.

"What are you thinking?" he asked.

"Nothing."

He continued to observe her while she chewed. She took another small chunk of bread and nervously tore it into tiny pieces. He watched her every move. Noticing it, she stopped and ran her hands over her shorts.

"I was thinking of gifts to buy for Nicky."

"When I was in St. George I got him a game, a train, and a couple of books."

She dampened down the flash of irritation and smiled sweetly. "You've thought of everything, haven't you?"

He looked at her in silence for a moment. "You're obviously upset."

"Why would you say that?"

"Your voice is too sweet and sugary. That is definitely not you. So what's upset you?"

"Nothing."

"Diana…"

"All right. Why did you buy Nicky gifts without consulting me?"

He stared at her, baffled at her question. "Why wouldn't I buy my son a gift?"

"You did it to gain an upper hand with him," she said, anger evident in every word.

He gave a short laugh. "You've got to be kidding. Diana, I know I have only known about him a short period, but I love him as much as you do. Of course I want him to love me and need me, but I'm not trying to usurp your position in his life. You are his mother, but I'm his father. I'll always be there for him."

"By buying him gifts?"

"You're being ridiculous."

Diana tensed. She jumped up. With her hands in fists by her side, she spat, "I'm his mother. I love him.

I won't have him hurt when you decide you're tired of playing father." She was being emotional and she didn't care. She didn't want to admit she was jealous of the bond between Trace and Nicky.

He stood to face her. He pulled her into his arms. She stayed stiff against him. He tipped her chin up with a long finger. "A lot has happened between us, Diana. Some of it I don't understand. Nevertheless, we decided to start our marriage off with a clean slate. It was uncalled for for you to insinuate I would leave my son. I thought you knew me better than that. You forget. We are married and…"

"We're married because you threatened to take Nicky away from me," she snapped.

He continued as if she hadn't spoken. "So I could be with him every day, not because I want to leave him or forget he exists. I would never hurt Nicky, and I don't appreciate you thinking otherwise. I'm in this for the long haul. You need to decide what you want out of this relationship, find a comfortable spot, and settle in it."

"I won't apologize. Everything has changed. I need time to adjust."

He sighed. "I understand. You're a mother and a bit territorial."

He was offering her a truce, time and space to understand he was in Nicky's life to stay. She wanted to believe him. She was strong enough to do so.

━◆◆━

They arrived in Asheville in the early afternoon. Trace scooped her up in his arms and carried her over the threshold. She was surprised and secretly delighted he remembered the traditional gesture. Inside the house, he slowly placed her on her feet while giving her a heated look and keeping his arms around her waist. Finally, he dipped his head, his lips searching for hers. The kiss was thorough and heated with promise of more to come.

"Welcome home, my wife," he said. His hands ran through her hair and held her head in place while he returned to her lips. She wrapped her arms tightly around his neck, giving him every emotion she was feeling.

"Daddy! Mommy!" Nicky squealed in excitement.

Diana tore her mouth from Trace and saw her son running toward them while Susan brought up the rear. Trace picked up Nicky and placed him comfortably in his arms. Diana leaned into him, giving Nicky a hug and kiss.

Susan said nothing. However, her wide-eyed grin had plenty to say.

"Did you bring me a present?" Nicky asked.

Laughing, Trace gave him a hug and set him on his feet. "Didn't I promise you we would?"

"You both look well rested," Susan quipped. She gave Diana a hug. "You seem to have found a way to alleviate tension."

Diana's cheeks burned. She spared a glance at Trace and saw his dark hair mussed and eyes still heavy with desire. He caught her expression, raised a wicked eyebrow, and then pulled her against his side with an arm looped tightly around her waist.

"It was nice." Diana looked at Trace for confirmation. He didn't say anything.

"Nice?" Susan frowned. "From the look on your faces, I believe it was a little better than nice."

"Susan." Diana gave her friend a warning look. Susan had the tendency to dig and be very blunt. She would have made a very good private investigator. The girl just didn't know when to quit.

Susan held up her hands in surrender. "Okay. All I was saying—"

"Stop it. I know what you were saying."

"I'm leaving before my foot gets jammed too far down my throat."

"Good," Diana said, and Trace laughed.

Susan bent to Nicky's level. "Goodbye, my love. I had fun. You must come and stay with Auntie Susan again, okay?"

Nicky put his arms around her neck and hugged her. Diana watched Susan close her eyes and absorb the love Nicky bestowed upon her. Diana swallowed a lump in her throat. She hoped one day Susan would find another man to love and give her the children she deserved.

Susan stood and cleared her throat. It was evident she was deeply moved by Nicky hugging her first. Diana put her arms around her friend and hugged her tight. Understanding passed between them. She gave Diana a bright smile, nodded at Trace, and walked out the door.

Nicky had a grip on Trace's hand. He pulled him quickly through the corridor toward the family room. This was one of the smaller rooms in the mansion. It was homey and very intimate. Diana and Nicky spent a lot of time in there. Although he had a huge playroom in the west wing, she allowed him to keep a few toys and books here. Diana sighed. She wanted to spend time with Nicky but knew how important it was for Trace to have quality time with him without her hovering around them. She decided to take a shower so they could be alone.

She stripped off her clothes, stepped into the shower, and let the water wash away her weariness.

I feel better, she declared silently as she dried off with a large towel. She grabbed another one to wrap around her body. Now that they were back at the mansion, how were they supposed to act? She thought everything was fine with them, but he still hadn't settled the question about Lisa Davenport. *Yes, he did*, her mind taunted her. *You just don't want to believe it.* All right, so he'd said he never slept with Lisa. For all she knew he'd been bedding the blonde-haired beauty during the five years they were apart. So what? She had been married to John and Trace had been a free man. But after all this time, it was still hard for her believe she was woman enough for him. A part of it was because she didn't have the social status or money that other women had. Was the other part because she was black? *Stop it.* She was a strong, confident black woman. She was starting a new life with Trace. Why then did she feel inadequate when it came to being with him? If she didn't get herself together her marriage didn't have a chance in hell of surviving.

Disgusted with her thoughts, she put on a pair of cotton slacks, and a short-sleeved top, and brushed her hair into a ponytail. She walked into the family room, where the sight that met her eyes stopped her in her tracks.

Trace and Nicky sat on the floor. He was showing Nicky how to put together the boat puzzle she had been working on with him for months. Nicky listened and watched his father assemble the pieces. He wore a rapt expression she had never seen on her son's face before. She needed to get used to sharing Nicky's affections with someone else. Not just someone. His biological father...who loved him as much as she did. It had been different with John. He always treated Nicky well, like an indulgent grandfather, but she'd never worried he would claim all his love.

Tears stung the backs of Diana's eyelids as she listened to Trace giving him calm but clear instructions, never showing frustration at Nicky's questions.

Trace looked up and saw her. He smiled and motioned her to come closer. Nicky followed his gaze. "Look, Mommy. Daddy finished the boat."

"I see that he did. Did you thank Daddy?"

"He doesn't have to thank me, Diana. I was glad to do it. I like puzzles. It's a way of relieving stress." He ruffled Nicky's hair. He stood and pushed the silent button on the intercom. "Nicky, it's time for your lunch and a nap. We will start another puzzle later, okay?"

"Okay," he said, grudgingly. Luca appeared at the door of the family room.

"Remember, eat everything on your plate, don't complain when it's time for your nap, and later you'll get your gift, plus a new puzzle. How does that sound?" Trace asked him as they walked to the door.

"Goody!" Nicky said and Trace laughed. Nicky grabbed Luca's hand and pulled her out of the room.

Diana shook her head in amazement. "You bribed him."

"You think so?" He closed the door, pulled her in his arms, and proceeded to place his lips at the pulse in her neck. "I want him to know there are conditions to some things you receive in life. It builds character." His arms pulled her even closer to his chest. "Your things are in my suite. If it's not satisfactory, I can move into your suite or we can choose another bedroom, okay?"

She nodded, surprised and pleased he would ask her permission. She had a hard time concentrating on what he was saying. "Yes."

He took her mouth in a deep kiss, using his tongue to dominate. She lost all coherent thought as she drowned in the passion.

Chapter 26

"The announcement comes out tomorrow," he said, his hands gently rubbing her back. His arms were wrapped around her and she leaned back in his arms on the loveseat. It was a lovely spring day as they enjoyed lunch on the terrace outside. It was quiet and intimate. Diana wished she could save this moment in time. Diana wished she could save this moment in time.

Food was arranged on the small glass cart beside the round dining table; an assortment of cold items and fruit were beautifully displayed, but they weren't hungry. They were so enjoying each other's company that food was the last thing on their minds.

She felt the fluttered movements of his tongue as he slid it up her neck. Her breath caught when his lips latched onto the smooth skin and suckled gently.

"Wh-what announcement?" Her voice was barely audible even to her own ears.

"Our marriage."

That brought her out of the stupor. "Huh? We've been married over a week and no one has bothered us. Why now?"

"We were married at the chapel on the grounds. No one except the staff, Dominic and Susan knew about the marriage. The minister was a long-time family friend. He'll not talk to anyone. It was carefully controlled."

"I see."

Feeling uneasy, she got to her feet. For a moment she stood looking at the spacious grounds of Raven's Nest, suddenly feeling overwhelmed.

"I don't think you do. After today, photographers will follow you everywhere. But you don't need to worry about it," Trace said.

"Oh, the invisible bodyguards."

"You might not like it, but they're necessary."

"I understand."

His lips curled faintly as he stood and walked toward her. "Good. It'll be the same as when you were married to John."

"No, it won't. John and I weren't together in public much. When we were, it was a conscious effort to be one step ahead of the paparazzi. It frustrated them, but I was able to lead a normal life. With you and your lifestyle, normalcy is out of the question."

"Once the newness of the marriage has worn off, they'll find someone else to hound."

She laughed. "Please. Don't downplay your appeal. The press has followed you all of your life. You being the dashing billionaire playboy has been a gold mine for them. The fact you married your uncle's widow will increase the frenzy. Our marriage has only sweetened the pot."

"They will never get near you. I promise you that," he said roughly.

She nodded and poured a glass of lemonade. She added lemon and lime slices and sat down at the table. He grabbed two plates and piled them with food. He placed one plate in front of her, scooted a chair beside her, and sat.

She took a deep breath. "Thanks." She grabbed a couple of grapes and popped them in her mouth.

"You can handle the press, Diana."

"I know I can."

A hint of admiration entered his eyes, warming her. "Nicky wasn't mentioned as my son." She looked at him sharply, surprised he was willing to keep it a secret.

"I didn't want them descending on him. He's too young to handle it. In due time, I will make an announcement."

"Oh." She dropped her head and pushed the food around on her plate.

"I'm proud to be able to call him my son." His eyes seared hers. "I would never deny him. I must think of what is best for him."

"I agree."

"Good. Your day-to-day routine will remain the same."

She frowned. "You believe we'll be able to do this?"

He gave her a wry look. "Do you doubt I can make it happen?"

She had to smile. "No."

He smiled at her in return, and her heart flipped. The space between them sizzled.

"We better eat before Nicky gets up from his nap. He will want to open his gifts."

He speared a slice of steak tartare on his plate and put it in his mouth. She nibbled on chilled shrimp. She believed Trace would move heaven and earth to protect them. Surprisingly, she felt safe.

❧

The announcement came and, true to his word, Trace kept the press at bay. There had been many calls to the office for exclusive interviews, but Trace had handled them like a pro.

The staff offered their congratulations. Although the extended Pisano family was chilly at the idea of their golden heir marrying John's widow, they knew where their bread and butter came from and were borderline cordial about the marriage and to her. Diana was used to the snide comments. It wasn't anything she hadn't experienced before. She learned to let if roll off her back. It was strange, but they hadn't heard from Crispina. She hadn't attended the wedding, which didn't surprise her, but Diana was curious that she hadn't put in an appearance by now.

The next few days followed a similar pattern with morning meals taken together, followed by outings with Nicky and nights of passion for them. When he gathered her close after a bout of lovemaking, she secretly cherished each moment.

They spent many quiet moments together. But she was always aware of his eyes on her, searching for something…what she didn't know. He always managed to find time for Nicky. For this, she was grateful. Nicky had come to worship his father. The connection between them grew ever stronger.

Where did she stand with Trace? Did he see her confusion? Was he testing her? Should she let him know how she felt? Maybe she should test him, but she knew such a move could be disastrous. She would not only lose the battle, she'd also lose the war.

And that would never do.

The following weekend, along with Nicky, Luca, and Susan, they flew to New York for a charity gala. Diana had begged Susan to come to New York for moral support. It hadn't taken much to convince her since she had family in the city. It would give her a chance to visit and enjoy home cooked Puerto Rican dishes made by her grandmother. Trace's attendance was required because he was on the board of directors for the charity. It was a black tie event. While they ate lunch in a café near the Pisano building, Susan apprised Diana of the need to wear something *stunning*.

Diana's nervous tension racked up to unbelievable heights during a shopping expedition at some of Fifth Avenue's exclusive boutiques for *the* gown, stilettos, and accessories. They eventually settled on a beautiful gown by Carolina Herrera in pale pink and eggshell silk chiffon. Full-length, the top hugged her small chest, leaving her shoulders bare. The bottom bore a sophisticated bias-cut overlay in pink over off-white.

Four-inch evening sandals and a beaded matching evening bag were added to the collection the driver stowed in the back of the Mercedes Benz.

Susan was in her element, clearly reveling in playing the fashion stylist.

Diana found it all a bit much as the evening hours drew near. She walked into Trace's Seventh Avenue penthouse, kicked off her heels, and set the bags on the floor. Susan followed close behind.

"You won't need much jewelry." Susan flopped on the sofa and shed her shoes. Rubbing her feet, she added, "The gown needs only a little adornment. Pull your hair back from your face in a sleek style, with the back hanging loose in big curls. A little foundation with emphasis on the eyes and the mouth and you'll be stunning."

"Okay."

"Whoa. Just like that, you agreed. Are you sick or something? You look a little peaked."

"I'm fine." Diana rubbed her eyes and slipped off her shoes.

"Are you pregnant?" Susan's eyes were piercing as they zeroed in on her.

Now that was a definite negative, or so she hoped. "No."

"Are you sure?" Susan continued to stare at her.

"Of course, I'm sure."

"Uh-huh."

"What's that supposed to mean?"

"Nothing."

Diana sighed. "Susan, don't you start."

Susan ran her fingers across her lips, indicating they were zipped.

"Are we done here?" Diana gathered up the bags and moved toward the bedroom.

"We are." Susan slipped on her shoes and gave her a hug. "Have a good time, and I'll see you in a couple of days."

"Okay." Diana returned the hug. "The driver will take you to your grandmother's house."

She rolled her eyes. "Please. I don't need a driver. I know how to get around the city. Remember, I grew up here."

"That's all well and good, but you're still going to use the driver. It makes me feel better."

"Okay, friend. I don't feel like arguing with you today."

"Good. See how easy that was?"

Susan laughed and walked out the door.

Diana went into Nicky's room. She was pleasantly surprised to see Trace seated in a chair while reading a storybook to Nicky.

Attired in black jeans and a gray cotton shirt, he looked totally at ease. She controlled her emotional reaction at the mere sight of him. Her need, basic and earthy, pulsed through her body but it wasn't sexual; it was a desire to grow closer to the man she loved.

She had only to look at him and they both understood the uncontrollable pull they felt to be with each other. In the past they couldn't get enough of each other, but this time around it was different. They were connecting on a higher level. They actually talked more and enjoyed each other's company. The future held a promise that made her heart skip a joyful beat.

"Mommy!"

"Hi, sweetheart." She hugged Nicky and settled him back against the pillow. "You're supposed to be asleep." She threw a mock frown at Trace. He smiled and winked at her.

"Daddy and I went to FAO Sch…" He looked to Trace for help.

"FAO Schwarz."

Nicky nodded. "Then we went swimming in the pool. And I had my dinner and a bath." His brown eyes widened. "And I brushed my teeth and said my prayers."

"Wow. I'm proud of you. You did a swell job," Diana said with warmth, including Trace in a smile of gratitude. "Thanks," she added quietly.

"No thanks needed. I enjoy spending time with him." He glimpsed the tiredness in her eyes. "A productive afternoon?"

"Yes, it was. Susan has impeccable taste. I spent a lot of money."

A wide smile tugged the edges of his mouth. "Really?"

"Yes, really. I bought new everything."

"I like the sound of that."

"Daddy, can you finish reading the story?"

Trace leaned forward and ruffled Nicky's hair.

"Just a little more. I promise I'll start a new story tomorrow."

"I like the ninja story."

"I think you've heard it before."

"It's my favorite."

Diana sat down on the opposite side of the bed while Trace finished reading, by which time Nicky had fallen asleep. Diana kissed Nicky, turned down the light, and left the room. Trace stood waiting for her.

"I'll take a quick shower and then meet you in the dining room," she said.

He laughed. "In about an hour or two, right?" he said.

"Ha, ha. I'll see you in thirty minutes." She rolled her eyes at him and strolled out of the room. She heard him laughing all the way to their bedroom. The sound of it warmed her heart.

A quick shower proved to be refreshing. She slipped on a short, lightweight jean skirt, pulled on a sleeveless cotton shirt in deep red, and twisted her hair into a loose knot. She decided against makeup, not even lip gloss. She felt fresh and relaxed.

Trace had ordered another one of her favorite dinners, shrimp scampi over a bed of steaming rice pilaf with a romaine salad and glazed brandied carrots, followed by fresh fruit, accompanied with a vanilla sauce. He was definitely on the right track to winning her heart. How could he go wrong with food?

While they ate, they shared their individual afternoon activities.

"What else did you and Susan do, besides shop?" Trace asked.

Diana took a sip of white wine and set the glass down before directing a pensive look at Trace.

"Why do you ask?"

He pushed his plate to one side and viewed her with speculative interest. "No particular reason."

"Well, let me see Susan and I had lunch in the West Village and then we ventured to Saks." She rested her chin in her hands. "Oh, I almost forgot. Susan asked if I was pregnant." She watched him closely.

Trace sank back in his chair. "And your answer was?"

"I told her there was no way possible I could be pregnant."

"Well, that's something that I can remedy," he said, smiling.

A sudden lump rose in her throat, and she swallowed it carefully.

"It's too soon to think about another child."

"I disagree." He shot her a look. "You haven't considered another child?"

"Of course I want another child…someday. But I'm more concerned about us. We need to know where our marriage is heading before we bring another child into it," she said, emotion clouding her voice.

"Our marriage is going to work. I won't accept anything less."

"Your arrogance is showing," she quipped.

"I don't care," Trace said stubbornly. "I've got everything I ever wanted in my life. I'm not about to lose it now."

Shocked, Diana absorbed what Trace had just said. Her brain was struggling to understand what her ears had heard. Did he love her? For the first time in their relationship, he was opening up his heart. Could she trust it? Before she could digest the impact of his words, he began to share more of himself.

"I want to be different than my parents. My father was so hurt by Crispina's coldness toward their marriage that he sometimes lost his way. I knew he loved me, but he was British and they express love a little differently…kind of distant. Nicky will never wonder if I love him or any of our other children. They will know because I will tell and show them." Trace's voice was forceful. "I need for *them* to know that. They'll never pay for the choices of their parents." He smiled grimly.

"You've already shown you're a wonderful father. Nicky loves you." She sighed. She might as well go for it. "I can't imagine anyone I would rather have as the father of my children."

Shock froze his features for a long span of time. "You honor me."

"It would give us something else to fight over," Diana teased. Something flashed in his eyes before it was successfully masked.

"I never wanted to take him from you. I only wanted to be a part of his life."

She sighed. "I know."

He reached across the table and enfolded her hands in his. Looking into her eyes, he brought her hands to his lips and bestowed gentle kisses on them.

She was held captive as he continued to worship each finger with his mouth. It wasn't sexual but humbling.

Later, in bed, he sprayed her face with butterfly kisses as she fought to hold back the tears that struggled to escape. She felt cherished…loved. Trace had never before made love to her more gently. He was treating her as if she was the most precious and fragile thing on earth.

Uncontrollable, her tongue involuntary changed the rules, slid against his own, causing a sudden hitch in his breath as she angled her head and allowed him free access.

His body tightened and he lifted her, eased her thighs apart, and then positioned her to accept his fully aroused length as he eased slowly into her slick heat. He surged deeply into her womb and she felt herself slipping. Each time they made love, she gave a piece of herself to him. Her vaginal muscles enclosed him and he began to move, creating a dance that lifted them both high until they reached the brink and then descended together in a splintering climax.

At some stage their breathing returned to normal, but barely. He smiled at her and eased onto his back, pulling her to sit astride him to start the dance over again.

His eyes darkened as she ran her fingers through the fine hairs on his chest. The movement caused her breasts to sway, and he traced their soft curves, teased the tender peaks. She gave a startled cry as he brought her down and took one nipple into his mouth.

Shock waves shattered through her body as he suckled, and a groan escaped from her lips as he caught the swollen bud between his teeth and rolled it with his tongue beyond pleasure to the threatening fringe of pain.

It made her acutely vulnerable, and she opened her mouth to plead with him to stop. As if he knew her mind, the pressure eased.

He wrapped his arms around her petite frame and rolled until she lay under him. For a long moment, he stared at her.

She moistened her lips, and he drove into her only to slowly withdraw before repeating the act again and again, increasing the intensity of the rhythm until she followed him in a climax more shattering and powerful than the first.

Afterwards he gathered her close and rested his lips against her temple in the lazy afterglow of spent passion. His lips pressed a trail of light kisses over her face and gently massaged her back.

She turned into him, settled her face into the curve at the base of his throat, murmured something incoherent, and then drifted into a deep, satisfied sleep.

Chapter 27

The gala event, held in one of the city's finest hotels, appeared to be sold out, with people from entertainment, fashion, and business coming together for a good cause.

The finest of New York society attended the evening in designer tuxedos, gowns, and exquisite jewelry.

Small groups gathered in the large foyer. Diana stood at Trace's side with a ready smile in place as guests mixed and mingled. She knew they were watching her. This was her first public event as Trace's wife. She wondered how many knew she had once been married to *the* John Pisano. How many knew Trace had married his deceased uncle's widow? She sighed, peeked at Trace, and kept her smile in place.

Tall, dark, and impeccably groomed, his tuxedo a perfect fit, he looked the epitome of the powerful man. He stood out from the rest, not only for his attractive features and perfect clothing, but also for the primitive and powerful aura he released. Some women simply flirted, but a few made moves—subtle, and not so subtle—that went beyond flirting. It didn't matter that Diana was by his side. Always insecure about her hold on him, Diana stiffened. He turned those mesmerizing eyes on her, seeing more than she wanted him to.

After greeting the last guest, his hand touched the small of her back. "Can I get you something to drink?" he asked as they moved toward the ballroom.

"Something cold but non-alcoholic," Diana requested with a smile and watched as he signaled a hovering waiter.

Her smile disappeared when Lisa Davenport headed their way. Diana frowned at her approach. Trace turned toward the beautiful, tall woman who had once been his lover. His face wore a blank expression. Only Diana noticed the slightly irritated squint to his blue eyes as he slipped a strong arm around her waist and pulled her close.

"Lisa." His voice was clipped as he gave the woman a pointed stare. Lisa tossed her bright blonde head and smiled the kind of sensual smile that had the power to blow most men's libido to shreds. She went to kiss Trace on the lips; it landed on his chiseled jaw.

Lisa laughed, not at all put off by Trace's coldness. "Trace. It's good to see you again. We mustn't go too long without seeing each other," she scolded. She ignored Diana, her full attention riveted on Trace.

"Lisa, let me introduce you to my wife."

"Your wife!" Lisa bellowed. Her eyes widened with shock. All color drained from her face. With pinched lips, she shot Diana a look of pure hatred.

"I didn't know you had gotten married."

"We were married a few weeks ago."

"I've been in the south of France, then Morocco, with friends. No one mentioned you got married, not even your mother." Anger vibrated in her voice while she tried to gain control.

Diana smiled.

"It was announced. But my mother has nothing to do with my marriage," Trace said in a cold tone.

"If Crispina knew, she would have told me. She must not know about this…marriage," she said in disgust.

"I don't give a damn if Crispina knows or not."

Lisa glared at Diana. "Weren't you married to Trace's uncle?"

"Yes, I was." Diana stared back, unflinching. Lisa Davenport was a bitch…and one in heat. If she thought for one moment that she was going to get her husband, she had better think twice. If she wanted a fight, she would certainly get one.

"It's a shame, darling, you had to end up with your uncle's leftovers," she fired at him. Diana gasped, surprised at such an open verbal attack. Trace pulled her against him to soften the blow.

"You're treading on thin ice, Lisa. Don't make me sorry I'm breathing the same air as you," he said.

"Tsk, tsk. My, aren't we protective of the little woman," she sneered.

Diana couldn't believe Lisa's audacity. "I don't need anyone to fight my battles."

"Lisa, I heard you had the pleasure of meeting my wife before," Trace drawled.

"No. I don't recall." She still didn't look at Diana.

She prayed she didn't explode because it wouldn't be a pretty sight. She fought hard to rein in the anger that was vibrating through her.

"Really?" he said.

Lisa gave a slight nervous laugh and offered a convincing pout. "Darling, I can't be expected to remember everyone I meet."

Diana gritted her teeth. Now Lisa had amnesia.

"Well, I certainly remember you, Lisa. The first time I met you, you happened to be sprawled across Trace's bed, naked," Diana spit out.

"I don't remem—"

Diana's laugh was brittle. "Come, Lisa. You don't remember how you demonstrated everything you and Trace had done? You described it in graphic detail."

"I'll not stand here and take this from her."

"Why not?" Trace's voice held a thread of steel. "You attack my wife but you can't take the same?" He laughed cruelly. "You're a piece of work, Lisa."

"I don't know what the hell you're talking about," she shouted.

"I want you to tell her the truth…now." Trace's voice held a tinge of something Diana couldn't define. He was furious. Diana knew it, but evidently Lisa hadn't picked up on the tone, or rather refused to acknowledge it.

"I'll not stand here and continue to be insulted."

"I seem to recall you got married last year to a man who is conservative and honest. I don't believe he would like to hear the stunts you've pulled."

She gasped. "You wouldn't dare."

"Try me." His voice was cold and unbending. He was sufficiently ruthless to enforce the threat should he have to, and with no regret. Diana got it. It was too bad Lisa didn't.

Lisa flattened her lips in disgust. "Nothing happened between Trace and me five years ago. I spilled a drink on my clothes and Trace let me come up to his apartment to clean the stain."

"And…" he said with force.

"He directed me to one of the guest bathrooms. He told me he wanted to take a quick shower and head to your place. I assumed he needed to be with you."

"Tell her the rest." The anger vibrated in his tone.

Lisa shot him a murderous glare. "We were alone in the penthouse. I thought, why not try and get him to bed?" She dropped her voice to a seductive whisper. "He's a fabulous lover."

He ignored her obvious praise and growled, "Tell Diana what you did."

"When Trace came out of shower and saw me in his bed, I know he liked what he saw. Given more time, I would have changed his mind." Confidence oozed out of her mouth.

He looked at her in disgust. "Not on your life, Lisa. We only dated for a month, and even that was too much," he said coldly.

"You're a cold and heartless bastard, Trace. You use women and then discard them," she shouted.

"You knew what type of relationship it would be. I told you going in that I didn't do commitment," he said.

"But you did with her," Lisa sneered.

"I knew the first moment I saw her that I wanted her for my wife."

Diana gasped softly.

"Well, she didn't feel the same," she snorted. "If she had she wouldn't have married your uncle. Do you concur, Diana?" she asked, finally giving Diana her attention.

Bitch.

"No, I don't. What Trace and I have can't be duplicated." The smirk on Lisa's mouth did it. Diana was tired of her. It was time for her to go. "Why don't you go find your husband, Lisa? You have become quite pathetic."

The arrogant tilt of her head and glib smile conceded nothing as the heiress turned with a slow, deliberately sensual movement and wove her way through the crowd.

"You were telling the truth," Diana noted quietly, relieved and, if truth be told, somewhat embarrassed. If she had been more secure in their relationship, they would have certainly stayed together, even if it were for the sake of the baby.

"And you doubted me."

"She's a—"

"Certifiable bitch and femme fatale," Trace said, "who thrives on playing games with the insecure and vulnerable."

Her chin tilted. "I'm no longer vulnerable, and I could've wiped the floor with her."

He laughed. "Ah...my fierce little lioness." He caught hold of her hand and brushed a soothing thumb over his rings that rested there. Then he lifted their joined hands to his lips and brushed hers lightly with his mouth. "You have nothing to be insecure about. I'm all yours."

Her heart jumped and refused to settle. She didn't move, could barely breathe. She hoped no one was watching them. She felt the press of his arousal against her thigh. It took considerable effort to focus on his face.

It was only a matter of minutes before Crispina wove through the crowd towards them.

Oh, boy. Can the night get any worse?

There was a frown on Crispina's face, but she still resembled the perfect Southern lady. She was attired in a designer gown in stunning black and white, a straight line cut that accentuated her height. From the top of her coiffured head to the tip of her light red lacquered fingernails, she exuded class and sophistication.

"Trace, my darling." The greeting was forced but polite. She offered her cheek to him for an obligatory air kiss. He met her halfway, pulling back before his cheek touched hers.

Uh-oh. This might be interesting.

"Hello, Mother. I didn't know you were going to be here tonight."

Diana shot him a quick glance. She detected a warning beneath Trace's pleasant tone.

"I decided at the last moment."

"Aren't you going to speak to my wife?"

Crispina stiffened, but spared a quick look at Diana.

"Diana," she said with pinched lips.

"Hello, Crispina," Diana said pleasantly.

"Mother, I assume you read the papers. Aren't you going to congratulate us on our marriage?"

"I wasn't invited to any wedding."

"Oh, that's right. I deliberately left your name off the guest list."

She ignored his off-hand rudeness. "I was in Europe when one of my friends called to tell me about it. I told her she was definitely mistaken. I didn't believe it until I read it in the paper for myself. I'm your mother, for God's sake. You couldn't have the decency to tell me instead of letting me read about it as if I were a stranger?"

"Not now, Mother."

"Is she pregnant? It's the only reason I can see for marrying her."

"You have overstepped the line, Mother."

"I have overstepped?" she said, incredulous. "What do you think you've done? You married your uncle's widow. The papers are having a field day with it. My friends are snickering behind my back. My only son has made me a laughingstock. I won't stand for it."

"We are done here." He took a hold of Diana's elbow and moved to pass his mother.

"I'm not finished."

"You were finished a long time ago," he snarled, and guided Diana out of the ballroom.

Diana didn't look at Crispina, knowing if she did, hatred would be brewing in her eyes. She didn't give a damn about Crispina, but she was concerned for Trace. He walked stiffly. His face was granite. A mask had covered it. She walked quietly beside him as he spoke to people who stepped in their path. It was a stop-and-go process. People were everywhere, and

Trace was recognizable to all of them. There were many congratulatory comments on their marriage. Whether genuine or not, Diana couldn't tell, but, like Trace, she took it all in stride.

"Trace, you can't leave. You're a board member," Diana said.

"We are leaving."

"But—"

"Diana, I have had enough. I want to go back to the apartment, have something to eat, and spend the rest of the evening with you…in peace. Do you have any objections?" He waited for her to answer.

"No."

"Good." He took a deep breath and continued walking.

They went through the foyer to the entrance. While waiting for their car, she saw Lisa with a tall gray-haired man holding her arm and talking earnestly to her. A Bentley pulled up at the curb; Lisa briefly looked their way and quickly darted into the backseat, urging the tall man to get in. Diana glanced at Trace, but he was talking to a gentleman she didn't know and missed Lisa's exit.

A few minutes later their driver came to a halt in front of them. He jumped out to open the door and they eased into the backseat. They were scarcely seated when Trace reached for her hand and threaded his fingers through hers. She looked at him in silent acceptance. There was no audience, no one to impress.

When they reached the penthouse, he lifted her in his arms and moved to the living room, setting her gently on her feet.

"I can walk," she assured him in low tones and heard his husky laughter.

"I know, but I wanted you in my arms. Why don't you go up and change and meet me in the kitchen."

Puzzled, she asked, "The kitchen?"

"Yes, the kitchen." He dropped a light kiss on her lips and walked away.

It didn't take her long to pull on a T-shirt and a pair of jean shorts that had seen better days. She scrubbed her face clean and brushed her hair into a ponytail. She looked in on Nicky and saw he was sleeping soundly. She walked into the kitchen and was surprised to see Trace standing in his stocking feet at the stove, cooking. He had removed his tie and jacket, and his shirt was hanging out of his slacks with the sleeves rolled up. He was devastating to the eyes, totally delicious. She moved slowly, not wanting him to catch her eyeing his profile. He turned from the stove with the skillet in his hand and smiled.

"Is there anything I can do?" she said.

"You can make the salad. I've set out the ingredients."

She reached for the cutting board and knife and began preparing the salad. She loved chopped salad, and noticed he had already cooked bacon in the microwave and had it draining on a paper towel. They were silent as they worked side by side, each lost in their own thoughts.

He placed perfectly cooked omelets on their plates. "Are you finished with the salad?

"Yes." She wiped her hand on a towel.

"Can you grab a bottle of wine?" She opened the pantry, took a bottle off the rack, and followed him to the dining room.

"Oh…" The table was lit with two candles. A beautiful bouquet of roses served as the centerpiece. He put the omelets on the table, took the salads out of her hands, and set them down. He pulled out the chair and assisted her into her seat.

"You accomplished a lot in a short amount of time. I'm impressed."

He smiled. "You're not a fast dresser. I knew I had at least a half hour to get things ready."

She rolled her eyes and sat.

He poured wine into their glasses and gave her a searing look.

She took a bite of the spinach and cheese omelet, savoring the richness of a spice she couldn't identify. "Wow. I didn't know you could cook." She took another bite.

"I learned the basics in college. I hated the cafeteria food so I cooked my own."

She sniffed, trying to identify the elusive spice.

"Its marjoram," he said, answering the question in her eyes. "It's similar to oregano, but milder."

"I'm impressed."

He smiled. "The ancient Egyptians considered it a symbol of happiness."

"Is that what we are, Trace, happy?"

"Right now, at this moment, I believe we're happy. I want it to be like this all the time. It's our decision alone to achieve it."

She lay down her fork, leaned forward, and placed her chin in her hands. "I'm sorry about your mother."

Trace leaned back with a slight frown on his face. "There's no reason to be. Crispina has been the same all my life. I don't expect her to change now."

"I know, but still, she's your mother."

He laughed mirthlessly. "This is the woman who sent me to boarding school at the age of six and forgot about me. I remember my first Christmas. All the kids went home except me. Finally, my father arrived sometime after New Year's and realized I never went home. He was furious. Their separation agreement allowed him every other Christmas. Since it was Crispina's year, he thought I had been home."

Tears swelled in her eyes. "Oh, Trace, I'm so sorry. I can't imagine how you must've felt."

A faraway look formed in his eyes and a small smile touched his lips. "That day he took me from that place. He enrolled me in a school a few miles from his estate in London. I saw him every couple of days. If I wasn't with him, I was at Raven's Nest with John. My father threatened to take her to court if she tried to get me back. It worked. Crispina loved her image. She didn't want the world to know how bad a mother she was. From then on, I saw her only intermittently."

They were silent as they resumed their meal. His comments had left her speechless. What kind of mother was Crispina? She swore the woman wasn't human. She should be shot for what she'd done to him. Tonight she saw a deeper side of Trace and felt his pain.

All at once he stopped eating and stared across the table at her. "I don't want to talk about Crispina anymore. I want to talk about you. You held your own tonight, Diana. I was proud of you."

"Thank you."

"You won everyone over with your elegance, intelligence, and beauty."

She grinned. "Why, thank you, sir. However, I think not everyone. I'm sure Lisa and your mother feel differently than you do."

He gave a hearty laugh. "I don't think they'll cause trouble again. Matter of fact, I'll make certain of it."

"I didn't realize Lisa was married until you mentioned her husband."

"She married an old family friend of her father's."

"He looked old enough to be her father."

"He is."

"Would you have carried out your threat and approached her husband?"

"Without a doubt. I won't let anyone hurt you."

"I can take care of myself."

"I never said you couldn't. But allow me this one small pleasure…okay?"

"I don't want to cause more trouble between you and your mother."

He took hold of her hand. "Diana, Crispina and I will never have the typical mother and son relationship, whether you're a part of the picture or not."

"But—"

He got up from the table and came around to her chair. He placed his hand under her arm, helping her to her feet. Trace placed a finger on her lips. "Shh, we have more important things to talk about than my mother or Lisa." To prove it, his mouth found hers in a searing kiss. Whatever she might have said was lost in the confines of his arms.

Chapter 28

Trace held John's private letter to him in his hand. He'd yet to open it. There was no better time than the present. He ripped open the envelope, pulled out the letter, and began to read.

By now, I hope you have met your son, Nicky. You'll find that he is so much like you in mannerisms, and, to top it off, he's your spitting image. He's very bright, inquisitive, stubborn, and lovable. I have told him about you. I tried to be a surrogate father until you came back. I think I did a pretty good job.

Please don't be harsh with Diana. One night she came to me begging for help. She told me she was pregnant but refused to let me call you. She threatened to leave town without letting anyone know where she was going if I did. I couldn't let that happen, so I suggested marriage to keep her and the baby in Asheville. I knew you wouldn't understand, but I promised to keep her secret. In time, I hope you come to forgive me and know I did it for you. I don't know what happened between the two of you, but I know she never stopped loving you.

I left Raven's Nest to both of you with the stipulation you would have to live together to claim the inheritance. I knew you wouldn't understand and that she would be furious. It was the only way I could bring you together so you would come to realize how much you loved each other. Nicky is the added bonus. Take care of them both. She is the daughter I never had, and you are the son of my heart. John.

Trace's heart contracted. All this pain over a misunderstanding, but it was over now. He wished John were alive so he could ask for his forgiveness. He would never get the chance. There had been too much silence between them. He would never hear his voice again. Pain shot through his heart. But thanks to his uncle, he had Diana and his son. He dropped his head and closed his eyes for a moment, wishing he could rewrite the last five years.

He had to stop. The past was finished. He had another chance with Diana and he would make sure he didn't mess it up. He stood and moved around his desk, opened the small fridge he kept in his office, and grabbed a bottle of mineral water. He went to the window and looked out over the city. The office was closed; most of the staff had left for the day. Even Diana had left to prepare Nicky for a costume birthday party at his friend Billy's house. He was seriously thinking about canceling his flight. He needed to fly out tonight to Chicago to meet with the project manager for a Montgomery Group high rise; he would be gone only two days, but already he missed Diana and Nicky.

He didn't want to go. He heard his office door open, turned, and saw Dominic walking toward him.

"Hello, cousin," Dominic said.

Trace frowned. "Can you at least let me know when you plan to show up?"

"Why would I spoil the surprise of my arrival?" He laughed.

"Real funny." Trace crossed his arms. "Why are you here?"

"Well, I heard about what happened in New York and thought you might need reinforcements. Plus, I have a meeting with the design department tomorrow."

"News travels fast."

"When it concerns a blowout involving Lisa Davenport and Crispina, all in one night, it certainly does. The gossip has Lisa screaming at Diana and calling her some unsavory names that can't be repeated."

"Never happened," Trace growled. "People should get it straight before they repeat something that is none of their business."

"Whoa, cousin, don't kill the messenger. You forget I'm on your side."

"Sorry, it's been a long week."

"Anything I can do?"

"No."

"Come on, Trace. You used to talk to me. You still can, you know."

He ran a hand over his face and gave his cousin and best friend a long look. Their great-grandfathers had been brothers. Even though Dominic had grown up in Italy, the two of them had always been close. They had gone to the same boarding schools and spent their summers together, either in Europe or in North Carolina. He trusted Dominic. He handed him the letter John had written. Dominic read it and gave it back to Trace. "I'm not surprised."

"Why not?"

"I always thought John treated Diana more like a daughter than a wife."

"You never mentioned that to me."

"Remember, during that time, no one could mention Diana's name without you biting their head off. I like my head too much, so I never voiced my suspicious."

"Why couldn't I see it?"

"You were hurting too much."

"Yeah."

"The great Trace Montgomery finally admits he has feelings."

"I never said I didn't."

"Diana has brought out the best in you."

"Yes, I believe she has." He sighed. "How long are you staying? I have to fly to Chicago tonight, but I'm going to see Diana and Nicky before I leave."

"I plan to stay the rest of the week. I'll bunk at your penthouse. Are you okay with it? How long are you going to be gone?"

Trace shook his head and grinned. "Although you didn't ask to stay in the penthouse, it's fine with me. I planned to stay two days, but I'm going to try and get back within a day."

Dominic grinned. "You can't stay away from her." His face turned sober. "Trace, I've got your back in this debacle with Crispina and Lisa."

"I know."

"Crispina by herself is hard to handle. She can be intimidating and manipulative. The two of them to-gether can be vicious. I wouldn't want to see Diana tangle with them alone."

"I think you underestimate Diana. She's fierce in her own right. But you're right, together they can be destructive. I'll not let them hurt Diana. I'll destroy them before they get the chance," he said without emotion. He meant what he said. He would not let Crispina or Lisa hurt his family.

"I believe you would," Dominic said. "Hey, I'm getting out of here. Go see your wife and son. I'll see you when you get back."

"Thanks, Dominic, for listening."

"Any time." He clapped Trace on the back and walked out the door. Trace stood thinking about the letter and his conversation with Dominic. Diana was his and had always been.

He swallowed the lump in his throat as he thought about how much he loved Diana. It was time he let her know what she meant to him. He picked up the phone, called the pilot, and cancelled the flight. Next, he called the project manager in Chicago to reschedule the meeting. Finally, he replaced the receiver, picked up his briefcase and keys, and walked out the door.

Diana and Nicky arrived back at the mansion close to seven o'clock. Nicky had enjoyed the party and chatted all the way home.

Entering the foyer, she helped him with his backpack as Luca approached. Seeing Luca, Nicky began to whine. "Oh, Mommy, do I have to go to bed?"

"You need to get your bath, brush your teeth, and pick out a bedtime story."

"Can I talk to Daddy before I go to sleep?" he asked, his eyes wide with excitement.

"Of course. We'll call him when you get in bed."

He placed his hand in Luca's and walked away.

The doorbell rang and she opened the door. Crispina glided in looking ready to do battle.

Diana hadn't seen Crispina since New York. *I don't feel like dealing with her crap now.*

Diana closed the door, pasted a smile on her face, and turned to Crispina.

"Trace isn't here."

"I know that. I came to talk to you."

Great. Just great.

"What can I do for you, Crispina?"

"What I have to say needs to be said in private." She left Diana standing in the foyer and walked down the corridor to Diana's sanctuary, the sunroom.

Diana entered the sunroom but left the door open. "All right, Crispina."

"What will it take to get you out of Trace's life?"

"Excuse me?"

"You heard me. John didn't leave you any money, so I know money could come in handy right now. What about two million? Is that enough?"

"You can't buy me off."

"Five million?"

"Stop it, Crispina. There isn't enough money in the world to make me leave Trace."

"Twenty million? Is that enough? I won't let you and that bastard child of yours ruin my son's life."

"You've gone too far. If you have a problem with me, deal with it directly. Don't you dare bring my son into this."

"Your son has always been in it."

"What are you talking about?"

"Don't play dumb with me. I knew from the beginning the boy was Trace's. I only had to look at him to see it. You snared my brother into playing the surrogate father. That was fine with me as long it wasn't my son." Venom infused every one of Crispina's words. "I don't think he'll take lightly you not telling him the boy is his."

"Trace already knows Nicky is his."

"You're lying."

"Why don't you ask him?"

"He never said a word to me."

"Why would he? You've never been a mother to him, much less someone he could talk to."

"You bitch!" Crispina growled and drew back her hand to strike.

Diana grabbed her hand before it connected with her face. "Not this time."

Crispina wrenched her hand out of Diana's. Her eyes glassy and lips pinched, she took deep breaths to regain control of herself. "I knew Lisa would mess it up. All she had to do was seduce him, get pregnant or at least pretend to be pregnant. Once that happened, he would have been so overwhelmed with guilt he would have willingly let you go. Next time I want something done, I'll make sure it's by a professional."

"Please continue, Mother." Diana and Crispina both gasped when they looked and saw Trace standing in the doorway. He was supposed to be in Chicago. He moved to stand near Diana.

"What are you doing, Trace?" Crispina asked the question before Diana had the chance.

"I decided to cancel my trip." He looked at Diana. "I didn't want to leave you and Nicky. I've rescheduled for the end of the week, and I'm taking you and Nicky with me."

Diana gave him a warm smile. "But Trace, this is going to put you behind on the project."

"I don't care. I want you and Nicky with me." He glared at his mother. The warmth in his voice was gone. For a moment, Diana thought he was literally shaking with anger. "You and Lisa schemed together?"

Crispina's face burned red with anger.

"Speak up, Mother. You were saying a lot when I came in, please do continue."

Diana watched a vein pop in his forehead and touched his arm to get him to calm down. He needed to remember she was his mother; not a good one, but, nevertheless, his mother. He looked ready to explode.

"Come now, Mother. Don't tell me all of a sudden you're speechless?"

"Women fall at your feet. You've never turned one down. You had already bedded Lisa when the two of you dated." She shrugged. "I thought, why not again?"

"How did Lisa know Diana would come to the apartment?"

"You had already landed and were on your way to the apartment when I called your secretary and asked her to call Diana. I told her to tell Diana you would be back that night. John always talked about how much you loved it when Diana surprised you upon your return from trips. It didn't take much to get Diana to the apartment. Instead of giving you the surprise, one was waiting for her. Since Lisa caught a ride on the jet with you, all she and I needed was to stage the scene and wait for Diana to arrive."

"Why am I not surprised at how devious you can be? You're my mother, but I want you out of my life. You don't know me at all. You don't have to keep hitting me on the head for me to get it." He shook his head in surrender. "You knew about my son and were willing to deny him to keep Diana out of my life. I'm glad he doesn't know anything about you. Someday he is going to ask about his grandmother and I'll have to tell him, but, until he does, he won't know anything about you. You have insulted Diana for the last time. You refused to accept the one and only woman I've ever loved because of the color of her skin. You deny your own grandchild because of your warped idea of the perfect pedigree. I want you gone from this house."

"Trace," Diana said, trying to get him to stop, but he was unrelenting.

"Fine, I'll leave, but I know eventually you'll come to your senses. When you do, you know how to reach me."

"No, Mother, I don't believe you understand what I'm saying. I want you out of my life...forever."

Crispina flinched but didn't back down. "I know you don't mean it. But I'll do as you wish. You'll come to your senses sooner or later."

Diana was stunned. "Trace, you don't mean that."

She turned to Diana and hissed, "I don't need you to defend me."

Diana recoiled and then tried one last time to get Crispina to understand. "I love your son. I always have. Can't you at least see that?"

"What does love have to do with anything? You'll ruin his life." She looked at Trace coldly. "You'll come to me and apologize. Until then, my mind won't change."

Trace closed the sunroom door and waited for the anger to leave his body. He waited for the sadness to come. It didn't. How could he be sad over something he'd never had? He felt the weight of wanting Crispina's love lift off his shoulders. After all these years, he was finally free to release his heart to a woman who wanted it.

"Are you okay?" His voice was gentle, soothing. He closed the distance between them, his steps timid.

"I should be asking you that. I'm so sorry. I know you—"

"Did you speak the truth? Do you love me?" He closed his eyes as though that could help him withstand the impact of her answer.

She smiled. The words escaped her lips in a husky murmur. "Yes. I love you. I always have."

He caught hold of her face and kissed her cheek. "Thank you. I love you more than you could ever know." He wrapped her in his arms. "I fell in love with you the first time I saw you. I knew there was something different about you and that you would change my life. I was so busy analyzing my feelings that I never stopped to tell you how I felt. I'm offering you everything I am and everything that I have." He tugged her a little closer, and her heart leapt as she yielded to that pull. "We have John to thank for us being together. I finally read the private letter he left for me."

She leaned back from him so she could see his face. "Really? What did it say?"

"He told me to take care of you and Nicky."

"Well, you're certainly doing just that." She smiled as she wrapped her arms around his neck, tilted her head up, and proceeded to show him how well he was taking care of her.

Epilogue

Diana sat on the terrace under a huge umbrella and let the laughter and conversation of her family wash over her. The Hamiltons, Pisanos, and Montgomerys had descended upon them three days ago.

She looked at Trace, the man of her dreams, sitting opposite her, and her attention was caught by the love in his blue eyes. Their son Nicky was happily playing on the lawn with his cousins.

"Give the baby to me." Her mother, not ashamed of interrupting their serenity, appeared at Trace's shoulder, her arms held out expectantly. Her father and mother had forgiven her once again, this time for not inviting them to the wedding. Diana had confided in them that the marriage had been rough at first, but now it was wonderful.

Diana gazed at Mia, who was six weeks old. She was cradled in Trace's arms and still wearing the lacy gown worn for her christening. He touched a gentle finger to her cheek. Diana's parents had come for the christening, but Crispina had been absent. They hadn't heard from Crispina since that fateful day in the sunroom. Trace never mentioned her name, but

Diana hoped for his sake that Crispina would one day accept her and the children.

Trace had adapted to the role of father of a newborn with the confidence and competence with which he did everything, and with the fierce love and protectiveness Diana was beginning to see was a part of his persona with the children. He pulled Mia a little closer. "She's asleep. I was just going to put her in the bassinette."

"Trace Montgomery, I can't believe you just lied to my face. You know good and well you were going to keep that baby in your arms. Now, come on, give her to me." Trace reluctantly relinquished Mia into her grandmother's hands.

Diana leaned into Trace and whispered, "I can't believe my strong and ruthless husband is afraid of a five foot, one inch grandmother."

He grinned and wrapped an arm around her waist. "She's ferocious. She would eat me alive."

Diana laughed and then sighed in contentment, happiness flooding her heart. She and Trace had been given another chance. She tilted her head upward and smiled at the clouds hovering above them. *Thanks, John.*

About the Author

Renee Wynn was raised Southern but now resides in the North. She began writing at the age of seven as a way to cope with the sudden death of her father. Always a daddy's girl, it was hard for her to talk to anyone about how she was feeling so she began to write what she felt on paper.

A creative writing class in high school helped her to begin a journal that also led her to channel the stories she made up in her mind. In college, she was a reporter for the college newspaper but never thought she could ever write anything of significance.

Thirty-two years after college, she's still writing. She works for a large scientific company and is in the process of completing another novel.

Renee has one son, who she calls her miracle baby. After thirty years of marriage, her husband, Michael, still makes her breath catch in her throat when she looks at him. They are a very close-knit family who enjoy vacationing together and having those small, intimate family talks.

2011 Mass Market Titles

January

From This Moment
Sean Young
ISBN-13: 978-1-58571-383-7
ISBN-10: 1-58571-383-X
$6.99

Nihon Nights
Trisha/Monica Haddad
ISBN-13: 978-1-58571-382-0
ISBN-10: 1-58571-382-1
$6.99

February

The Davis Years
Nicole Green
ISBN-13: 978-1-58571-390-5
ISBN-10: 1-58571-390-2
$6.99

Allegro
Adora Bennett
ISBN-13: 978-158571-391-2
ISBN-10: 1-58571-391-0
$6.99

March

Lies in Disguise
Bernice Layton
ISBN-13: 978-1-58571-392-9
ISBN-10: 1-58571-392-9
$6.99

Steady
Ruthie Robinson
ISBN-13: 978-1-58571-393-6
ISBN-10: 1-58571-393-7
$6.99

April

The Right Maneuver
LaShell Stratton-Childers
ISBN-13: 978-1-58571-394-3
ISBN-10: 1-58571-394-5
$6.99

Riding the Corporate Ladder
Keith Walker
ISBN-13: 978-1-58571-395-0
ISBN-10: 1-58571-395-3
$6.99

May

Separate Dreams
Joan Early
ISBN-13: 978-1-58571-434-6
ISBN-10: 1-58571-434-8
$6.99

I Take This Woman
Chamein Canton
ISBN-13: 978-1-58571-435-3
ISBN-10: 1-58571-435-6
$6.99

June

Inside Out
Grayson Cole
ISBN-13: 978-1-58571-437-7
ISBN-10: 1-58571-437-2
$6.99

2011 Mass Market Titles (continued)

July

The Other Side of the
  Mountain
Janice Angelique
ISBN-13: 978-1-58571-442-1
ISBN-10: 1-58571-442-9
$6.99

Holding Her Breath
Nicole Green
ISBN-13: 978-1-58571-439-1
ISBN-10: 1-58571-439-9
$6.99

August

The Sea of Aaron
Kymberly Hunt
ISBN-13: 978-1-58571-440-7
ISBN-10: 1-58571-440-2
$6.99

The Finley Sisters' Oath of
  Romance
Keith Thomas Walker
ISBN-13: 978-1-58571-441-4
ISBN-10: 1-58571-441-0
$6.99

September

Except on Sunday
Regena Bryant
ISBN-13: 978-1-58571-443-8
ISBN-10: 1-58571-443-7
$6.99

Light's Out
Ruthie Robinson
ISBN-13: 978-1-58571-445-2
ISBN-10: 1-58571-445-3
$6.99

October

The Heart Knows
Renee Wynn
ISBN-13: 978-1-58571-444-5
ISBN-10: 1-58571-444-5
$6.99

Best Friends; Better Lovers
Celya Bowers
ISBN-13: 978-1-58571-455-1
ISBN-10: 1-58571-455-0
$6.99

November

Caress
Grayson Cole
ISBN-13: 978-1-58571-454-4
ISBN-10: 1-58571-454-2
$6.99

A Love Built to Last
L. S. Childers
ISBN-13: 978-1-58571-448-3
ISBN-10: 1-58571-448-8
$6.99

December

Fractured
Wendy Byrne
ISBN-13: 978-1-58571-449-0
ISBN-10: 1-58571-449-6
$6.99

Everything in Between
Crystal Hubbard
ISBN-13: 978-1-58571-396-7
ISBN-10: 1-58571-396-1
$6.99

Other Genesis Press, Inc. Titles

Other Genesis Press, Inc. Titles (continued)

Other Genesis Press, Inc. Titles (continued)

Other Genesis Press, Inc. Titles (continued)

How to Write a Romance	Kathryn Falk	$18.95
I Married a Reclining Chair	Lisa M. Fuhs	$8.95
I'll Be Your Shelter	Giselle Carmichael	$8.95
I'll Paint a Sun	A.J. Garrotto	$9.95
Icie	Pamela Leigh Starr	$8.95
If I Were Your Woman	LaConnie Taylor-Jones	$6.99
Illusions	Pamela Leigh Starr	$8.95
Indigo After Dark Vol. I	Nia Dixon/Angelique	$10.95
Indigo After Dark Vol. II	Dolores Bundy/	$10.95
	Cole Riley	
Indigo After Dark Vol. III	Montana Blue/	$10.95
	Coco Morena	
Indigo After Dark Vol. IV	Cassandra Colt/	$14.95
Indigo After Dark Vol. V	Delilah Dawson	$14.95
Indiscretions	Donna Hill	$8.95
Intentional Mistakes	Michele Sudler	$9.95
Interlude	Donna Hill	$8.95
Intimate Intentions	Angie Daniels	$8.95
It's in the Rhythm	Sammie Ward	$6.99
It's Not Over Yet	J.J. Michael	$9.95
Jolie's Surrender	Edwina Martin-Arnold	$8.95
Kiss or Keep	Debra Phillips	$8.95
Lace	Giselle Carmichael	$9.95
Lady Preacher	K.T. Richey	$6.99
Last Train to Memphis	Elsa Cook	$12.95
Lasting Valor	Ken Olsen	$24.95
Let Us Prey	Hunter Lundy	$25.95
Let's Get It On	Dyanne Davis	$6.99
Lies Too Long	Pamela Ridley	$13.95
Life Is Never As It Seems	J.J. Michael	$12.95
Lighter Shade of Brown	Vicki Andrews	$8.95
Look Both Ways	Joan Early	$6.99
Looking for Lily	Africa Fine	$6.99
Love Always	Mildred E. Riley	$10.95
Love Doesn't Come Easy	Charlyne Dickerson	$8.95
Love Out of Order	Nicole Green	$6.99
Love Unveiled	Gloria Greene	$10.95
Love's Deception	Charlene Berry	$10.95
Love's Destiny	M. Loui Quezada	$8.95
Love's Secrets	Yolanda McVey	$6.99

Other Genesis Press, Inc. Titles (continued)

Other Genesis Press, Inc. Titles (continued)

Path of Thorns	Annetta P. Lee	$9.95
Peace Be Still	Colette Haywood	$12.95
Picture Perfect	Reon Carter	$8.95
Playing for Keeps	Stephanie Salinas	$8.95
Pride & Joi	Gay G. Gunn	$8.95
Promises Made	Bernice Layton	$6.99
Promises of Forever	Celya Bowers	$6.99
Promises to Keep	Alicia Wiggins	$8.95
Quiet Storm	Donna Hill	$10.95
Reckless Surrender	Rochelle Alers	$6.95
Red Polka Dot in a World Full of Plaid	Varian Johnson	$12.95
Red Sky	Renee Alexis	$6.99
Reluctant Captive	Joyce Jackson	$8.95
Rendezvous With Fate	Jeanne Sumerix	$8.95
Revelations	Cheris F. Hodges	$8.95
Reye's Gold	Ruthie Robinson	$6.99
Rivers of the Soul	Leslie Esdaile	$8.95
Rocky Mountain Romance	Kathleen Suzanne	$8.95
Rooms of the Heart	Donna Hill	$8.95
Rough on Rats and Tough on Cats	Chris Parker	$12.95
Save Me	Africa Fine	$6.99
Secret Library Vol. 1	Nina Sheridan	$18.95
Secret Library Vol. 2	Cassandra Colt	$8.95
Secret Thunder	Annetta P. Lee	$9.95
Shades of Brown	Denise Becker	$8.95
Shades of Desire	Monica White	$8.95
Shadows in the Moonlight	Jeanne Sumerix	$8.95
Show Me the Sun	Miriam Shumba	$6.99
Sin	Crystal Rhodes	$8.95
Singing a Song…	Crystal Rhodes	$6.99
Six O'Clock	Katrina Spencer	$6.99
Small Sensations	Crystal V. Rhodes	$6.99
Small Whispers	Annetta P. Lee	$6.99
So Amazing	Sinclair LeBeau	$8.95
Somebody's Someone	Sinclair LeBeau	$8.95
Someone to Love	Alicia Wiggins	$8.95
Song in the Park	Martin Brant	$15.95
Soul Eyes	Wayne L. Wilson	$12.95

Other Genesis Press, Inc. Titles (continued)

Other Genesis Press, Inc. Titles (continued)

Things Forbidden	Maryam Diaab	$6.99
This Life Isn't Perfect Holla	Sandra Foy	$6.99
Three Doors Down	Michele Sudler	$6.99
Three Wishes	Seressia Glass	$8.95
Ties That Bind	Kathleen Suzanne	$8.95
Tiger Woods	Libby Hughes	$5.95
Time Is of the Essence	Angie Daniels	$9.95
Timeless Devotion	Bella McFarland	$9.95
Tomorrow's Promise	Leslie Esdaile	$8.95
Truly Inseparable	Wanda Y. Thomas	$8.95
Two Sides to Every Story	Dyanne Davis	$9.95
Unbeweavable	Katrina Spencer	$6.99
Unbreak My Heart	Dar Tomlinson	$8.95
Unclear and Present Danger	Michele Cameron	$6.99
Uncommon Prayer	Kenneth Swanson	$9.95
Unconditional	A.C. Arthur	$9.95
Unconditional Love	Alicia Wiggins	$8.95
Undying Love	Renee Alexis	$6.99
Until Death Do Us Part	Susan Paul	$8.95
Vows of Passion	Bella McFarland	$9.95
Waiting for Mr. Darcy	Chamein Canton	$6.99
Waiting in the Shadows	Michele Sudler	$6.99
Wayward Dreams	Gail McFarland	$6.99
Wedding Gown	Dyanne Davis	$8.95
What's Under Benjamin's Bed	Sandra Schaffer	$8.95
When a Man Loves a Woman	LaConnie Taylor-Jones	$6.99
When Dreams Float	Dorothy Elizabeth Love	$8.95
When I'm With You	LaConnie Taylor-Jones	$6.99
When Lightning Strikes	Michele Cameron	$6.99
Where I Want to Be	Maryam Diaab	$6.99
Whispers in the Night	Dorothy Elizabeth Love	$8.95
Whispers in the Sand	LaFlorya Gauthier	$10.95
Who's That Lady?	Andrea Jackson	$9.95
Wild Ravens	AlTonya Washington	$9.95
Yesterday Is Gone	Beverly Clark	$10.95
Yesterday's Dreams, Tomorrow's Promises	Reon Laudat	$8.95
Your Precious Love	Sinclair LeBeau	$8.95

Order Form

Mail to: Genesis Press, Inc.
P.O. Box 101
Columbus, MS 39703

Name _____
Address _____
City/State _____ Zip _____
Telephone _____

Ship to (if different from above)
Name _____
Address _____
City/State _____ Zip _____
Telephone _____

Credit Card Information
Credit Card # _____ ☐ Visa ☐ Mastercard
Expiration Date (mm/yy) _____ ☐ AmEx ☐ Discover

Qty.	Author	Title	Price	Total

Use this order form, or call 1-888-INDIGO-1

Total for books _____
Shipping and handling:
  $5 first two books,
  $1 each additional book _____
Total S & H _____
Total amount enclosed _____

Mississippi residents add 7% sales tax